The Hacienda Mirage

A Novel

Howard Wallman

ISBN: 9798375445038 (paperback)

Thoughtfully Edited by Cynthia Katz

"We're all just walking each other home."

~ Ram Dass

The Hacienda Mirage

A Special Place for Special People

Live Independently where you can age with grace and dignity without the pressure of daily obligations.

The Hacienda Mirage is a privately owned community built around your comfort, happiness, health, and well-being.

You'll have time for the things you enjoy — learning, growing, exercising, developing relationships, experiencing new things, and living your very best life.

Up to three meals a day; assistance with personal care. Help with medications, housekeeping & laundry.

Social and recreational activities to suit your lifestyle.

And should your needs change —
we can help relocate you to our adjacent Assisted Living Residences...
or the Meadowlands Nursing Home in nearby Santa Maria.

Four Days in February 2019
San Luis Obispo, California

Part 1

Saturday

Chapter One

Gavina McVey

I shall explain my outfit as I am certain you are curious about what I am wearing, especially if you are one to go by appearances. Judging books by their cover. First impressions. That sort of thing. Well, when I was getting dressed for lunch, I felt my countenance going from gray to angry. From moody to red. Now, if you are a person who does not understand that colors are emotions and you wish to call me nasty names — or look at me as if I am completely nuts instead of just a little eccentric — if that is you, we are not going to get along. Unlucky folks who nonchalantly write me off do not fare well is all I am saying.

Gray. Red. Gray. Red. Not good. So to brighten my spirits I decided to wear these orange and green floral-print pants and a sky-blue blouse — a very comfy, V-neck polyester with short sleeves even though there is still a chill in the air. As far as I am concerned the month or the weather should not dictate your wardrobe. Your mood should.

This is not my usual week-day monochromatic guise because Saturday is Festive Day at The Hacienda Mirage Rest Home for Curmudgeons and Crones. Why is Saturday the day to dress up? Because I say so! And it is not about wearing my traditional Scottish tartan skirt, shawl and ghillies. Notice the long, happy, sun-yellow pashmina that Quinn gave to me because he knows yellow is my favorite color. 'Tis making the other wrinkled old gals at my lunch table yellow with envy. Not that it is any of your business — unless you really want to understand me — but I always dress according to the day of the week. Monday, Wednesday, and Friday are primary colors. Red, yellow, blue only. Head to toe. Tuesday, Thursday, and Sunday are secondary. Orange, green, violet. Saturday, I wear whatever suits my fancy. Thank you very much. 'Tis because of this extensive wardrobe that my studio apartment is sporting its own titanic wall-to-wall armoire rather than the microscopic, old, built-in-the-wall closet that comes with the typical studio-size apartments. My special closet is big enough for my sassy thrift shop clothing along with a body if one needs to be stashed away should I decide to vent my occasional rage instead of taking my medication.

Let us get one thing straight. Shall we? Something I learned from the illustrious psychiatrist, Doctor Arnold Felden. It is *not my fault* that I seem to have trouble with just about everyone, often even Quinn. 'Tis the fault of my so-called parents, abject poverty, poor hygiene, backward schools, other kids, slimy politicians, shipyard closures, and winters with more smog clogging the air than snow falling from the heavens.

Am I confusing you? Well, do not expect me to feel sorry for you. I am always confused. How do you like it? The only one who ever understood my confusion — or for that matter, my anger — was Doctor Felden, who abandoned me by up-and-dying quite a while ago. Sure, I have tried other psychiatrists since then, but not a one of them appreciated me or knew what to do with me. Doctor Felden, on the other hand, was sympathetic whenever I explained such things as how acutely aware I am of people like you watching me. I very well know if someone is scrutinizing me. Thank you very much. No matter how near nor faraway they may be. Should they be many miles distant, they may not be *watching per se*, but they are surely cogitating about me. Pondering. Scheming. Judging. My nostrils begin to itch, interior up into my brain, and an image of their face appears in my mind whether or not I have actually seen their visage afore. 'Tis a foggy vision of their face floating through the universe, behind my eyes and into my brain. If it is someone familiar, I can smell them and hear them breathe. Not their perfume or shave cream. Their essence. Some poor souls smell like rotten prunes or dead rodents. The benevolent ones might conjure lilac or other romantic or lyrical flora. If it is a person or persons I do not know, I itch from a prickliness in places that are private — sometimes only for minutes, sometimes for hours at a time and I catch myself holding my breath. Of course, if they are near, I see them hovering and gawking — their gaze fixed on me and then moving away in a failed attempt to pretend that they were not examining me at all. The nearby ones' eyes penetrate the part of my body that they are scrutinizing, and you might find me hiking up my pants to hide the little stretch of pale pink flesh peeking out over the waistband or I may be drawing my dressing gown tighter to better conceal my admittedly no-longer-buxom bosom. I will find myself patting down my head of still thick but gray hair, often braided down my back so as not to intimidate the other females. Point being — Gavina knows you are watching. Enough said.

See that man over there in the fancy all-too-white shirt? He is clearly a dangerous visitor. He is sitting at The Manager's lunch table occasionally looking my way and muttering things about me as if to say, 'And she ... this. And she ... that.' His beady eyes are on me while he is taking notes. He is jotting things down in a little notebook as if it is 1919 instead of 2019 and iPhone Notes have not yet been invented. The two of them are trying to decide what to do with me once Hacienda Mirage is brought to the ground. My nose is itching. I am holding my breath. And you do not have to point it out — because I very well am aware — that I am nervously wrapping and rewrapping the yellow scarf as if I am a mummy swathing itself.

I am not going to say anything to the other girls. I am not! I promised myself. Especially not that stuck up Cookie Nussbaum who thinks she is better than anyone. The other old bats at my lunch table have a bad habit of ignoring me when I share one of my insights. Cookie usually smirks or giggles like one of the schoolgirls who taunted me as a child on the playground in Scotland. As for now, I am intent on not letting on that I know anything about the facility being sold and the plans to level our so-called 'rest home' in order to build high rise condominiums above a sleek modern boutique shopping mall with underground parking. Up until now, my lips are sealed on that, and I have thrown away the key.

Then again, sometimes promises made to oneself are not kept — out of respect for the greater good. I am always concerned for the greater good! I do not like keeping secrets when the telling of them might be the humane thing to do. I, myself, do not relish being kept in the dark for what too many people call *my own good.* Falderal!

But I cannot take it anymore. My Rueben Sandwich is swiftly going from lukewarm to chilled and my cup of coffee is shaking in my hand when Cookie Nussbaum opens her Jezebel-Red, piehole lips and asks, "What's wrong, darling? You look upset. How are you feeling? Would you like to lie down? Can we get you a sedative?"

The bright sunlight is streaming through the windows of the dining hall. Management calls it the Windsor Dining *Room* but — having been incarcerated and confined in less glamorous situations than the plush Hacienda Mirage — I very well know that this is just a good old mess hall for old people. The sun's rays creep past the insufferable, shimmery, gold drapes, and the light inches across the patterned, flat, industrial carpet beyond the other tables and heads toward me until it hits the sauerkraut leaching from my sandwich, the golden apple cider in my glass, and the pale-yellow banana I took for myself while roaming through the kitchen against all rules.

Okay, I see now that *yellow* is the color of cowards, not envy or jealousy. I had gotten it wrong about the envious females turning yellow when they saw me dressed in all my splendor. I stand corrected. Are ya happy now? I am not beyond admitting when I am wrong. *I* was turning *cowardly yellow* in my fear of telling them what I knew. And *they* were becoming *green with envy* like Wicked Witches of the West. All stands corrected.

"I am fine, Cookie," I say in my best ancient Scottish Cailleach hag voice. "I do not need a sedative. I am not one of your alleged patients from twenty years ago. And as I have told you a thousand times, you are *not* my therapist."

But I am trembling with the withholding of my secret. And the others deserve to know that they will be without a home in a couple of months at best. Perhaps their immediate families know. But people without siblings or other kin, like me and Cookie, will be up shit's creek without a paddle if I do not speak up.

"Listen," I say. "There is a man over there ... do not look. 'Tis a man sitting with The Manager. I have seen him for the past week or so. He is from the corporate office!"

"There's no corporate office," Cookie says.

I explain that Hacienda Mirage is going to be torn down and a monstrous shopping, parking, and condominium complex will be built upon the hallowed ground. The destroyers will tear it all down and probably chip or burn the old, sanctified wood for fuel or backyard BBQs. And Lord only knows what will happen once that blasphemy happens.

"We are all going to be kicked to the curb," I continue. "It will not be my first time homeless, but I know that you, Cookie, will have a hard time and I do not know how you other girls will manage. But I worry about all of you."

"Well, isn't that a whole lot to swallow," Cookie says — her mouth curling into a condescending smirk.

I doubt that any of her lipstick-stained pearly teeth are real.

The other two hens are in various stages of disbelief, shock, or ennui. I cannot remember either of their names. Why should I? The fat one next to me — I call *Butters*— keeps on eating. The skinny one, *Twigs*, fidgets a while and then pulls her walker up to her chair and scoots herself up and across the floor to the exit. They might be sisters. Both are still Independents who have each other, but they are well on their way to becoming part of the Assisted. They pretend that they don't hear me. Or maybe they're as deaf as they claim. Butters always has the same blank expression on her mug like my drunk Uncle Ian used to have on his face before Quinn killed him in Scotland over thirty years ago.

"*I'll* just go over there and ask," Cookie says, running her knobby fingers through her thinning and bleached blond hair as if she were a fashion model. Her fingernails are painted blood red and look like talons.

"Please do not do that," I say, imagining myself stabbing her in the heart.

"I'll just ask politely whether or not the rumor's true," Cookie says, looking at me with a pained expression as if she reads my thoughts.

"'Tis not a rumor. 'Tis a premonition," I declare.

Dr. Cynthia (Cookie) Nussbaum PhD.

A premonition indeed. I simply can't find the words to express how over her I am. I'm generally a very patient woman. I've had to learn to accept average or sub-par individuals like Gavina — otherwise I would have been without a career and wouldn't have a cent to my name. Granted, there are some days when she sits quietly at my table in the dining room. But most other times, she talks about supposedly growing up in some god-forsaken village in Scotland, or her adventures in New York and Los Angeles during the Nineties, or one of her clairvoyant experiences. Admittedly somewhat entertaining if I'm in a rare mood for such gasconading even if it's — let's face it — mostly unbelievable. Sometimes she goes on and on about her nameless special manfriend, whom no one that I know of has ever seen or met. When challenged she says that he's very secretive and she can't give us personal details about him. Just details about their supposed romance. And then there are days of complete gibberish spewing from her dry, chapped lips. I've offered her some elegant lip balm, but she flatly refuses any such niceties on my part.

Right now, I'm trying to eat while having to view this woman who dresses like a bag lady yet carries herself like the Queen of Scotland. The only thing Gavina has in common with Mary Queen of Scots is that they were both born in 1542. If I had my way, I would do her a favor and take scissors to that rat's nest braid of hers just to knock her down a few pegs.

Gavina is the worst of the impoverished studio apartment residents. Most of the Medi-Cal folks are harmless and I get that not everyone can afford to pay for a one-bedroom and private bath. But please. This Gavina chick should be in Assisted, and none of them should be eating with Independents. I say that for her and everyone else's own good. But then again, I'm not managing The

Hacienda. Although things would work better if I did. But I no longer have that kind of energy.

"Nice scarf," I say to her, trying to be friendly by complimenting the thing around her neck instead of reaching over to strangle her with it.

"No need to be sarcastic," she says.

"I wasn't being sarcastic. I was complementing you. The yellow brings out the jaundice in your cheeks."

"Do you think I do not know what jaundice means?" she replies, leaning forward with both hands on the table like she's about to pounce.

Although she was here before me and is perhaps a bit younger in actual years, that's not the point. She acts like she reigns over the whole damn place. But I can assure you Gavina is *not* the Queen Bee of Hacienda Mirage. People stay out of her way and generally humor the poor thing.

With her around I sometimes feel like I'm sixteen-years-old again, having to put up with girls like Judy Johnson when we were both on the Beverly Hills High School newspaper. And just like back then, no one here gives me the respect I deserve. I am after all, Doctor Cynthia (Cookie) Nussbaum PhD, dethroned Hollywood Psychotherapist to the Stars. Having had thirty-plus years in private practice. Over thirty-thousand hours in session. Three hundred plus boxes of Kleenex — mostly soft anti-viral. Proudly having served twice as many total patients as tissue boxes.

I've therapized individuals, couples, families, groups. Celebrities of all shapes and sizes. Athletes, politicians, actors, actresses, models, writers, directors, producers, agents, managers, publicists, and photographers. Trust Fund Babies and self-made icons. There's no end to the variety of the rich and famous I've nourished and mentored. No limit to the range of emotional problems I've treated. Anxiety. Depression. OCD. ADD. BPD. And of course, a bevy of narcissists and their co-dependent partners that would make you lose sleep after being in their invasive presence.

These are the patients who gave me the reputation of *Therapist to the Stars.* I didn't ask for it! And you can bet your bottom dollar I know things about people you admire or idolize or get yourself off to! I can't tell you *who* because of therapist/client privilege but I can assure you that I could put your Facebook and Instagram selfie photos and brags to shame in comparison to *who I know* personally.

And now, here I am. Anonymous. Nearly invisible while living amidst and among aged, average schmos.

Unfortunately, because of one snitch, I lost my license and had to retire because of my allegedly *inappropriate therapeutic interventions.* If I ever run into the patient who reported me to the Board of Behavioral Sciences, I will strangle him — regardless of the consequences. After all, my sexual assignation with him was consensual, no matter what he claimed. And once the gig was up, I went a little downhill and eventually gave in to my need for Independent Living because of what was a low score on instrumental activities of daily life. It's humiliating. I've never gotten a low score on anything. I was valedictorian of my 1960 high school graduating class, received my Master of Psychology degree from Nantucket School of Higher Education in 1970, and passed the State of California LCSW licensing exams after only three tries — on Halloween believe it or not — in 1975.

My doctor said I'd scored low on matters such as paying my bills myself, cleaning my house, cooking, and socializing. Can you imagine the foolishness of making *socializing* a requirement of healthy daily living? And if you must know, they now say that *hoarding* is far more pathological than having a messy house. I don't agree. But then, I don't concur with a lot of diagnoses that were listed in the DSMIII. And don't go lecturing me on the fact that there are a few changes to the disorders that were popular back in my day. I was never a big fan of labels. Yet, living at Hacienda Mirage, I can tell you that this place is like a complete volume of the Diagnostic and Statistical Manual of Mental Disorders. Which is possibly why I love it — and hate it — here.

"The scarf was a gift from my manfriend," Gavina says, deciding not to lunge at me while I pat my lips and carefully place my silverware onto my plate. That's me. Always a well-mannered lady with the tongue of a viper. Need be.

Her Majesty Gavina is churning out her delusions about The Hacienda being torn down. The other women at the table are no longer interested in anything Gavina has to say. They remain nameless to me. One's fat. Another's skinny. Both seem to be hard of hearing. They've either resigned themselves to the Grim Reaper or have reached some sort of nirvana or enlightenment leaving blank expressions on their faces. I have nothing against these women. But for some unknown reason, I don't think they like me. Probably due to whatever their station in life was compared to mine.

Gavina is staring at the new gentleman across the room with one of her piercing eyebeams of which no one would want to be the recipient.

"I'll just to go over there and inquire about this," I say, pushing my chair back with the muted groan that is only possible from a hardwood chair struggling against substandard carpeting. Gavina doesn't want me to take charge, but if it's one thing I can't stand it's being relegated pleb status by a fool who thinks she's royalty.

Elmore Fingerton

Identical over-sized, wooden Windsor chairs surround every table, unless one is pushed aside to make room for a wheelchair housing one of the self-entitled Assisted Living residents. The extra-long, pinch-pleated drapes drag onto the flat sculpted carpet like a mud slide. Dreadful yellowing trans globe chandeliers hang in odd configurations. I'm not going to be able to digest my lunch properly with the décor the way it is. It's time for redecorating. Being put out to pasture is bad enough, but with nothing to do, I tend to obsess about my digestive track deteriorating, my spinal stenosis, and my surly mood making me feel like punching someone — which is a very old and I thought retired impulse. Up until now, I've been way too busy to feel this way, but with a lack of useful work my ego is beyond frayed. Putting a workaholic like me in a place like this — where time stands still — is not good for said-workaholic's physical or mental health. I need to get my hands on some reupholstering fabric or wool carpet samples before *I go nuts* with nothing to redecorate. And you don't want to see me nuts — as the old British prince might say as he dismissed his valet from helping him on with his dress pants.

The man across from me at my table is looking down at an enormous Rueben my ego is suffering something awful. No one else is in the other two chairs. I'm feeling quite isolated as I jot some notes in my journal. Perhaps it's a bit premature since I've only been here a few weeks, but I can't help but ask my shy and silent lunch companion about redoing the place. They call him The Manager. I'm not sure the manager of what.

"So, I was wondering ... don't you agree that we're in need here of some upgrades? Some professional interior design?"

This heavy-set old gentleman may have worked his way up in the elder living world from emptying bed pans and reassembling walkers to the exalted position of The Manager. He's probably been in service most of his life and I can certainly respect that. I think of myself in that way, although making living space come alive is not quite the same as helping the elderly feel like they're among the living.

Even if he was younger, he is totally not my type. Not because of his physique but because of his manner, which is that of a bewildered, ridiculed fop from a Nineteenth Century romance novel. I prefer a more manly man, regardless of age. I pride myself in maintaining a decent, age-appropriate shape even though I'm nowhere near where I used to be when I was a dashing young East Coast Queer, or a debonair—middle-aged Californian.

I don't like feeling like such a bitch today. It must be something in the air. Or in the food. Or within the tacky beaverboard walls.

"Well, Sir," The Manager responds. "Go on then."

"Please call me Elmore," I say to the top of his head, while he slices his sandwich, spreads an inappropriate and unnecessary amount of butter, and winces as if I'm annoying him. He has a disheveled Einstein look about him, grey hair venturing wherever it chooses as he moves his head back and forth in disapproval. The man is much too old to really be managing the place if you ask me. Something is off kilter here.

"I've already priced the dining room upgrades," I say. I inform him about my having been a very well-known interior designer in my day and still having a lot of contacts in the biz. Don't get me wrong. Being here is a godsend since I can certainly use some assistance with things like cooking meals and cleaning house. I figure I can practice my craft and also partake of a touch of help in daily living, while I get some stimulation by fixing the place up. Right now, my only stressor is not having any stressors if you get my drift. I don't miss Nervous Nellie clients who harangued me with complaints about the wrong color legs on a wingback chair or those who tried to haggle prices down. But I do miss the good clients with challenging decorating needs.

"I can get it for you wholesale," I continue. "Remember that show? Of course, you do. It was Streisand's debut at around nineteen. I'm not suggesting that I did any design for her. And even if I did, I'd have to keep it strictly confidential."

"Who's Streisland?" The Manager asks.

"Streis-and. No L and no extraneous A in Barbra."

"Oh," he says shyly, as if he has just awoken from a dream. "Funny Girl."

We share a laugh, and that — along with thoughts of Babs singing *people who need people* — seems to lighten my mood. Our giggling seems to draw one of the inmates across the room over to our table. I know I shouldn't call them inmates because now I'm one of them, but I'm not a man who always says or does what he's supposed to. This is a rather elegant looking woman weaving her way past the other lunch tables. She has carefully styled silver hair framing her once-pretty face. Her Ralph Lauren satin straight-leg slacks are well worn, having been sat in beyond their intended lifespan. There are impenetrable creases across her lap. And her matching beige blouse hangs in places that once held that old garment up, up. Up.

"Excuse-moi," she purrs, while looking at me and then taking her time to address The Manager. "We were wondering not only who the new gentleman here is, but what his intentions are for our home."

"How you feeling today, Cookie?" The Manager asks her, as she eyeballs him under her manicured eyebrows with suspicion or perhaps plan old nosiness.

"I am feeling quite chipper. Any time I can catch crazy Ms. Gavina in one of her lies, it's a good day."

"I'm sorry?" The Manager says, scratching his head, seeming unable to digest what this woman is saying.

"I'm Elmore. New resident," I say, carefully standing and reaching out my hand. It takes me a while to do those two things in concert nowadays. "Pleased to meet you, Cookie."

"I hate this first name thing. I wish you would call me Doctor Nussbaum," she says.

"You're not *the* Doctor Cookie Nussbaum are you?" I ask.

"Yup." Cookie glows in the light of recognition. I know her type.

"Therapist to the Stars! We shared a couple famous clients when I was redecorating for them. I'm not supposed to know, and you're not supposed to say. But they bragged about you being their therapist. Said you were the best. Edgy. Direct. Hard Core. Some of the words they used to describe you. Did I say *edgy*?"

"Why thank you, Elmore. That's very kind. You'll have to give me their names. Perhaps this evening after dinner."

"Sounds good. I don't suppose they would mind. Not sure. Let me think about it."

"I love to hear about old patients of mine. I'm hoping to find one in particular who did me wrong."

"*I've* been done wrong," The Manager mumbles.

"Are there plans to tear down the place?" Cookie asks.

"Huh? What?" The Manager stammers. "No. No. No. Can't be. This is our home!"

"There just might be a little redecorating however," I say, as if the decision has already been made.

Chapter Two

Quinn Adamsdaur

The bleak Hacienda Mirage Garden gives me the creeps what with its patches of lemon grass and expanse of endless gravel. But I prefer to meet Gavina outside instead of inside. I can't stand going into the place. It smells like a mixture of burrito farts, sour Elsy Louder perfume, black mold, and Bengay. I'm going to have to add a budget item — called either *fumigation* or *smudging* — to the production costs before we begin filming.

There's a stray gray and white cat purring next to my feet and staring up at me — judging me and begging for food that I don't have. Don't you just hate hangers-on? Careful not to dirty my prize Nike Air Flight Huaraches, I kick the pest away. And when I do, it feels like slivers from the drab wooden bench stab me. The last thing I need is to get splinters in my ass.

This film I'm gonna do is important and will go down as a boon to the dying culture of great filmmaking instead of adding to the pablum and pulp that's being shoved down the throats of the unsophisticated public nowadays. The world needs another Quinn Adamsdaur motion picture and I am determined to make inroads today even though you can sneer at me for being a little hung over. Like you've never had too much to drink or stopped off for a bump on your way to visiting a sick or old — or old *and* sick — relative or friend.

I'm visiting the ridiculous Gavina, waiting for her to make her entrance. In the meantime, I want to check out the grounds to make sure there will be room for all the buses, trailers, production gear and food trucks. Anyway, Gavina is calmer in the open air than she would be in her room. Excuse me. I should say her *studio apartment.* The one she's convinced that I've helped pay for over the past decade. As if.

Meeting this way has me waiting for her to arrive *after* I do, so she feels important. Let her have it. Truth be known, it's a power thing I've employed myself on occasion, although it's a ploy that has less and less clout with all the wrongly enabled millennials in charge of too many things these days.

I've been visiting Gavina every so often for the past ten years or so as she used to unintentionally inspire me from time to time with ideas that led to creative breakthroughs. And the fact that *Scottish Mistress* took Sundance by storm back in the day secures her with a special place in my heart. What I mean by *a special place* is — that although the bat-shit-crazy bitch has been kinda like my muse — she *did* try to kill me when we were both in our thirties.

Gavina and I grew up in Scotland and after her Uncle Ian committed suicide, she made up this thing in her mind that I *killed* the guy and ran off to America without her and with the money he left *me* — not *her*. No Comment! She also had a bizarre belief that I was her boyfriend! Which is completely off the rails. She was a mess as a teenager and never looked any better when she tracked me down in L.A. with jiggers of poisoned Vodka that knocked me out but obviously did not snuff me out. But it did turn out to make for a great film. Eventually we became what *she* likes to think of as friends. And as I said, she can be amusing and comes up with nutty ideas that are often food for thought. A handy DVD of *Scottish Mistress* is waiting for you to dig it up somewhere if you're interested in that whole story.

I'm hoping for some possible input from her on this latest project, *The Home*, a slasher being written and directed by yours truly, about a murder in a surreal nursing home. I want to use the Hacienda Mirage dining room for a couple of months as a location. It's perfectly spacious and out-of-date. Plus, it has an eerie Hitchcock Psycho vibe to it that has made it semi-infamous. My main concern right now is getting approval from the manager of the place to let me film here. Maybe Gavina can help in some way. I'm not sure. You can't ever know with people. I seldom even know what I can count on even from my own self.

Like now. Here she is, stepping up to me and already talking crazy. I'd expect myself to maybe be a little excited, but I feel instantly annoyed. I guess I'm just an eternal optimist destined to be disappointed by the walking dead that inhabit the earth.

"That man is here. He was at lunch," Gavina says, before she even sits on the bench.

"What man?" I ask, scooting over to make plenty of room between us.

"Why are you moving away from me?" I imagine she learned somewhere — in one of the zillion books she's read — that it's cute to extend her lower lip like a pouty child. The bitch reads so much she thinks some of the stories are about her. Cleopatra: look out.

"Um. I like to see you when we talk," I say.

"Okay. I guess I get that. I sure like to look at you, too. You get more and more handsome every time you are here."

"Thank *you*."

"Thank you, yourself. Notice anything about my outfit?" she asks – again with the coy downward glance.

"You look very pretty," I say, already wishing I was somewhere else. But where?

"The scarf, you scoundrel. The yellow scarf."

"Wasn't that the name of a weird Polish movie about an alcoholic?"

"I do not know, Darling. But you gave me this shawl a while ago."

"Oh, of course. It looks good on you."

I don't remember ever gifting her a stupid scarf, but if I had, it would have been something that looked a whole lot better than the rag she has spun around her neck.

"Well, that man was at lunch."

"What man?" I ask again.

"The pretentious eejit from the corporate office who wants to tear the place down."

"I don't know anything about that. I need to shoot a movie here. They can't tear the place down. I haven't even approached anyone about shooting. And anyway, it would only be the dining room and only for a couple of months."

"Do not lie to me, Darling. What are you really up to?"

Every time Gavina calls me *Darling,* I just want to puke. I have PTSD from the time in that sleezy Los Angeles hotel in Koreatown in the Nineties, where she tricked me into meeting her only to find out that she wanted to murder my ass.

"You never told me you were going to make a movie right here," she continues. "I knew you were up to something. Are you in co-hoots with that guy in the white shirt?"

"No, Gavina. But I only plan shooting for a few months and only in the dining room. And actually ... I want to talk to you about some ideas for the final script."

"Do you have to smoke?" she says, as I light another cigarette.

"Don't get all up in my face about me smoking. I'm outside. Get over yourself." Cigarettes never killed anyone. That whole lung cancer shit is bull. And anyway, it's a free country. I can do whatever-the-fuck I want. It calms my nerves and improves my creative process.

"Where will I live when they tear the place down?" she asks, as if to end the no-smoking discussion with what's in all probability a fake coughing spell.

"Tell you what ... I'll talk to management about that when I contract for the location."

"I think it is time for me to live with you after they tear down Hacienda Mirage, Darling."

I'm up — standing and flinching back away from her, nearly tripping over myself into the weeds.

"Live with me?"

Rudy Schneider

The little kitty purrs as it rubs my leg when I stop at the main entrance of the Hacienda. I have an uneaten piece of power bar in my pocket which I offer her along with a good petting. Hopefully cats like to have a shot of mid-day plant protein.

I'll do my thing with Cookie first, while my man Elmore's taking his daily after-lunch nap. Elmore's schedules are *unfuckwithable,* so it's a safe bet that he'll be in bed resting while I'm in bed doing Cookie — *not* resting. There're pluses and negatives for good-old Cookie and Elmore both now living in the same old folks' home. On the good side, it's a two-fer-one drive and easy stopover from Los Angeles to San Luis Obispo. It saves on gas. And it lets me squeeze in a visit to the first and original Obie's Gym, where I like to pump up before going to see them. And I can crash for one cheap, inexpensive overnight at the handy ResTight Motel before heading back home to L.A. Win Win. My favorite thing. Advantages to all parties evolved. Like when your favorite restaurant is right next door to your laundromat, so they both get more business when you've got dirty clothes or feel like an authentic burrito.

Also, by visiting Hacienda Mirage, I can practice my strategical moves and acting skills. I gotta be careful not to let either of 'em see me sneaking from one of their apartments to the other. And I can try acting out different personages while I'm at it. Today I'm wearing a Dodgers cap and big sunglasses so I'm unreckonable. Don't get me wrong. I think that Cookie and Elmore are both basically really good people — who I didn't mind doing the nasty with years ago when they were not elderly and slow. But let's face it, there's a bigger difference in ages now, what with me only being fifty and them pushing eighty.

Both of 'em don't expect that much from me anymore, so most of the time it's sweet. If you get my drifts. They basically want the same things now. A back massage. A few hugs and kisses. Maybe a lap dance once in a while. In return, Cookie provides enough bank for some of my rent. And Elmore gives me enough for car insurance. It's a great way to fill in the rest of my income from personal training gigs, while continuing my twenty-year-watering-of-the-dog-shit-garden that's been my acting career. If only Hollywood would realize I'm not just a good-looking mug and well-built physicality. I have acting chops that haven't been given a chance to dig their teeth into and show their bite. Come see. Come saw. If you don't mind my French.

When I get to her apartment at The Hacienda, Cookie snaps at me with, "It took you long enough to get here." Misfortunately she immediately recognizes me in the hat and glasses. Sometimes things start out that way with her. She doesn't like to be kept waiting and I'm admittingly a few minutes late because I decided to squeeze in a few more reps on arms at Obie's since Cookie and Elmore both like my guns. A lot.

Luckily, as soon as I open my shirt, Cookie mellows out like an organtic fruit smoothie. She's wearing something only right for a Victor's Secret Model — not someone her age — but ya gotta admire the woman's spunk.

"I guess you're worth the wait," she says. "You're lookin' good, Rudy."

"Aim to please," I say, slowly removing my shirt over one pumped-up-and-ripped shoulder at a time. My stripping days are over, but I sure do miss it. It's a different feeling doin' it for one person alone verse doin' it in front of a howlin', appreciatin'audience with cash in hand when the adrenalines are pumping and pumping, and you feel like you could go on all night and don't even need drugs or alcohol. Of course, I'm getting older and beginning to wonder if I need to do some re-evaluation of my limits and parameters.

"Can we talk for a minute?" Cookie asks.

"Of course, Love. We can do whatever you want."

"Remember back in the day when we stopped all the talking and communicated how much we liked each other without words?"

"I'll never forget," I say, as I sit beside her on the bed and lightly massage her spongy neck and back — the fabric of her frilly nightie bunching between my fingers, wishing she felt more solid. More trim and athletic? It looks like we're maybe gonna have a remembering for a while like she likes to do by conversating about the good old days.

We used to make out on the couch in her office, after some of my therapy sessions back when I was degenerating myself for being Bi. She said that she didn't care if I was fucking men, other women, or my pet iguana. Which I was not! I didn't believe she didn't want me to herself and that still makes me nervous because she was an important person in my life. Still is. Thanks to her I was able to swallow my sexual orientational urges and be accepting of myself for being who I am. And don't think it's just for the money now. Although I've never done much stuff like this without some sort of cash numberation.

Now, if Cookie found out about Elmore, she might cut me off. She might be thinkin' we have some sort of love relationship. She sure isn't getting any lovin' from anyone but me. Wish she would have a real boyfriend to put her in a better mood. Even though I'd have to really hustle to make enough dough to make all my ends meet if I had to do it all on my own — like my father used to say I could never do since I was such a dope.

"I'm a little worried," Cookie says.

"About what, Baby?"

She loves when I call her that. Always has. It's my *cha-ching* word. Like when a cash register goes *cha-ching* when you put money in it or when money comes out of it. Ya know.

"There's a rumor going round that Hacienda Mirage is being sold and torn down," she says. "Now don't get me wrong. I heard it from crazy Gavina, but nevertheless, it's gotten me worried. Maybe it's time I got out of here and we got our own place. Surely, we can be together by now. No one is interested in our story anymore."

Well, there is no story. There was no scandal. But she sometimes does have illusional thoughts about us having a romantic relationship that was in the tabloids. I was for sure not famous enough for anyone to care who I slept with twenty or thirty years ago. And Cookie was well-known with only a small group of Hollywood types before someone reported her for being a no-good therapist.

When she says that we ought to move in together, I panic. I stop stroking her hair, jump up from the bed, and step back like I'd been stung by a bumbling bee.

"A place of our own?" I repeat. And then to buy some time, "You heard this thing about a tear-down from that crazy Gavina woman you talk about so much?"

"I don't talk about her *that much*, Rudy."

"I didn't mean it that way. I thought you liked it here."

"Rudy, my love ... I hate it here."

"You need a lot of care, Baby. You need to be in a place where they can take care of you. I can't."

"You can't? Or you won't?"

"I can't."

"If we had gotten married long ago you would have *had* to take care of me."

She goes on and on, then asking that if I don't take care of her now, how do I expect her to take care of *me*?

"Let me check into the rumor," I say. "I'll talk to the manager and find out what's really going on. We'll work it all out. I promise."

That's me being quick on my feet. I learnt that in boxing class years ago and from watching old Cassius Clay film clips of him dancing like a butterfly and stingin' like a bee.

By the time my shirt's off, and I'm standing in front of her for one of her favorite lap dances, she has forgotten about the fantasy of our being some sort of lovers living together. She's sitting on the bed and leaning forward with her head on my chest and her sweet, age-spotted hands exploring my body. It tickles more than anything else.

Almost finishing my striping and gyrating, Cookie's eyelids close and I help her lay down and fall fast asleep. I leave a note telling her that I'll find out about the tear-down, etc. and get back to her. Signed *Love ya, Baby.*

I step out into the hall and quietly close her door, careful not to bring any unwanted detention my way by rattling the rafters.

And with Cookie off to dreamland, I head to Elmore's apartment at the end corner of the other side of the rest home. I'm pretending that I'm a building inspector of some type and walk down the halls with the confidence of someone who inspects buildings — acting like I'm inspecting this and inspecting that with a stern, serious building inspector type look on my face.

Elmore — that sweet, old, once-pretty man — is about as goofy as Cookie. He's suffering from the hope or maybe the belief that he's been admitted to Hacienda Mirage to redecorate the place top to bottom. The guy needs to be here for the Independent thing because of his condition, but there's been no agreement to put him to work redecorating. I know because I helped get him accepted when it became crystal-like clear that it wouldn't be long before he won't be able to make big decisions himself. I even had a lawyer, who I was servicing, draw up a Power of an Attorney's paper that said I am in charge. That part was at Elmore's insisting. There's no one else in Elmore's life that looks out after him the way I do. He's a good guy. He's sure done a lot for me. He was the one who got me some auditions by strong-arming one of his interior design clients who was a commercial casting gal way back when. She got me the Fiddle Faddle Chocolate Bits spots. Remember my famous '*Look Good and Eat Bits*' tag line? It got me a few other commercials.

When Elmore opens his door, I rush in so we can quickly close and lock it. If anyone found out that there was what Elmore calls '*hanky-panky*' going on, who knows what they'd do? And it's fun anyway to be bad boys together and break the rules. Reminds us of the days when Elmore used to parade me around to gay clubs showing me off. It feels now like a real transgressioning.

"The poor old folks are left to shrivel up and rot here without even a private smooch," Elmore says. "If it wasn't for you, Rudy ... I would join them in the endless loss of all the joys of youth."

I wrap my arms around the old man and kiss him on the lips.

"Don't talk that way. You've got a lot of life left into you, my friend ..."

"None of this for none of them," Elmore says, after he returns the kiss and hug. Then we stand that way for a while until I help him sit and then lay on the bed just like I ended up doin' with Cookie. He's dressed in a white shirt and jeans, rolled up at the ankles like James Dean. Without shoes or socks it's easy to pull off his pants and then my own.

"I had lunch with the man they call The Manager," Elmore says, as he watches me climb onto the bed and lay next to him. "He didn't seem all that interested in hearing my ideas for the redecorating. I'm not sure he'd appreciate a fine linen drape or plush carpeting which—come to think of it—wouldn't work anyway. The old commercial carpet they have on the floor should be replaced with birch planks so the wheelchairs can glide instead of struggle. Shouldn't life be made easier for these folks? I know that when I end up in a chair, I want it to float across the floor like I'm in the Rose Parade."

"You are a parade float in and among yourself," I say.

"Are you listening to me? I was talking about the redo of the dining room."

"I'm listenin', but I'm also mostly interested in how you're feelin' and if you're getting what you need here."

"What I need is to be fifty again, like you. So you can like me."

"Elmore. I like you. I've always liked you."

"One of the dames here interrupted my breakfast asking about Hacienda Mirage being demolished instead of redecorated."

"Really?"

This rumor is taking hold and catching on. But I can't let on that I've already heard it. Right? Cause, you remember, I can't let on that Cookie told me the same thing. So I say to myself in my own mind, *'Don't act like you already heard this, Mister. Cause there's no way you could know about this rumor otherwise Elmore might find out that you've been with Cookie who he may or may not even know.'*

"I doubt that there's going to be any tear-down," I continue, as I massage Elmore's frail body. I'm a licensed masseur BTW. Esalen Massage School 1995 and Western Horizon's physical therapy school dropout.

"That feels nice," Elmore says. I check his pulse and breathing to make sure he's just fallen into a nap and nothing more serious.

Chapter Three

Quinn

As I think I maybe said a little earlier — unless it's a strategic power play on my part — I hate waiting for anyone. Especially in tight quarters with low ceilings that cramp my style. But since I have to do everything myself for this film, here I sit — outside the office of Kevin Vernkowsky, manager of The Hacienda Hell Home — while eating the disgusting pastrami, cheese, and avocado sandwich that Gavina gave me. God only knows when or where she got this thing. Probably lifted it from lunch when one of the shower-capped servers turned their head away from the chow line. The buttons on my shirt are screaming and ready to pop as I swallow. At sixty-five years of age, I've seen better days before my once-toned, athletic body went into hiding behind a layer of too many burgers, fries, and chocolate sundaes. Fuck me if I ever end up in a place like this. I'd rather die on the side of a road, under a freeway overpass or beneath the Santa Monica Pier.

This manager clown has to let me shoot the dining scenes here. Why wouldn't he? People like him and the old geriatrics who live here love to be part of anything Hollywood. Their lives are winding down and not exciting enough to take them beyond mere day-by-day survival. This should be easy. I'm sure the guy's a push-over.

Since I abhor wasting time, I'm on my phone watching a series of movie clips saved for inspiration to help find ideas to polish up my script. It's my firm — or could be naïve — belief that my muse or more likely *my nemesis* Gavina will do or say something to trigger a revelation in my still fertile but unfunded screenwriter/director's mind.

Okay. Here goes. If you *must* know the truth, I haven't had an actual movie deal in the past decade, and the prospects are razor thin for my newest attempt which — I don't remember if I said — is both being written and will be directed by me. I don't actually have even one name seriously attached to this project or any other, after being turned down and literally laughed at by the agents and managers of stars such as Vanessa Smith and Felicia Stropp, even though I knew them personally from directing *Scottish Mistress*. Women like those two divas seem to relish holding a grudge.

Thing is, I can still be quite commanding and influential. When I want something, I've been known to get it. That's how I managed to conquer the film business during the 1990's before the drugs, alcohol, and various STDs got the best of me. True confessions. Happy now?

When the door to the general manager's office opens, a buff fellow greets me with a self-important smirk that makes it impossible to finish the sandwich that I wrap and toss into the trash can.

"Please come right on in, Mr. Adamsdaur," Kevin Vernkowsky says, in what sounds to me like a forced deep tone of voice. He can't be more than fifty, and I think I'm right in my plan to cast an egotistically aerobicized next-door-neighbor type like him for the role of the manager/slasher of the old folks' home in my film.

Vernkowsky's office is not much larger than the waiting room. He squeezes himself behind his desk and slips into the chair. There are two visitor seats facing the desk and a tiny bookcase against one wall. I select the chair nearest the other wall to his right and fold my hands in my lap like I used to do when beginning one of my pitches to the executives at the big movie studios. Positioning myself like this gives me the deceptive look of a hat-in-hands type of guy even though I'm nothing of the sort. Once I get going, I've been known to take the room by surprise with my commanding presence. Boom.

"What's the sign mean?" I ask, trying to break the ice, motioning to the wood carving on the desk.

Don't stop growing just because you're no longer a tree.

"I'm not too sure. My stepfather told me that I'd understand it when it was time. He's a bit of a philosopher of life."

"Whatever."

"Anyway, thank you for finally coming in. I hope we can iron this out," Vernkowsky says.

Having no idea what the man is talking about because I never said I was there to ask about using the dining room as a location — but in the spirit of seal-the-deal negotiating, I say, "*Work* it out. I think you mean."

"Iron. Work. Whatever. In any case, your portion of Gavina McVey's monthly fee has not been paid for months now, and we can't overlook it any longer. Medi-Cal only covers so much. And it's fixed. Gavina's shortfall has been paid for years until now and we hope you haven't run into a problem."

"I have no idea, Sir. I haven't paid Gavina's way since she got in here. That's not why I'm here."

"Then who's been making those payments?"

“Fuck if I know.”

“Really? That’s odd. Well then ... why else have you come to see me?”

Vernkowsky sports one of those current white-sidewall haircuts with an up crop on top that he sometimes probably wears in a fucking manbun. Today it’s casually flopping from side to side belying his formal manner. As the manager of a nursing home, he’s most likely used to speaking slowly, carefully, and a bit too loud.

“There’s a couple of things I want to discuss,” I say, bouncing my folded hands in my lap to punctuate my words.

“Shoot.”

“Gavina heard a rumor that Hacienda Mirage is going to be demolished. Says you told her at lunch that she had to find another place to live.”

I unfold my hands and lean forward in the chair, resting my fingers on the desk. It’s a slight invasion of his space and the right move for establishing the hierarchy between us. The clown doesn’t flinch.

“First of all, Sir ... I *never* eat my meals with our residents. Imagine how many times I would be interrupted with one concern or another.”

I lean back.

“Additionally,” Vernkowsky continues, “We are certainly not going to put anyone out on the street regardless of what anyone says.”

“Okay. Good. I will tell Gavina that.”

"Some of the folks here are more Independent than others. We've always let everyone dine together even if they live in separate wings. A few have what you or I might consider strange beliefs or misconceptions. Aches and pains. It's part of growing old. It could happen to any of us someday."

I'm grateful that I've been put in the *someday* category — even though I'm close to twenty years older than Vernkowsky.

"I would like to use your dining room as a location set for some scenes in one of my forthcoming motion pictures, and I came to ask you how to go about making that happen."

"That can't happen."

"I can pay handsomely."

"You can't even pay your share of Gavina McVey's keep."

"I'll try to get that all straightened out."

"I hope so."

"You're saying no to the location shoot?"

"Yes. I mean yes ... I'm saying *no*."

"But I haven't even made you an offer."

The guy is annoyingly lining up his pens and pencils on his desk like they're surgical tools and he's about to operate. The tension between us is so deprecating it's beginning to deaden the leaves of the already limp Ficus plant in the corner. It's an atmosphere that I've experienced far too many times in the past decade. The rejection digs at my skin like termites. I feel my rage itching to be released whereas I admit it's usually controlled with marijuana, cocaine, vodka, Xanax, and lots of sex with lots of girls — whether they truly agree to it or not. This Vernkowsky character is no different than all those high-ups that have taken charge of the studios and networks. He's just as big an asshole as all the super cool, stuck up, full-of-themselves bastards who have rejected me.

"Please, Sir. There's nothing to offer or discuss. This is an Independent and Assisted-Living home. Our residents cannot be uprooted."

"So you're only concerned with Gavina's overdue bill."

"That is a very crass way to put it."

"You think you're pretty important, don't you?" I ask. I can feel my mouth going dry.

"Not at all. Not one of my weaknesses actually."

"Well, who else can I talk to who might have real authority in this god forsaken pokey?"

I find myself standing as I speak, just as I did against my lawyer's advice in the stuffy courtroom when facing off with the young prosecuting attorney in the 1990's civil suit against me — the air hot and muggy and this guy ranting on and on about what a schmuck I am — defaming me and disgracing my name.

"I'm the manager of The Hacienda. The buck stops here," Vernkowsky says, running his fingers through the full, thick portion of his floppy, young mop of hair. It seems like the walls are closing in and I'm about to be crushed. The piercing sound of his voice is penetrating my eardrums.

"And like I said, no need for you to be crass."

"You want to see crass? How about this?"

When my fist decides to make contact with Vernkowsky's nose, there's a slight squishing sound as he slides below the desk, his head hitting the chair on the way down.

Rudy

I hope that the manager will put the tear-down rumor to sleep. I sure hope it's not true. The place is perfect for Cookie and Elmore, and I need to know they're taken care of properly. I don't wanna to have to deal with a big change. I've just gotten used to things being practicable and could use some stableness instead of constant change in my life.

The door to the office is open wide, so I slowly step into the little room imagining that I'm walking on hot coals like a swami in one of those fake old flicks from India. I sometimes do this to play out a role that I come up with in my mind and then act it out in real life. Exorcising my actor chops like I said before when I was being a building inspector before I became this hot-coals swami.

There's a groaning sound and a hand appears from under the desk followed by an arm and then the head of a man — maybe a little younger than me — with a very cool haircut but a bloody face. And I gotta say — electrical blue eyes that snap me wide awake like as if I was not totally awake before. Sparks go flying as they say.

"Oh my God," I cry. And then embarrassed by my girlish shrieking, I check myself and dart around the desk to help the hot guy up onto the desk chair. I'm weirdly sucking in air like I'm the one who's injured.

"I think he broke my nose."

"Oh, shit. That's terrible. Let me take a look. Try not to move your face. Where can we get some ice?"

"Dial O on my desk phone."

I've seen my share of broken bones. I'm always freaked out by the idea of bones cracking. Slips and falls of people in the gym. Not to mention the busted wrists after walls are punched or ankles crumpled when a husband or wife has gotten ragey after walking in on me and their cheating spouse.

After calling for ice packs of which there are plenty in a place like this I figure, I sit on the desk facing the injured man and say, "Just try to not move around too much and we'll get you to a doctor."

"We have a nurse on site in Assisted Living," he says, resting his head forward on his hands folded on the desk. He's inches from my thigh.

I hit the button on his desk phone, and after talking to the nice lady again about what I've found, I turn to Kevin Vernkowsky and quietly say, "Okay. No more talking. Just try to relax, there's ice coming and a wheelchair to get you to the infirmary or whatever you call it here. No more talking. Can you *write* answers to a couple questions? Like, who hit you?"

Quinn Adamsdaur.

"A resident?"

Visitor. Gavina McVey's friend.

I lightly massage Kevin's burly back. The muscles in his shoulders feel well-pumped through his shirt.

"Okay. That's enough," I say. "I'm sure we can find this guy and figure this out. Right now, here comes the wheelchair. Just keep breathing in and out through your mouth."

Who are you? Why are you here?

"I'm visiting Elmore Fingerton and dropped by to ask you a couple questions."

Go ahead.

"All that can wait. I'll ask around and find Gavina's friend. I've got time. I'm staying in town."

Just go grab dinner and forget about it. I'm alright.

"I won't forget about it, but where should I have dinner in town?"

It's kinda weird that we're kinda having a casual conversing while all this is going on.

"Padre's Bar & Grill," he says out loud suddenly able to speak, as a tall blond person in professioning medical scrubs rushes in. The nurse can't fit between me and Kevin, so I lift my legs and spin around like a top to get out of the way. It's sort of fun to do but I know I shouldn't go 'round again under the circrumtrances. The stern look on the nurse's face convinces me that I should be serious. But Kevin watches me like he knows that I want to spin. A hint of a smile hides under his red cheeks.

"You guys go ahead and take care of Kevin," I say. "I'm gonna find the guy who did this."

I take off and then realize when I dart into the dining hall that not only have I called the manager by his first name but I've left my hat and dark glasses in his office in my hurry to capture the mugger. 'Dumb,' I say to myself. But then since I'm tryin' not to downrate myself these days since I'm tired of feeling like I've done something wrong when it's probably no big deal, so I shake it off and go on ahead on my mission.

There're a bunch of tables and chairs spaced all around. Most of the residents are here enjoying — or if not enjoying, at least eating up — their dinner. When I call out "Gavina McVey," all eyes pivitate toward me. "I'm looking for Gavina McVey."

Three people immediately stand up. The first must be Gavina — a super plain woman who looks more homeless than resident. And then Elmore and Cookie. A little man with a friendly face who's probably staff, stops cleaning up a broken plate by the fireplace and leans on his broom. Everyone else stays seated. Some continue eating. But most of the residents— happily watch the scene that's about to unroll, as they probably haven't been to a good show in years.

Gavina

A stunning young man interrupts our dinner and calls out my name. At first I think it is Quinn, but he had already run off to figure out how to make our living together finally work. He was overly excited when I suggested it. He repeated the idea. 'Live with me!'

But now, when I instinctively stand at the sound of my name echoing through the dining hall — hoping it is not the Lord calling me home

— I see that it is not Quinn at all, but a strikingly handsome man with olive skin and eyes as black as onyx. He stands like an Aztec Warrior frantically calling his beloved from the other side of a rushing river. And the name he speaks is my own. Thank you very much.

I have no idea why Cookie and the fancy man who is having dinner at the table with The Manager also stand up at the sound of my name. But before you know it, the corporate spy man and Cookie are both walking toward my soon-to-be lover. They make no polite effort to lower their voices and I simply stand my ground, listen, and wait.

The old, paneled windows shimmy, blink and chuckle while orchestrating the scene, amused by what is taking place and acting like they had nothing to do with it. The drapery undulates like waves of the ocean. The floor quivers.

"What do you want with Gavina, for God's sake," Cookie shouts, as if she knows the beautiful intruder. The way she is acting you would think he had just shouted a horrible profanity instead of crying out for his sweetheart. He is ignoring her and looking at me. Thank you very much. That certainly is getting her goat.

"Who's Gavina?" the fancy man asks, also seeming familiar with the paladin looking for me. Now that he is up and around — instead of sitting at a table eating — the corporate chap looks rather cute for an elderly person. He has the kind of mischievous grin that always tickles my fancy. So, if you are thinking *the fancy man is tickling her fancy* then you are correct. If you are *not* thinking that, I have probably over-estimated how clever you are, although I am not sure it really matters.

"Do you two know each other?" the tall dark young stranger asks.

"I just met Elmore today at lunch," Cookie says.

"Do *you two* know each other, Rudy?" the fancy man — evidently named Elmore — asks the gorgeous man — evidently named Rudy. Do you not just love how people seem to fit their given names? Except for those like Engelbert Humperdink or Puff Daddy. I surely have grown into Gavina, which means *white hawk* in case you did not know. A symbol of peace and harmony. Other worldly do you not think? I do not know who named me that. My mother never paid even enough attention from the day I was born to select a proper name. She might have called me Mistake or Curse. I wager a nice nurse at the hospital picked my name.

So the three of them stand here. Everybody knows everybody. They know one another. And once that becomes clear, Rudy, Cookie and Elmore just freeze in place, ready to either slap each other silly or give a hug.

"Look, we can sussex this out later. Right now, I have to find the man who was visiting Gavina," Rudy says, as he looks across the room and sees me standing there like a damsel awaiting her prince. I thought Quinn was magical, but *this guy Rudy* gives *braw* new meaning — even if his English could be improved.

I am destined to be his prize.

Standing with a bit of a sway and my most demure presence, I watch him approach with the other two trailing behind like mad dogs fighting over a bone. Rudy is flustered and in a hurry. And to prove that we are soulmates, I simply answer his query before he says anything more.

"My manfriend left earlier today. The last I saw him he was on his way to meet The Manager to discuss the film shoot and the demolition, which Mister Elmore here knows all about. I am sure. The Manager is right over there at the table near the grand antique inglenook. Go ask him about it. And just ignore whatever the big mouth fireplace has to say."

"That's not Kevin Vernkowsky," Rudy says, as The Manager waves at them.

"Gavina, enough already," Cookie shouts. She is upset about something deep from within her soul. It is not about me. She has the expression of an unloved girl who has caught a lover cheating on her. Or the look I sometimes see in the mirror, of a girl abandoned or betrayed by her own mother.

She continues ranting.

"Everyone in this place knows that the poor sap that we all call The Manager is not the manager at all. He is just a very kind and sweet dementia patient who loves believing that he still runs the place."

Cookie Nussbaum is jealous that she is not the center of attention and is trying to deflect Rudy's focus on me.

"We shall just see about that!" I say, hoping to show Rudy that I am a powerful woman — someone to be reckoned with.

"Wait," Rudy tries, as he follows me. "Where did your friend go?"

We are now all at The Manager's table. He is still seated and looking terrified as if we are killer bees about to swarm and sting-ravage him.

"Did my friend come to visit you or not?" I ask him, hands on my womanly hips to show this motley crew that I mean business.

"Good day, Gavina. 'Tis Gavina, right?" The Manager says.

“Yes. As you very well know,” I say.

“And welcome back, Sir.” The Manager continues. “Hello, M’am. How are you feeling today?”

“Not now,” Cookie snaps. “I’ve grown very tired of supporting you in your delusions. Until just this moment I thought it was harmless and none of my business.”

Rudy interrupts, saying, “Her friend attacked Kevin Vernkowsky and ran off. I think he has some explaining to do,” Rudy says. He holds his head high — fitting for the fierce protector he is.

“So this is not the manager of the place,” Elmore says, motioning to The Manager, who now seems to be crying.

“Oh, don’t cry,” I say.

I go over to The Manager and put my arm around him. He has always been extra nice to me. Not everyone is. As far as I am concerned if he or I occasionally think he is The Manager, so be it. If I need to iron out any administrative issues, I go see Kevin Vernkowsky, who is also very nice to me. You see, we are all old, some more than others. But we mean no harm. Well, I doubt that Rudy or The Manager means anyone harm. I am not sure of Cookie or this Elmore character. And let us face it, I myself have been known to harbor a murderous streak when especially frustrated, disrespected or crossed.

Cookie

I’m just not having it. This Elmore guy is looking at Rudy with such lust that it makes me want to puke. I’ve always said — trite as it sounds for an educated person like myself — that a leopard can’t change its spots. Who did I think I was kidding? I helped Rudy accept his bisexuality and I naively thought that he would be faithful. Or that at least we had something special. What's wrong with me? Does growing old make one more gullible instead of wiser?

I'm paying for sex. I've not fully realized it. Well not really *sex* at my age, but I *am* paying for the attention and whatever pleasure I can still manage without breaking my back or cracking a rib. And Rudy has been a most attentive lover in the past. Or should I finally admit — escort? Companion? Hooker? Masseur? In my own way I love the man. And up until now, he has helped me feel younger than my years. But I never wanted to feel *this* girlish — like a jealous teenager. I had enough of that drama in high school.

My major focus right now is *not* Gavina's *manfriend* having decked Kevin Vernkowsky. And I can't be overly concerned about The Manager. I don't have much of a social life here anyway and I'm sorry if I offended him. It's not the first time I've raised my voice or gotten a bit brusque.

You'd probably call it a problem with anger management. But truth be known, I know that I have an impulse control disorder. Always have. I once fired a patient on the spot and physically escorted — or should I say shoved — her out of my office when she told me she was seeing another therapist who was 'better than me,' then called me the C-word, and spilled black coffee on my beige couch and carpet.

My anger started to become inward rage when I was around ten and my father left — soon to be replaced with my mother's boyfriend from hell. I began to wear my anger like armor under my skin with it taking more and more shape every time that man seduced me into playing Guess What — the game he invented where we would each touch each other with eyes tightly closed. Every time he put his own finger somewhere on my body — instead of a pencil eraser, troll doll, tinker toy, pillow corner, or some other inanimate object — I'd love and despise the whole thing, and another sheet of metal would take shape to try and contain the complex feelings inside me. How's that for self-analysis?

So, as I stand here at The Manager's table — between Rudy and Elmore — I wait for my humiliation and rage to impulsively find its full expression. In my mind I imagine the digital display on my blood pressure monitor going up and up. I take a deep inhale. They are all staring at me now. It seems they're waiting along with me for my explosion. Elmore and Rudy each take a step back. Gavina takes her hand off The Manager's shoulder and steps *toward* me. My armor rattles in my ears and I scoff at Gavina, turn, and walk out of the dining hall toward the library where I intend to cool off, sit quietly, and figure out how to deal with my feelings.

Elmore

Doctor Cookie Nussbaum storms off like a woman scorned. Hell hath no fury like it. Rather than mad, I myself feel the synapses of intrigue gleefully firing in the theater of my mind. I never expected Rudy to be exclusive or devoted only to me. And I certainly always assumed he was Bi and capitalizing as much as he could on his tight pecs, big guns, solid abs, bubble butt and magnificent dick and balls. So, if he was doing Cookie *and me,* so be it. No hair off my chest. Rudy is always going to be somewhat of a player for as long as he can. Why shouldn't he? The fact of the matter is I am now dying to hear the whole story. Well, hopefully not actually *dying.*

"How do you know that woman?" I ask Rudy, who is frozen in place with the look of a child caught engaging in self-gratification.

"Um. She used to be my therapist."

"Really? You've been to therapy?"

"Is that so hard to believe?"

"No. Not really."

"It was a while ago. I'll tell you about it when we're alone."

I don't blame him for wanting to get out of here. The Gavina woman has moved on from The Manager and trying to console Cookie, who rebuffed her kindness. Now she's next to Rudy trying to hold his hand. I know he won't be able to deny her, so it's up to me to come to his rescue from her pawing at him like a neglected puppy.

"Okay, come with me," I say, as I literally pull him from her impending grasp.

"I need to find the asshole who punched the real manager," Rudy says, as I bid adieu to Gavina and lead him out of the dining room back to my suite. Rudy used to call me *Daddy* but right now I really do feel like a father to him, rescuing and protecting him from harm.

"Take a load off," I say, once we are back behind closed doors. "Mind if I have a drink?"

"You have liquor?"

"Rudy, Honey. How long have we known each other?"

"Probably twenty years."

"More. I was about your age when we first met. I had liquor then and I have liquor now."

My suite has a small kitchen and it's well stocked thanks to Dimitri, the adorable delivery boy from Kadoto's Liquor store in downtown San Luis Obispo. I'm a vodka man myself. Always have been ever since my San Fernando Valley School of Interior Design days when I got quite sick of mixing Manhattans and was done thinking they were the most sophisticated drink around. I can still picture the lone cherry floating aimlessly around the surface of the nasty brown liquid.

"Did you sleep with Doctor Cookie?" I ask. Rudy is mixing me a vodka martini and pouring himself a 7-up on the rocks. I'm settling into my recliner, exhausted. I kick off my shoes and release my throbbing feet — two old dogs that are not aching from dancing all night like they once did when I was clubbing.

"I used to ... as you politely say ... *sleep* with Cookie. And I still sort of do. But she can't screw or anything anymore. Just stuff like we do."

"Different equipment. Same expiration date."

"Very funny."

"It doesn't matter to me, Rudy," I say. "I still get to look at you and you've always been very kind to me. How did Cookie and I happen to wind up in the same old folks' home?"

"If you'll recall, Elmore, I am the one who told you about this place."

"Oh, right. I thought it was because of the redecorating."

"There is no redecorating, Elmore. You are here just like everyone else. A resident."

"But, Rudy, my boy ... I am not like everyone else. I'm going to redecorate the whole place and make them pay, or I'll have to revert back to my old habits and break a few kneecaps."

"Right, Elmore. You're a real badass."

Gavina

When that fancy old homosexual drags my Rudy out of the dining hall, I sit myself right down in his empty seat at The Manager's table, interlock my fingers in lady-like fashion, and give myself a think. I remember being alone at times with my Uncle Ian, when I visited him and he let me sleep over for one night maximum because he was afraid of what his sister — my mother — would do to him if I was gone for more than one night. He need not have been afraid. She only noticed if I was not with her after two nights before she thought of me as missing. And even then, she did not do anything about it. I liked staying at Uncle Ian's house. He was polite to me and of course, as you know, Quinn was in the bedroom right near the living room couch where I slept. Just being near him was a thrill even though he was quite the crabbit and paid me no never mind. So after dinner, there I would sit, watching Ian drink without speaking and Quinn disappear into his room.

Eventually, I address The Manager who is unnecessarily adding more butter to his garlic toast and glowering at his spaghetti and meatballs like a hungry lion.

"Well does that not take the cake? What are we going to do about all this?" I ask him. "Something has got to be done."

The Manager carefully places his knife down next to his plate — butter oozing off the utensil onto the table like a slow oil spill. And after watching it for a while, he looks up at me as if I was an alien just landed before him from outer space.

"Do about what?" he asks.

"Do about Cookie and the new guy. And the obvious sexual misconduct going on with the handsome stranger. Not to mention someone punching Kevin."

The dining auditorium has cleared out. We are the only two left and the cleaning crew will sweep through here very soon, nosing around and not doing their job while hoping that some old biddy has dropped an expensive broach or some folded cash. But something important is about to happen. I know because my teeth are chattering, and my fingers are tapping the table with a message being sent from The Beyond via SOS — the code developed by Samuel Morse and myself way back before telephones were invented. The glass in the windowpanes is alternating the colors of the rainbow and planting an Eagle's tune in my head about a hotel where you can check out but never really leave.

"I'm not the manager anymore," he mumbles.

I cannot believe my ears. Sometimes people just flat out surprise you. I have never heard this man utter more than a sentence or two in the past few months or so. And I am rather sure that he has been at the Hacienda longer than I have. As a matter of fact, it occurs to me that this relic of a gentleman was indeed The Manager when I first got here. Once upon a time.

"Yes, I realize that you are not really the manager. At least, not anymore. *Sometimes* I know that. But I get befuddled and confused."

"I made too much butter," he says.

"I think you did. 'Tis okay. They will clean it up. Do not worry."

He is focusing on the knife and then back at me, like someone caught doing wrong. The confused look on his face is the same one I sometimes see in my own mirror. It is the expression of a walloper idiot trying to sort out and delineate what is happening. Talking to him is akin to having a conversation with myself. I feel bolted to the chair. You might say *mesmerized* or transfixed like we are pulled together by a strong magnetic force as Franz Mesmer, a close friend of aforementioned Sammy Morse, used to explain to me. Some of us are just simply oppositely charged objects surrounded by an electric field that pull us toward one another. You never know who might become a dear friend or a mortal enemy.

"I'm dying," The Manager says.

"As are we all," I reply.

"Help me, please."

"Help you what?"

"Help me die."

Cookie

I must say, the library here is to die for. Unlike the rest of the place, the atmosphere in this over-sized room is warm and comfortable. Good-old-fashioned bookcases climb from floor to ceiling on one whole wall, even though not many of us ever venture up the ladder to get a book from the high shelves. Once you reach a certain age, just the thought of going up a ladder makes your frayed nerves shriek at the mere idea of it. It's another reminder that I won't be climbing much of anything anymore.

I made the book wall my own project about a year ago, bringing all the best and most popular reads down to reachable levels, like restocking retail shelves with a focus on the middle range. Nothing spectacular on the bottom or very top. Kingsolver, Morrison, Tan, etc. smack dab in the middle — eye level. Even Updike, Palahniuk and Roth for the few erudite men who might be sequestered here — most of them against their will and at the insistence of their wives or daughters, who ran out of patience with their enlarged prostates and bloated egos.

I keep hoping I'll meet someone reaching for one of my favorite reads, but most of these oldsters don't even come in here. I've tried talking to those who read eBooks, but not much luck with those slackers either. The last biddy I asked about what she was reading squawked, 'The Best of Reader's Digest.'

Dimitri, the hot delivery guy from the liquor store, helped me restack the books and do the heavy lifting on his off days. A short, sturdy young man of mysterious ethnicity. He worked for generous tips and wore tank tops and ultra-stretch shorts with the clear intent to tease the hell out of me. "Reach higher," I'd say. Or "bend over."

In addition to the awesome wall of books, there are comfortable cushioned chairs and reading tables. The recessed lighting is gentle and there are plenty of floor and desk lamps. And on my insistence and generosity the library offers good internet, wi-fi outlets and plenty of charging stations. It makes me feel less like a savage in a cave. What else is all my money for nowadays except for eyeballing boys like Dimitri, upgrades for the Hacienda, and of course Rudy — who really should get better at standing on his own two feet instead of accepting money from me.

In addition to arranging tangible improvements such the ones in the library, I've also put myself in charge of interviewing the front desk volunteers to make sure they have all their marbles and are Independents, not prime for Assisted or Nursing Care.

One of these Welcome Ladies now ambles into the library, followed by Elmore Whatshisname. The old woman hands me a note and without saying a word, turns and retraces her steps, sheepishly heading back to her duty-station or her room to watch The Great British Baking Show or call out the wrong questions on Jeopardy.

"There you are," Elmore says, eyes wide to the note in my hand.

"Nosey, aren't you," I say.

"Not nosey. Curious. I got a note that looks just like that when I woke up from a very tiny nap. I bet I can tell you what it says."

"Go on."

"Spending the night in town. Back tomorrow to make sure you're okay."

"Close. He wants to make sure I'm not *too mad*. See for yourself." I hand him the message with a bizarre but welcome feeling of kinship rather than any jilted lover rage.

"He's such a sweetheart," Elmore says.

"I was so angry when I saw what I saw between you two. I feel a lot better after sitting here for a while than I did when I was on display in the dining room or hall, or whatever they want us to call it ... where all the plebians could witness my humiliation."

"They had no idea what was happening."

"You're probably right about that."

"Place needs some redecorating, don't you think? Especially the dining hall, if they want to call it a dining room," he says, as he pulls a chair up next to mine and lowers himself into it like the old man that he is. The fun thing though is that he is dressed more like James Dean than Walter Matthau. He's sporting a too-tight, white T-shirt with a paisley bandana tied around his neck. Deck shoes. No socks.

"They call it the Windsor Dining Room. It's more like a Mini–Alcatraz Dining Hall," I say.

We both get a laugh out of that. His teeth are whitened. As are mine.

"I wonder who did *this* room. It's very Edith Wharton," he says.

"I did the book wall."

"You did?"

"Well, not physically. I had some help, but I financed it. I don't know who designed the room. We must find out."

"I'm going to redecorate. Starting with the dining chamber. No need to touch *this* lovely space."

Letting go of my studied posture, I feel physically relaxed. This homosexual is no threat to me. None of them are. Back when I was a person, I always enjoyed *my gays*. I think my gay friends hated being called that as much as I hated being called a fag hag. I hope it's not too late for me to become more woke, although nowadays it's exhausting to try and understand what is socially acceptable.

"Redecorate? Do say," I sound like Maggie Smith in *Downton Abbey*.

"Maybe you can help me out. Give me some feedback. No one I've met here has the right taste. And The Manager doesn't seem interested. He's not really the manager, is he?"

"No. Kevin Vernkowsky is the manager. You need to talk to the actual powers that be. You and I know that if you don't deal at the top, you just waste your time."

"Well, that's for damn sure. I get rather tired easily these days, so I'll have Rudy look into it."

"What is he, your slave?"

"Be nice. He's hardly anyone's slave."

"He's bisexual," I say, looking around the library to make sure no one is here but us.

"No shit," Elmore says.

"I don't think we're supposed to have non-relatives of the opposite sex in our apartments."

"That's naive."

"Right. So you can have Rudy in without anyone being concerned."

"I'll tell anyone who asks that he's my son. No hanky-panky here," Elmore says. "Don't want anyone getting suspicious."

"Rules are made to be broken. I don't know about what goes on with you and your so-called *son*. But me and my ... let's call him *my nephew* ... still enjoy some top-notch, senior citizen chicanery."

"Senior porn."

We both chuckle at our self-depreciating jokes. The constant nagging in my back that often radiates from between my L4/L5 down my legs disappears. I sit back up straight in my chair like the Dowager Countess of Grantham.

"We were going to share war stories about patients and clients. Maybe name names," I say, leaning forward and looking both ways again as if we're in an elevator with others instead of alone in a deserted library. "I'm looking for some raucous drama since the tenor of my life has become as boring as that of a church mouse."

"You want to talk about Rudy or our clients?" he asks.

"What more is there to say about Rudy? I love him dearly."

"Me, too."

It appears we have the same taste in men, libraries, and mischief. I feel like I'm on a date as a high school senior with Monty Silverman, who eventually became known as Polishta Silver — first runner up on Season One of RuPaul's Drag Race.

"So. Name names," I say, with an excitement that comes with a *premonition.*

"There were two of my clients that I believe were your patients at one time."

The first name he mentions is that of a woman he claims was a well-known casting agent whom I never heard of, or perhaps I forgot treating that person. I shrug it of with a side-to-side turn of my head to indicate *no.*

“Name another one.”

“He was a movie mogul. All washed up now. Born Scottish. Named Quinn Adamsdaur.”

“You’re kidding,” I say.

“Why would I kid about that?”

“That bastard.”

“Yes, not a good person. Stiffed me out of half my fees,” Elmore says as if this fact is always top of mind for him, just as Quinn has been for me. Funny, isn’t it? If Elmore is anything like me, he can’t remember why he goes from one room to the next but has a clear memory of how someone did him wrong years ago.

“He’s the bastard who reported me and got my license revoked,” I say, with all the righteous indignation of the innocent victim that I am.

Chapter Four

Quinn

I should not have decked that motherfucker. It hurt my hand. It's making it hard to manipulate the steering wheel, so I drive slowly which is fine because I know that when I drive agitated — at the very least, I lose my way and at the worst, very bad things happen. According to my research on the area, Padre's Bar & Grill is San Luis Obispo's most famous pub, constructed in 1920 on the corner of Washington and Saint Paulo, immediately across from the old mission. Actually, I think it was built around the same time as was the original Hacienda House which was a large family home that eventually became the stupid rest home.

I'll stop by for a drink before checking into the ResTight Motel next door. Not for what I'd hoped would be a celebration, but instead — thanks to the unfairness of the world and its selfish inhabitants — for another typical drowning of a bad-luck break topping off a shitty day.

It's still happy hour but the bar is empty except for a couple tourist types, two men in work clothes, and a very attractive girl — younger than the ones I'm used to picking up these days. But after spending time with Gavina and being inside that depressing mausoleum, I sure don't feel like fucking anyone over forty. Who am I kidding? I hope to Jehovah that she'll be interested in me. The older and fatter I become the less chance I think I have with females. I'm giving the term *washed up* new meaning. I'm not feeling sorry for myself or trying to garner your sympathy. I'm just trying to be honest about how unfair life can be. I'll feel a lot better once I have her in the sack.

There are two stools between us. Bitch doesn't notice me, until I move one closer. Her blondish hair is pulled back and tied with a purple scarf. She moves the long sleeves of her tailored blouse up past her elbows as if she is about to eat a plate of ribs or get into a brawl.

"Stay there," she says out the side of her mouth.

"I wouldn't think of coming any closer without an invitation," I say. "I'm not an animal."

Glancing my way and catching me rubbing my knuckles, she asks, "Been in a fight?"

"I wouldn't say a fight. The other guy deserved it. I lost my temper. I never lose my temper, but I did."

"Am I supposed to ask what he did to make you lose control?"

"I wish you wouldn't."

"What did he do to make you lose control?"

I'm in love. This girl is feisty, pretty and drinks alcohol. How much better can it get? I motion to the bartender to bring us both another drink. He looks almost as ancient as the bar itself, but he's immediately on it even without words being spoken to him. And the cliché unfolds neatly with me moving over one more seat, as I explain the loss of my filming location.

Sometimes I feel like I'm in a bad movie instead of inhabiting my real life. I play out the scene just like I've watched it countless times on the big screen. I feel numb and will continue to feel nothing until my morning hang-over kicks in. But I do it again and again anyway. No amount of therapy has helped me overcome my addiction to sex. The problem is that my taste in women is still for ones who are too young to dig a guy over sixty unless he's rich or famous. I always thought I would be both. But — alas. Females only like you when you're on top of the world.

She arches her eyebrows at the sound of the word *filming.*

"Why were you doing your own location scouting anyway?" she asks. "Isn't that a lowly job for a PA or scout?

"You sound like you know something about the business," I say, choosing not to answer her question.

It's ridiculous that I have to find locations and don't even have a real film to shoot which no one needs to know and I'm probably going to rue the day I mentioned it because I can sense your smug judgment of me already as if you've never lied, punched someone, or forced yourself on a person weaker than yourself.

"I know a lot about the business," she says. "What did you say your name is?"

"I didn't say." Once again. No need to share too much information with my prey.

"Well, I'm Crystal. I'm an *Actor.*"

She pronounces the word in an annoying Shakespearian manner. I wish she had said *actress* like in the good old days. These liberated chicks can be more trouble than they're worth. I learned that the hard way a while ago. You have to be careful or you can get fucked big time in the world of sexual harassment, even if it's just verbal. I let her say whatever she wants, however she wants to say it.

"Nice to make your acquaintance, Crystal," I say, careful not to touch her. I'll wait until she moves in on me.

"May I ask who your agent is?" I continue. That's how you find out if a person is legit or a wannabe.

"I'm with Paradine. Valerie Mann."

"Impressive."

"She's great. So far I've only done some small supporting roles. But fingers crossed."

"Ever heard of *Scottish Mistress*? Two-thousand Sundance Grand Jury Prize winner."

"No, sorry. Cannot tell a lie. Can't say that I have."

"That was my film."

"Very cool."

We chat for a while, but this isn't going well. She's not really flirtatious or overly suggestive. I'm imagining those buttons on my shirt popping and unveiling my belly. I run my fingers through my hair and notice that there's more scalp than mane. And things really hit the skids when she turns all her attention to the leading man type who sits down at a table away from the bar. He's tall, dark, and handsome to say the least. I'm out of luck. He's around fifty years old. Not sixty-five. And they obviously have a pre-arranged meeting or she's just trying to get away from me. Could be a Tinder thing.

Rudy

After leaving my friend Elmore napping under the blanket that his mother knit just before she died at the ripened old age of ninety-five, I left a note for him letting him know I'd be back. I do what I can for him but once again I'm relieved that he's in Hacienda Mirage and getting the care he deserves.

Elmore:
I am going to spend the night in town.
Be back tomorrow to smooth out stuff and make sure you're okay.

There was no reason to wear a disguise anymore, so I just left the note and hurried past the library with my head turned away. I knew Cookie was in there stewing. I went to the front desk to ask the nice lady there to get a note to Dr. Nussbaum please. She gave me the stirred-up eyes and hungry grin I sometimes get from women of a certain age and said she would be pleased to do so and would deliver it herself.

Cookie:
I'm going to spend the night in town.
Be back tomorrow to smooth out stuff so you don't stay mad.

So on Kevin's recommendation, after turning tail from The Hacienda, I stop by Padre's Bar & Grill conveniently located next to my motel to unwind from my busy day and figure out what my responsibilities are toward everyone — including Bloody Nose Kevin and the guy who plugged him — not to mention Cookie, who I'm maybe supposed to get a patch-things-up gift like a flagrant candle or a Elsy Louder perfume. And Elmore, who would be happy if I just brought him a bottle of vodka. I want to make sure that I dot my eyes and cross my tease.

I know that when I feel all mixed up like this, I should *not* be drinking. After being sober for the past ten years, that doesn't mean I don't still want to divulge myself into at least two or three Seven and Sevens before bed. But I've worked too damn hard and don't want to disappoint Cookie any more than I already might have, since she is the one who got me to go to AA in the first place. And I don't have the self-discipline like Elmore— stopping after one shot of booze. At eighty he should maybe only be drinking orange or prune juice anyway. Or whatever he wants. I don't know.

While I'm persuing the menu to decide what to eat, a pretty woman comes up to the table and says, "Is this seat taken? Can I sit here for a minute and finish my drink? I need to get away from that creep at the bar ... and I'm sure the bartender will bring me my check."

She's real good-looking and gives me an ear-to-ear grin as if we know each other.

"Hello. Sure. Sit," I say. Then I can't help myself. "You look familiar."

"So do you."

"You live in L.A.?"

"Part of the time in L.A. and part time here," she says. We both have that puzzled where-do-I-know-you-from look on our faces. It's fun. And it's *real* because we're trying to remember if and when we met before.

"I'm just going to finish this drink, pay my tab and get out of your hair," she says, looking at me as if to figure something out. "This is silly."

"Not silly. We must have met before. Maybe in L.A.?"

I'm pretty sure this is that thing called coinseedent or sinkrominity.

She has a friendly face but looks kinda sad at the same time. Like somethings bothering her besides trying to think about how she might know me. She has the look of someone who has had a drink or two for drowning some bad stuff. I feel bad for her.

Then she bursts out, "Kibbles and Bits!"

"We'd never feed our dog anything but!" I answer.

"Oh my God. We did that commercial together. I played your sister or something. Holy shit."

"Rudy," I say again, holding out my hand, taking hers in mine and holding onto it —acting all hetero and challant. Her wedding ring is very thin, but I'm used to checking that sort of thing, especially with unhappy women in case they need to pay for someone's shoulder to cry on. But for some reason, I don't feel like doing that sort of thing tonight.

"Oh my God. How are you?" she asks.

"I'm good."

"What was the dog's name?"

"I have no idea. How are *you* ...?"

"Crystal. I'm fine, too. Been doing a few *real* acting gigs lately. Nothing big yet."

"I'm still pluggin' away. Nothing even little yet ..."

She glances toward the man at the bar then back at me and says,

"Looks like we're all in The Business in one way or another. That creep says he's a movie maker."

The guy comes over and offers to shake my hand. He has defined, furry forearms — something that usually turns me on no matter who it is. He's about a decade older than me but has what I call a sexy Papa Bear vibe. But for some reason, I feel turned off, not on by either of them.

"I think the little lady ran away from me," he says.

"That would mean she's not interested. So ...." I give him my stay-away-from-my-woman look.

"Please go about your business," she says to him.

After staring at us both with non-belief, he turns, slaps some money on the bar, and leaves, looking back at us for a sec. If he had a long tail, it would be curled between his legs.

"Sorry about that," I say.

"Guy's a dick. Pardon my French."

"That's something I say."

"That guy's a dick?"

"No ... pardon my French. You're supposed to say it when you cuss and you're not sure if the other person you're talking to is going to be off-ended."

She asks the waiter for a coke, which I think is being polite since it's obvious that I'm not drinking alcohol. And we talk about acting and auditions for a while. She says she lives in L.A. going on endless auditions or as an extra in one of Steven Slanders films.

"They like to put me in and give me one speaking line. Watch this," she says.

She stands, hikes up the sleeves of her blouse — exposing aerobicized arms and says, "Don't mean to bother you ... sorry ... is this seat taken?"

I applaud, saying, "Great acting."

After she does a few more stand-up improvs, I do a few of my own. When the bartender suggests we tone it down or take ourselves out of there, we head for the exit door.

"That troll who was hitting on me ..."

"Yeah?"

"He was just in a fight, so you're lucky he bolted out of here."

"A fight?"

"Bruised knuckles."

"You don't say. Really? Well maybe he's the lucky one who got away *from me*."

She puts her hand on my arm and I pull back, and she takes her hand off me. She looks sort of wounded and turns to walk away. I am — by choice — going back to my motel alone, hoping I didn't hurt the poor girl's feelings 'cause even though I don't know too much about sexual rejection, I *do* know what it feels like to be disappointed and then think maybe you did something wrong when it wasn't about you at all.

Part 2

Sunday

Chapter Five

Rudy

I wake up on Sunday morning tucked under clean white sheets, alone in my comfy, ekonominal motel bed where I slept like a baby. People say that *slept like a baby* thing when there's no way you could really know how it feels way back then and I sure as heck don't think I ever slept all that well when I was a little kid what with all the unhinged goings on around me.

I'm proud of myself for being a gentleman with the sexy woman last night, although I've been feeling a bit more toward the *gay* than the *bi* spot on what Cookie used to call 'the continumin of sexuality' ever since I met Kevin, who I hope I'll see again today. I slept deep and to perk up, I'll allow myself one strong cup of java and then head straight to the gym. I'm sure you know that too much caffeination is not good for you. It can make you jittery, give you headaches and jump up your blood pressure. I don't ingest any caffeine except on Sunday mornings and I crave a shot more than usual. Since I'm not at home, I'll have to go out for my Cup o' Joe before heading to Obie's for my workout and then back to The Hacienda. I'm stoked to be alone in the motel room without having to deal with anyone from the night before. I can get it together without worrying about anybody judging me or grabbing at me. No hands on me or expectancies of me. It feels good sometimes not to be in service, or have to worry about what to do, how to act, or what to wear. I wonder if that's one of the perks that come with growing *really* old and feeling free of pressure and combrances like that.

When I was a kid, before I moved in with my sweet *abuela*, Sundays were all about church. They'd force me into a stupid shirt and tie after giving up on pressing me into a jacket. My unsaintly mother would hoot and whoop all about what was wrong with me and how dumb I was. "*Eres tonto como un poste*. You're as dumb as a post. You can't even utter a complete sentence in Spanish," she would yell at me. *"El estúpido! Que Dios te ayude."*

If I was so brainless, why did I know that putting on a suit jacket wouldn't make me any smarter? Am I right?

There's no way now to get me to dress up for much of anything. Specially not coffee and the gym. So after a lovely dump — followed by a good face-washing and electronic teeth brushing — I'm out the door in my work-out shorts, old Obie Gym T-shirt and hoody, ready to continue my search for the bastard that hit Kevin-With-The-Square-Jaw.

Guess who I run into on my way to my car.

Right. Papa Bear is loading up his little old grey Prius in a get-away hurry. He's not happy to see me, 'specially when I give him the famous Rudy ear-to-ear face beam. I can't help it. Sometimes I get so happy to see people even if I don't know the person at all. I've only seen this guy at the bar but it feels like I've been looking for him.

"Off already?" I ask, surprised at my own self again for being so chipper, when he was so rude last night.

"Got to get back to L.A. I've a film to put together."

"How 'bout a cuppa wakey juice? There's a nice coffee shop nearby."

He throws his small suitcase into the trunk and slams it shut as if we were having an argument instead of a friendly morning-after chat.

"I don't think so," he says.

"Did I do something to piss you off?" I ask.

"No. No. You did nothing wrong. I just have to go."

"I'm not gonna take no for an answer. Just a cup and anything else you want. It's on me. My treat. You can jump in my car, and I'll swing back by to drop you off. You need to chill, Man."

This guy looks like he's been caught *stealing* the old car. But I really don't think he has because the keys are in his hand — oddly shaking I might add. Shaking from what? Fear? Fear of what? Me?

"Are you okay?" I ask, stepping toward him but careful not to come too close in case he's one of those supposedly straight men who's spooked by my just standing near them.

"Okay. All right. I guess I could use some breakfast," he says, looking at me as if I'm strong-arming him.

"We'll take my car," I say. I want to keep my eye on him.

"Let me lock mine up."

"Have you checked out of your room?"

"I prepaid when I check in."

Papa Bear looks different in the morning light. He's wearing slacks and a polo shirt as old as his Prius. His handsome face is slightly red and swollen and he's sporting a tiny, botched goatee. Recessing hairline. But I could overlook all that if he didn't look so worried and districken.

By the time we're settled into a little table in the corner of the SLO Cafe, he's chill enough to have a conversation. In the short drive from the motel, he hardly said a word while I rattled on and on about how I was an actor and longed to be in a real movie. Not too sure if he was someone worth pitching my talent to.

"How about that chick last night, though? Your girlfriend?" he asks.

"No. But you should have left her alone," I say.

"Christie?"

"I believe she said her name is Crystal. Not really your business though."

"Can we move past that?" he asks. Looks like he wants out, but the dude thinks twice 'cause he's without a car.

The guy is now depressingly eating his egg and cheese sandwich and gulping his coffee. It's like watching a hog at one of those long emptied out wood things with slop in it. For some unknown reasoning, I'm thinking about the handcuffs that I have in my sex-toy goodie bag in the trunk of my car as if I was going to need them very soon. There's almost like a voice whispering to me to pay attention.

"I have a friend, well not really a friend ... a woman I knew since I was a kid, who lives in the nursing home up the hill from here. Sometimes I visit her. Maybe once a year or two," he says.

He's talking fast and hyper. My brain unclogs and clears. And I get more angrier and madder with everything he says about the woman *named Gavina* and how he lost his temper with the guy who runs the place because he won't let him shoot some movie scenes there.

I grab his wrists. Tight. He can't get away from me and we'll be locked in place like this for as long as it takes for me to figure out what the heck to do.

"You're Quinn Adamsdaur!" I say, imagining steaming puffs of rage coming out my ears. I'm not acting.

Gavina

I miss Rudy and wonder about Quinn. Or do I miss Quinn and wonder about Rudy? Have they found each other? Are they fighting over me? I tug the library ladder over to the stacks and climb up to return Emily Dickenson's *Because I Could Not Stop for Death* to the very top shelf where I found it weeks ago — the thin work hidden between two Russian novels. The personification of death as soothing.

Euthanasia and physician-assisted suicide refer to deliberate action taken with the intention of ending a life, in order to relieve persistent suffering. That is a direct quote. I looked it up. Thank you very much. I research lots of things in the library when Her Majesty Queen Cookie is not in here hogging space pretending to be reading one of the books — all of which I have already read. Or she is monopolizing the internet connection for herself. She spends a suspicious amount of time in this basilica to literature and information. Hopefully, she is not plotting to steal my thunder by becoming the merciful Angel of Death *herself* before I get my act together. 'Tis happened to me before when I have been excited about an idea or invention and someone beats me to the punch. Like the time that Johannes Gutenberg claimed he invent the printing press — but he stole the idea I spoke of during a soiree at Andreas Dritzehn's estate where we sat chatting in Andy's massive library surrounded by books shelved to the ceiling. I cried with indignation for many nights after I heard that Hans had stolen my rightful place in history.

These stacks of books in The Hacienda are meant by Cookie to intimidate me, but what she does not know is that books are my friends. Each one has taken me on a voyage to somewhere beyond the stupid places where I have been in this planet space. And my increasing mastery of the interwebs gives me superpowers that transcend those I have already been blessed with or acquired over the years. I prefer an old hard-bound book that has had fingers flipping the pages, like mine itch to do. I love this old room with its oriental rugs and wood accents everywhere. There is a universal smell to the books in this library, as there is in all places where paper-bound stories live. And yet each tome you pick up encircles you with its unique musty odor of pulp. Embracing you like your mother was supposed to. Its pages hug you securely and whisper magically woven words that soothingly blanket you.

When The Manager mentioned his wish to end his life, he knew just who he was talking to. 'Tis the solution for those of us who will be homeless once they demolish The Hacienda. Some of the residents here do not have family to turn to or are too sick to be relocating and starting over. For instance — the oh so very sophisticated, delightful, and worldly Cookie Nussbaum. She has no one and all her money will not buy happiness at her age. This new homosexual, Elmore, naturally has no one and he will die alone. Both of them think they have Rudy looking after them. But even I know what a gigolo is. And do you really think that I believe that Quinn is going to look after *me*? And The Manager — such a sweet, quiet old soul who is now blatantly entrusting me — intuiting that I am just the right person for the job. We are all being interwoven into one mass — like string being wound into an orb or a snowball becoming larger as it rolls downhill. 'Tis not an accident. 'Tis fate. I feel sorry for you if you cannot suspend rational thinking and accept inexplicable coincidence or the work of a magical old building on Chumash land. If you think that makes you sane and me crazy, so be it.

I have two pure dead-brilliant ways to get this done, both easily accessible. The first is the Baby Blues Cocktail where I substitute antifreeze for the Blue Raspberry MD 20/20 and mix it with vodka and crushed ice. Baby Blues are good for those like Elmore, who will never turn down a bevvy. Non-drinkers depart more easily with a certain food preservative used legitimately for curing meat. My favorite website that delves into assisted suicide is called SergeSaysGo.com. It is the most fun because it has good graphics and funny cartoons.

I am not sure I can pull it off *alone,* so I have been thinking of asking Quinn for assistance. The idea might appeal to him since it solves his problem of how to clear out the place and shoot his film before the demolition. If he agrees to help me and invites me to move in with him, it will be our little secret. If he does not, I will simply add his name to The List, along with my own and anyone else who belittles or disrespects me. Or most importantly, anyone who asks for my help in getting them out of this life, should they be suffering mind or body pain.

Elmore

Cookie is not in the library after Sunday brunch, but Gavina is here in front of the computer with her face about three inches from the bright screen. She looks a bit Helen Kellerish — hoping to be able to see better if she positions her nose within inches of the monitor. I can't help but think of my Aunt Bea who took me in when I was thrown out of the house as a teen. Bea was farsighted and also a little loopy, but she claimed to clearly see who I was and what I wanted. Fact being, *I* didn't really have a clue as to who I was or what I wanted. Except I did want to be around the building super who we both enjoyed watching while he puttered under the sink or reached way up toward the ceiling fan in the kitchen.

> *"You might have to lie yourself down to see under the sink," Aunt Bea would say.*
> *"Let us know if Elmore or I can help in any way."*
> *"Could you please reach your hand way up to the fan there and reconnect the cord."*

I'm pretty sure that he knew Bea often pulled the cord off the fan herself, so she'd have to call him. We would enjoy viewing him — each of us with a can of Coke in hand — while he worked. I wasn't sure what was going on with me, but I somehow knew that to be a boy so excited by a man in his work pants and tank top was bad, not normal, and — after the rage of my father — should never be spoken of.

Now, as I quietly step past Gavina, I think about how Aunt Bea used to dress up in odd thrift store finds. Her outfits were scattered around the house in make-shift piles, and she might have known that I sometimes borrowed her diaphanous violet scarf, tying it around me in various configurations. Or an occasional clip-on earring or wide-buckle belt. Shiny gold. Red leatherette.

According to Rudy, Gavina's manfriend was the one who punched Kevin Vernkowsky in his handsome, young face. And I know Rudy is out for justice. He's a Libra, you know. Maybe I can be of some help if I find a way to engage this Gavina character.

I thought that Kevin worked for The Manager, but now I see that I was wrong, although I admit I'm still a bit confused. When I'm confused about fact versus fiction, I'm quite pleased that I'm in a rest home rather than out and about trying to negotiate the changing world. But when I'm feeling so-called normal, I still crave variety and newness — that is when I'm not enjoying stick-to-predictable-routines. I want something to do and then I don't feel like doing anything. I'm trying to find a regular activity here at The Hacienda and so far, I only have the library as a place of solace. Eventually, I will give in and try drawing and/or scrabble. Hopefully, those are non-speaking goings-on and I'll be able to get into both since I don't believe socializing is required for either.

Be that as it may, I leave Gavina to herself and settle into a chair with a copy of *Tales of the City*, which I prefer reading rather than watching reruns of the original television adaptation — although who wouldn't fuss over hottie Marcus D'Amico as 'Mouse?' God knows, I couldn't get through the new version with a middle-aged Mary Ann and all the *thems, theys and thoses* of the new generation of gender queers. But I digress, as I'm told I do from time to time.

So, I'm casually sitting here — dressed in my Sunday best pleated chinos and polo shirt while peacefully ensconced in my book — when I look up to see Gavina standing so close I have to move my feet away to avoid getting stepped on. She's not speaking. Just spooking.

"Last night at dinner ..." she eventually says.

"Could you please pull up a chair or step back a little?"

She snorts. She actually splutters. I don't mean sighs. I'm telling you she makes a grunting sound like a sow. She's dressed in a lose-fitting, violet t-shirt and roomy, matching, cotton slacks. Purplish canvas shoes that could only have come from some vintage shop. I hear there are shopping days provided here when they load up The Hacienda van and take the ladies into town. I bet the few hetero-normative men folks don't go.

"Like my shoes?" she says, catching me looking at her feet as she steps back and pulls up a chair a few feet in front of mine like she's going to interrogate me. She smells a bit like gum turpentine.

"You are a vision of lavender today," I say in my most complimentary tone.

"I tie-dyed the slippers myself. Although I should say I *dyed* them because obviously you do not twist and turn and *tie* them, do you? I mean you *tie* sneakers, but not like you tie up a t-shirt or such."

"I suppose not," I say.

"Have you been to arts and crafts, Mister Elmore?" she asks, lowering herself into the chair.

"It's Elmore. Elmore's my *first* name. And no, I don't go to arts and crafts. It's not my thing."

"Cookie goes. I know you and the not-so-good doctor would love to tie-die some outfits together. You could be matchy-matchy. People like her just love the gays."

"Right? We're like little pets."

"Excuse me?"

"Never mind," I say.

"Last night at dinner ... when you and Cookie were toadying over Rudy, I nearly lost my lunch."

"You mean dinner," I correct her.

"Shut up."

"Really?"

Aunt Bea used to say *shut up* to me when she meant *you're kidding*. But I'm not sure Gavina is being friendly or teasing me. She's not smiling and the light behind her makes her look rather ominous resulting in a sudden chill, reminding me to more frequently carry or wear my old-man sweater.

"After you and Cookie were done fawning over Rudy, I was left alone with The Manager," Gavina says.

"Yes. The Manager."

"You know he is not really managing this place anymore."

"Yes. I know. Now. What do you mean by *anymore*?"

"Thought I would come over and properly welcome you. I have been here the longest. At least, I am the longest standing and talking resident here. Some of these folks were here when I arrived but I do not really count them because they are on their last leg over in Assisted or moved out to Nursing."

"Not the most sensitive, are you?" I ask, squinting from the light from the window surrounding her.

"Shut up."

"Really? Again?"

"Look ... there are a few things you need to know."

"Shoot."

"Do not say such to me or I might fill you full of bullet holes."

"You're talking to the wrong man. I used to be known as ... how-do-you-say ... Mafioso."

"Oh, if only that were true. It would endear me to you forever. Those guys rule."

"*Us* guys."

"Whatever. If you are mafia, I am the Queen of England."

"Your Majesty," I jest.

"First of all, Quinn could not have punched Kevin Vernkowsky. He was not even here. Second of all, I like your taste in men and I am giving you the heads-up that I can take Rudy away from Cookie, no contest. You can keep copulating with him, or whatever you are still able to do at your age. And third and final, if you cannot cope when they close this place and rip it to its foundations, I can help you *off yourself* neatly without much suffering. I am willing to do that for you."

Cookie

It might surprise you to learn that Sunday brunch is quite nice here. There's a full buffet for those of us who can manage to move our bodies up and down from our chairs, as well as make decisions about what we want instead of holding up the line. I'm not saying it's a Four Seasons experience, but the scrambled eggs are kept hot, there's bacon, sausages, and ham for those who want to clog their arteries even more than the march of time has already done, and there are three types of potatoes — roasted, hashed, and boiled. And to give credit where it's due — oatmeal, yogurt, hard-boiled eggs, and a plethora of fruit according to season and harvest. The stout women who man the buffet all wear health department mandated hair nets and gloves. And there's plexiglass like nobody's business installed by that cute little man — with all the keys clipped to his waistband — who is always screwing in light bulbs, sweeping up the floors or raking in the garden when he's not shuttling us into town on shopping days.

I like a buffet because it keeps me moving and helps limit my calories, since I have to think before I go back for more. I can't stay healthy with a paltry Hacienda Stretchercise Class in the crusty, old, ill-named, tiny *fitness center* led by some Independent Supercentenarian who fancies herself some sort of wellness guru.

Looking down at my thighs as they spill onto the chair, I wonder whose fat legs have attached themselves to my body. It's amazing how suddenly you go from being the Hot Hollywood Therapist to the Wrinkled Retired Matron with someone else's flabby and often achy body.

Today I've decided to eat at The Manager's table, where Elmore is already sitting. He greets me by slowly standing as if expecting me and graciously pulls out a chair informing me that he's enjoying the buffet also. Mostly he says, because of the tofu scramble — which is a rare addition I've frankly never seen before.

I inquire regarding his night's sleep as is customary around here. We're always checking in on one another's nocturnal aches, pains, and miscellaneous nighttime challenges. Then we usually do a detailed and descriptive review of our health with an emphasis on specific preventive measures and hopeful cures. I find I can delightfully skip this with Elmore, who jumps right into normal conversation.

Elmore seems like a standard variety neurotic. I'm sure once I get to know him better, his issues will become more apparent and more specific. He taps his fingers like early Parkinson or simply good ol' generalized anxiety.

"Slept good," he says. "Learning my way around the place. I went to the library looking for you but found Gavina instead. Now that was a trip!"

When I was in private practice, I would *not* have taken on someone as severely disturbed as Gavina. But since Elmore might be someone I can talk to and trust, I admit to him that I sometimes find her amusing, since she is *not my* responsibility. I'm hoping she'll move to Assisted where she belongs and can have her own shrink. I've seen goofy Doctor Edelstein on the first Friday of the month — his blond hair tied back in a ponytail and his shoulders slouched — creeping up the wheelchair ramp and down the hall toward Assisted as if he was Quasimodo. Heard he's a good clinician, but oh my, he looks quite nuts himself.

"Gavina's more than a trip. You're being tactful," I say to Elmore.

"I guess she does seem rather dangerous," he replies.

"Oh no. She's harmless."

"She does *not* seem harmless. I'm telling you. I've had my experiences with sociopaths and criminal minds. Don't ask me where or when ... or who."

"Well, Elmore. *You* seem pretty harmless."

"I am not only harmless, but loveable. That is ... unless you seriously cross me."

With that I invite him to join me for some more food.

"If you're really a violent man, I'll eat my hat," I say to Elmore. "That's a phrase I think made popular by Charles Dickens who wrote, *'If I knew as little of life as that, I'd eat my hat and swallow the buckle whole.'* You can check with Gavina to see if that's true. She claims to have read the original manuscript of *The Pickwick Papers* when her friend Charley asked her to edit it."

Elmore and I chuckle and approach the granola jug like we're the only ones there — both of us obviously proud of our momentary erect posture. The wide mouth of the glass jar calls for us to grab a scoop of the crunchy treat.

"I love me some seeds, rolled oats, sugar and of course, nuts. Love my nuts," Elmore says, loading up a bowl.

"Looks like we have similar taste in foods," I say.

"Would you like to share some grains and nuts, or should I take the last of it?" he asks, holding up the line forming behind us.

"Happy to share. I took too much food. And anyway, we already share nuts and stuff."

"Pardon me?"

I look at him conspiratorially, waiting for him to decipher my meaning. And when he does, we have another delicious moment together.

Seated back at the table we're practically howling, drawing some angry mumblings from the humorless inmates. Even The Manager is laughing in a low growl without the slightest notion of what's going on. Gavina has eyes on us in a truly chilling glare. And then she pads her way toward us like a prowling panther — albeit one with an aging bad knee or two. Step by step. Inch by inch.

"Hello," she says clearly addressing The Manager and ignoring Elmore and myself as she sits in the one vacant chair. She rests her hand on The Manager's arm. "How're your delicious-looking eggs?"

He looks at her and nods.

"I've made some real progress on that thing we talked about yesterday for when they evict all of us," Gavina says, now patting his arm reassuringly. He nods again with a hint of excitement at what she's saying. "And there's every indication that these two here will be on my list to be liberated along with you."

She stands and leaves without a word to either of us directly. But if looks could kill!

If this woman was a client of mine back in the day, I would ask for details on a threat like that to determine if I was supposed to report her for portending to harm herself or others. Not that I always did so when I should have. Like that one time when the lover of a super famous athlete suggested she would have to burn his house down, which it turned out she *did* even before I could have tried to stop it. You probably read about it in the newspapers, back when we all read newspapers and believed most of what we read.

"What was that all about?" I ask Elmore.

"She won't let go of her thing about them tearing down the place and she claims The Manager here ... asked her to help him die."

I look over at The Manager who is finishing off a huge muffin as best as he can with shaky hands. He looks oblivious to it all.

"Whatever. Let's go right now and ask Kevin Vernkowsky himself about the tear down bullshit."

"Does he work on Sundays?"

"We'll find out. We need to see how he's doing anyway, after yesterday's fisticuffs."

Chapter Six

Rudy

Some of the people in the coffee shop glance our way probly 'cause there's a lot of tenseness going on back and forth with me and Quinn. I'm holding onto his wrists so tight he's squealing like a little piglet caught in a bear trap. My boxing coach once told me that the toughest guys show their true Weak Willie Nature once you have 'em hog-tied. I didn't get his point 'til he explained that it was a fig-your-speech for backing someone in a corner where there was no chance to get away. I wish people would just say what they mean instead of trying to prove how clever they are. The more big words and needless elabratoring the better, and I find the nicer person it is who just speaks clear. I had too many teachers like that in El Paso — like my know-it-all mother with her handy wackadoodle wooden spoons — who thought their job was to correct my grammar and humleate me in front of the other kids. I remember being a rapidly developing teen thinking *I'll say whatever I say how I select to say it and if you have a problem with it, you can go F-U-C-K yourself which we all know is litrally just not possible.* Then I'd go work out, lift weights, or run a few miles. When I got big enough, I moved out — easily carrying what was maybe a fifty-pound duffle bag of my things in each hand.

Quinn is the type of fellow who acts all bigshotty until he's cornered. I'm already very, very mad — clear that this is a bad guy, who must be dealt with.

"Just sit there," I say.

"What have I done to you?" he almost whispers, as if he's talking to someone else. Someone in his own brain from way before right now. It's like he's watching a movie in his head of something that happened a long time ago. Maybe when he was a kid? "Why are you doing this to me?" he asks.

"You're the guy who punched Kevin Vernkowsky, a very nice man who hardly deserves to be slugged. A very *hot* man, I might add."

"I lost my temper with Vernkowsky. I can explain."

"Okay, then spill."

"Can you let go of me?"

"No. But we can go to the car, and I can cuff you and we can talk back at the motel in my room, since I haven't checked out."

"I'm not going anywhere with you."

My grip tightens, and I say, "I'm not going to hurt you."

"You're already hurting me. Let me go."

"Stop being such a baby. I won't hurt you, but I can't let you run off, until we straighten a few things out."

"Why do you have fuckin' handcuffs in your car?"

"Some folks like to be dominated a bit. I never really harm anyone, but you never know when someone might want to be chained to the bedpost ... even though there aren't a lotta actual bedposts around nowadays. *Bedframes* I guess is more accurate."

Quinn looks around the place and then bows his head like he's thinking. I'm hoping he's not the masosistic type who *likes* to be bound up and punished. That's sure as hell not gonna happen. I once met a guy that wanted me to piss on him and that sure wasn't gonna happen. Why would anyone want me to take a leak on their chest? Excuse my French.

"Everyone's looking," he says to more his breakfast plate than to me.

"They'll just think we're lovers," I say.

"Fuck that. No."

"Well, your choice. But we're gonna sit here or walk out with everyone thinkin' we're holding' hands. Cause I'm not lettin' you go."

"Okay. Let's get out of here. We'll talk in private. Can I take what's left of my sandwich?"

Of course, I don't have to tell you that I got stuck with the bill, and as soon as we get near my car, Quinn tries to make a break for it. My arm goes up when he tugs on it, but he's so weak that I don't budge from where I stand. I look like one of those floppy blowup giant figures at car dealers standing firm with an arm flapping but not moving from the spot. So then he stands next to me like a bad kid who's afraid someone might see him misbehavin'. Then once we're on our way after failin' his escape, he aims to open the child-proof locked door — as if he has the guts to jump out of a moving car. We don't talk. The scenery is nice on the short drive, so it's okay with me if I don't have to conversate with this dude. There are old brick buildings and artsy graffiti on some walls. I like colorful street art. I'll admit I've sprayed a few excellent pictures of bright green cactus on walls of Venice California. If I painted hangable art instead of unmoveable wall drawings I might be able to sell some and make a few bucks.

When we get to the motel, I easily hold onto him, grab my toy bag, and drag the bastard into my room, bolt the door, cuff him, put him on the bed, and sit myself down in front of the locked door. I'm such a badass. Right? Or at least I'm a damn awesome actor recreating some sort of Tony Soprano gangster role. The fingers of one of my hands is wrapped around the fist of my other hand.

"You know I'm a big film maker," Quinn says, as he resignates himself to being held captive.

"Well, imagine that."

"And you are either the toughest, most slick, good-looking tough guy around or an amazing actor."

"I'm both, my man."

"I'd love to cast you in my next movie."

"That's what I'm hoping."

"I'm not kidding. You impress me."

"We can talk about that later. Right now, you know what I wanna hear."

"Can I have my sandwich?"

"Are you nuts? Your leftovers are in the car. Start talking or I'll beat it out of you."

Quinn tells me that he went to Kevin to arrange shooting some scenes for his movie. He goes on to complain that he decided to scout locations himself, since the team that usually does it for him costs too much and he has to trim his production budget. He throws in the idea that a newcomer like me could save him actor fees on talent. He says that Kevin flatly refused him. And then Quinn Adamsdaur begins to cry. Fake sobbing — I'm telling you.

"Truth is ... I used to be a big deal," he mumbles, changing his tune and trying to butter me up. "Now everyone turns me down. I took it all out on poor Vernkowsky after *he* turned me down which was right after Gavina told me that she wanted to come live with me when they close the facility."

"That's what Cookie said to me," I say.

"Cookie?"

"I have a friend there, too."

"I knew a shrink once ... named Cookie. Went to her for my sex addiction years ago when I hit the skids. Had a bit of sex with her myself."

"Doctor Cookie Nussbaum?"

"You heard of her? She was well-known back in the day."

"She was *my* therapist."

"Are you playing a scene. This is ridiculous."

"I'm not kidding."

"You're telling me that we had the same fuckin' therapist? Both slept with her? And she's now a resident at Hacienda Mirage? That's insane," Quinn says.

Then he laughs. He's litrally rolling on the bed, handcuffed, and cracking up. And then *I'm* in stitches. The back of my chair knocks against the door with each round of laughing.

"We need to go back there," I say — all serious now, which proves I can act out emotions and turn around on a dime.

"I can't," Quinn cries. "I squealed on Cookie for being a rogue therapist years ago and she got her license taken away. She retired after that. She hates me. She once left me a message that if she ever saw me again, she would murder me. The woman always scared the shit out of me."

"I used to have sex with her in her office," I blurt.

After another laughing fit when hearing my confessing, Quinn stands up and between giggles he says, "I probably sat on the same couch. This is true synchronicity."

"I know. Right? It's like stuff is related but has no real reason for connecting."

"Uhm, yeah. That's what I said."

"I liked Cookie. I still like her. She's a handful, but she's always been very good to me."

"As long as you're fucking her."

"I am not fucking her." I am not laughing anymore now — for real. This guy is crude. "We need to find out how much you really hurt

Kevin," I say, not sure if I'm acting or becoming the cool dude I pretend to be.

"You can do that without me ..." he says.

"No. You're coming with me."

Quinn

This would be comical if I wasn't being held prisoner and about to be forced to confront Gavina, Vernkowsky and Cookie Nussbaum. How the fuck did this happen?

I guess Hollywood is a small world. At dinner parties you'll often hear conversations where people brag about their stylist, or doctor, or decorator, or therapist. You'll hear the rich and/or famous tout *'he's or she's the best.'* And you can bet everyone's in the market for the best of everything. Before you know it, everyone's sharing resources over their third glass of Pinot Noir while breaking their diets with two-hundred calorie bacon-wrapped dates from Saudi Arabia. When I was relevant, I was at a soiree hosted by Vanessa Smith where the conversation led to the best Independent or Assisted living facilities in Southern California. You guessed it — The Hacienda Mirage Rest Home.

"Brad's mother went there and was happy as a clam. Until she died that is."

"Tom was there for the last couple years of his life."

"Anna is there now, in case any of you wonder what happened to her."

So, I'm not surprised to find out that most of us in The Hacienda Crowd find ourselves with one degree of separation. We seem to be linked together. But it's still comical.

"How about I let you blow me and you let me go?" I politely ask Rudy. You can imagine how freaked out I am if I'm offering *that*!

"Be quiet!" he says. "I wouldn't touch you with a tin footpole."

"A tin footpole? You mean a ten-foot pole?"

"Whatever."

"I wouldn't let you do it anyway. I'm not *that way*."

"Will you please just shut your pie hole! I'm trying to think," Rudy says.

"I'll go back to L.A., and you'll never see or hear from me again," I plead, trying to get through his thick skull.

Rudy's not responding. He's quiet but clearly straining his limited intelligence to come up with a plan. It's bright daylight and I suppose I don't look that good to him right now. After a little while, he gets up off his chair and grabs my handcuffed hands and leads me into the bathroom, where he unlocks the cuffs and relocks them with my arms raised high to reach around the shower rod that is firmly affixed to the wall.

"I'm not into any kinky stuff," I say.

"If you don't stop talking, I'm gonna make whatever you did to Kevin look like children's play."

"I think you mean *child's play*." If I have to keep correcting this moron's use of the English language, I will lose my mind. If I haven't already.

Rudy ignores my English lesson as he strips naked, steps into the shower, closes the curtains between us, takes his shower, comes out, dries off and dresses. He moves around like a man who knows what the fuck he's doing, not the caveman who trapped and shackled me.

Then he finally speaks. "We'll go back to The Hacienda, get Kevin to let you shoot our movie there ... and ask my friend to help fund our project since he has lots of money and loves me.

"So now you're fucking *another* oldster at The Hacienda ... and it's *our* movie?"

"You said you would cast me in it."

I think I might be sick. Between the booze last night and all this drama, my stomach is trampolining. But deep down I know I'll be alright. I've certainly been in a lot more complicated and dangerous shit than this. My entire life has been nothing but mega highs and rock bottom lows. And believe me, I've come out alright after dealing with characters more dangerous and powerful than this gigolo. Of course, it's true I was younger then. But I've still got *it*. I am going make this work. I'm okay. Don't worry.

Rudy said something interesting about his friend financing the film. If I can get some seed money, the chances for *Old Folks* increase exponentially.

"How much money does this guy have?" I ask, hands still up over my head even after he's dressed and ready to split.

"I don't really know. How much do we need?"

I tell him that we could make an award-winning Indie Film for half a million. The truth is if we got a hundred K I would be a happy camper. I explain that I've already written most of it and I'll direct. We need the location and will cast some extras from The Hacienda. I mention that he won't make much up front, but he can cash out after distribution and box office. I explain that we could hire some real actors. He doesn't like that.

"I'm a real actor! And after I get you down from there, your hands stay cuffed."

Gavina

After Sunday brunch, lunch — whatever you want to call it — no one else is in the library. The large room is pure dead-brilliant — what with all the lovely books piled up to the roof and the dark colors and classy decorating that brags from the walls and furniture. 'Tis the place I like to go to when I have silent, secret incantations to do — like the spell I have cast onto Quinn, Cookie, Elmore, Rudy, Kevin Vernkowsky and anyone related to them biologically or through marriage. My favorite magical formulation of interconnection between these people is taking shape. Abracadabra, Alakazam, Hocus Pocus, Open Sesame and Sim Sala Bim.

I use the computer sometimes when I am alone here without having to look over my shoulder while shopping online or doing my research. I rotate the usage of the various credit cards I may have nabbed from a few of the other residents who have lost most of their marbles and would not know I had taken their little plastic jewels. 'Tis not only residents but also visitors who sometimes leave purses lying near their soon-to-be departed loved ones. I am like a ghost — in and out with wallet in hand which I return anonymously by leaving it on the front welcome desk for whatever old crow is manning it at the moment. I do not need any thanks or reward for finding and returning the wallet. Yesterday, I used Butter's Visa card for my online shopping. I saw her full, actual name when I completed the purchase of the food preservatives for my Angel of Mercy Plan, so that's the name I'll add to my P.O. Box in town. I got a surge of pride and satisfaction about me ordering what I need and doing something about the situation instead of only moaning and grumping or expecting Quinn or someone other than myself to fix things. I know I should not be telling you all this, but you know how I get about keeping secrets and I am pretty sure you will not bust me because no matter how cocksure and arrogant you are, when push comes to shove, you are no braver or better than me or anyone else and you had better keep your mouth shut is all I am telling you. You are no saint yourself.

The antifreeze I can get in person when I ride to town in the shopping van to pick up my paraphernalia for my first two methods promised on a rush for tomorrow.

The third method I would like to perfect is the stranglehold that I am strengthening with the Fit-It Grip Extender — a hand exerciser that increases performance, power and stability in your wrists and elbows. Of course, I will not be able to strangle *myself* if I decide to join those that are on The List. At the thought of it however, I begin to chuckle quietly, picturing me struggling to release myself from my own grip while another part of me insists on yielding to my strong hands. Is that not hysterical? Go ahead and have a laugh on me. I do not mind in this instance. Thank you very much.

'Tis been way too long since I have had this sense of purpose. It feels so much better to take charge of my own life and to help others who are not as savvy as I am. People just bury their heads in the sand when things are going down that they do not want to accept and face. But every day there is something or someone out to ruin your good mood or trick you into being compliant and complacent while they plan to tear down the facility in which you live without a care in the world about what it might mean to you if you have to relocate and adjust to a whole new living environment and way of life in a different place with new people or no people at all because you are alone and no one cares or understands you like when you were a dirt poor kid growing up in Wester Hailes with a lunatic mother and no father.

All the while, people like Cookie Nussbaum or Elmore Whatever hook up and become bosom buddies and form cliques that exclude you just because they think you have no money or do not wear trendy clothes because you have your own fashion sense and style. Those two vultures are just plain orphans like me and Quinn. They have no family and might as well go the way of The Manager. And to prove what a good person I am, I am willing to put them out of the misery of being kicked homeless to the street. Everyone else can fend for themselves because I just do not have the stamina to deal with every single old person here.

And then there is Rudy. Thank the Lord he has come into my life because the thing with Quinn is beginning to feel one-sided and at this later stage of being I think I am done with unrequited and non-reciprocal love. Quinn can either prove his devotion to me by moving me in with him so we can finally live together, or he can just go right onto The List, and I will carry on with Rudy or go ahead and strangulate my own self. 'Tis good to have options. Is it not?

Elmore

Now Cookie and I are off together on a mission to visit Kevin Vernkowsky and get the real scoop. Far be it for either of us to go skipping down the halls of The Hacienda holding hands, but that's what it feels like even though we're actually ambling along like tortoises — her arm interlocked around mine as if I could hold both her and me erect. I've often found that those with the most frail bodies have the strongest minds.

Doctor Nussbaum is one tough Cookie. You know I couldn't help saying it. Someone had to. One of the things I'm learning to like about her is she's not about to take crap from anyone and she goes after what she wants. I've always been like that myself. It's not easy to find folks like that to pal around with because most people just go with the flow and too many just end up somewhere with something they didn't plan on, or they simply drown in their own complacency. Or they ignore the warnings or blessings that are placed in front of them. It's only by my own wits, guts, stamina, and willingness to trust the signs along the way that I survived being a deeply closeted gay man when it was extremely forbidden and dangerous.

When we finally maneuver our way to Mr. Vernkowsky's office, Cookie immediately asks him, "How come you're here on a Sunday?"

He's sitting behind his desk, elbows on the desktop and forehead in hands.

"I came in to get my mind off things at home," he looks up and says.

"How's your nose?" Cookie and I both ask in unison.

"It's okay. Hurts a bit but nothing's broken. Does everyone know about my little incident yesterday with Gavina's friend?

"Everyone who's interested and still has their wits about them," Cookie answers.

"You're Mr. Fingerton ... new here, aren't you?" he asks me.

"Elmore," I say.

"Elmore. Please ... both of you take a seat. How can I help you?"

His nose is red and there's a Band-Aid on it. But even with that little bandage, he's a real stud. Not the Rudy type of hunk handsome. More the nerdy, intellectual Clark Kent type. More Bring-Home-To-Mother than Down-Low-Man. As if I could ever bring a man home to my mother back when.

I already know I have to talk fast if I want to get a word in with Cookie around.

"What's going on at home? Is everything all right?" I ask.

One of the few benefits of old age is you get to say and ask what you want without worrying if it's proper. Especially if you've given up the popularity game as I have. If you don't like me, you can just be on your way which is a polite way of saying *bugger-off*.

"Fight with the wife. You know how it is," he mutters.

"Not really. Never *had* a wife," I say.

"Not really. Never *been* a wife," Cookie says.

We both get a chuckle out of that, while Mr. Vernkowsky simply watches us with a confused look on his damaged and suckable face.

"Oh. Right. Sorry. Assumptions."

"Never assume. You know what they say, Mr. Vernkowsky," I tease.

"*Assume* makes an *ass* out of *u* and *me*. And please call me Kevin."

"Kevin ..." Cookie says, leaning forward as seductively as an eighty-year-old woman can. This broad has balls. Hopefully just a figure of speech, but who knows? "Are you sure your nose is all right? That Gavina Man sounds dangerous. Violent. Why on earth would he do that to you?"

"What's going on with the wife at home?" I ask.

"You both have a lot of questions. Can we slow it down a bit here? I'm sure you didn't come into my office to talk about my marriage or my nose."

"We most certainly did come here to see if you were feeling okay," I say, with as much indignation as I can muster.

His office is small and stuffy. You can bet I'm already redecorating in my mind. There would be a more open feel with a mirror on one wall, and his desk moved sideways at the tiny window — that does not need blinds making his little chamber even darker than it already is. As a matter of fact, the window needs to be enlarged and the walls painted in a nice bright eggshell white. We could even take out a wall and shrink the waiting room. There are no family photos on his desk, so there's no information about his personal life. It's obvious that he didn't mean to share anything about his trouble at home. We just must have caught him in a vulnerable moment. I can tell he needs a hug. If I was thirty years younger, I would have already made it around the desk, kneading his sinewy, tan neck.

"Your office could use a little touch up," I say. "I could easily add it to the work order once someone around here initiates the invoice for the redecorating."

"I'm not sure what you're talking about now," Kevin says.

"I'm going to update some of your interiors here at The Hacienda. Who do I have to talk to in order to get this design project going?"

Cookie faces me and reaches over to pat my arm with a welcomed look of understanding. She nods and smiles, as I look into her eyes. They're very blue.

"Is that your therapist smile?" I ask her bitchily.

"Yes, Elmore. It's my look of compassion. Empathy and understanding all rolled into one lovely smile of support. I'll help you work out the interior design assignment. But right now, we're here not only to make sure Kevin is okay, but to put the tear-down rumors to rest."

We both turn to Kevin Vernkowsky whose head is back in his hands just as we found him.

Chapter Seven

Rudy

Quinn's hands are still bonded together but he's a squirrelly one and might be bigheaded enough to try to open the passenger door and jump out, so I switch on the child safety proof to stop him from abscowding from the car during our short drive back to The Hacienda. I'm still acting all macho and gangster. It's method acting but good enough for Brando so good enough for me. The dude is talking a mile a minute and I could shut him up if I want but I'm thinkin' I might as well know what's goin' on in his mind. And why not get to know him if he's gonna direct me in our upcoming film where I'll play the Kevin Vernkowsky role?

"I don't want to do this," Quinn pleads.

I don't answer.

"I don't know *how* the fuck to do this," he continues. Gavina wants to move in with me because she's convinced that they're tearing the place to the ground. Whoever *they* are."

I don't answer. Eyes on the road.

"I can't stand Gavina. She makes me sick to my stomach. But the old battleax is in love with me and thinks I've been paying for part of her keep because I love her ... which is total bullshit ... since I was blackmailed into it years ago and only did it for a short while to avoid being sent up the river for various and assorted reasons that are all in my past. Now she's in the rears. Hasn't paid lately. Don't know how she's gotten away with it all these years of me not paying."

"Go on," I mutter so that he knows I'm listening and evaluating what he's saying. But I'm not showing any emotion because I am now totally in Brando/Pacino mode. Quinn is over-the-top rude and obnoxious, and I really want to slap him but refrain myself because I want to star in a movie. I'm only human after all. And I'm not at all sure what I feel about poor old Gavina except *no one* should talk about *anyone* like he is.

He says, "And what if Cookie sees me and recognizes me as the guy who turned her in and caused having her therapist license to be revoked? I am afraid of that woman. She hates me!"

I nod as if I know what a revoke is.

"I *can* apologize to Kevin Vernkowsky if he's not hurt real bad," Quinn continues. "I think I can finesse that."

Now Quinn stops talking. I can tell without even looking at him that he's tryin' to figure out and plan his next move. And the truth is, he has brought up a lot of good points for considering. Mostly these are *his* problems, not mine.

I pull the car over, take out my phone and call The Hacienda.

"Is Kevin Vernkowsky in today?" I ask the woman who answers *yes* in the confirmative. "Please ask him if Rudy — Elmore Fingerton's son — along with Quinn Adamsdaur can come to see him as soon as possible .... Yes, I'll hold."

Quinn is silent, watching me as if waiting for the dials to click while breaking into a safe. I think he's afraid of me for real.

"He'll see us. Okay, good," I say. "Please tell him we should be there in about ten minutes to apologize and set things right."

"Did you just say you are Elmore Fingerton's *son*?" Quinn asks, as if I just told the woman on the phone that I was the damn pope.

"I'm not really his son. Elmore and me told them that so they wouldn't suspect we were sexing around together against their rules."

"But you *do* know him," Quinn says.

"He's the man I plan to ask for money to back our film," I say.

"Elmore the interior decorator?" Quinn asks, hanging his head down like an exhausted prize fighter in the corner of the ring with no more fight in him. "I don't think that's gonna happen."

"Why not?"

"Um. I sort of know him, too."

"What the heck? You sure do get around. Do you know everyone?"

"Um. I don't think Elmore likes me."

"What are you talking about now?" I ask. I'm breaking character and sounding like the regular person I am. This is all getting too confused and jumbled. And all the ironicals are overtaking me. I feel like a twelve-year-old boy being teased in class and punished at home for not being able to answer the teacher's questions or figure out what's going on around him.

"He did some decorating for me a long time ago. A *lot* of interior design actually. I sort of ..."

"You sort of *what*?!"

"I sort of didn't exactly pay him all of what I sort of owed him."

Gavina

I am pacing the floor of my studio apartment and beginning to wonder what difference it makes about the tear-down when there are other things to worry about. You are probably wondering why I have not gone to Kevin Vernkowsky sooner to confront him about the tear-down. 'Tis because he doesn't know anything. He has become merely a puppet of the Billingsby Ultra Care Homes of The Americas. He is one of at least ten thousand employees managing a network of rest homes all across the once-called United States. And with companies like BUCHA only the men at the top know what is coming down the pike. They sit in their ivory towers in skyscrapers in cities like New York or Chicago and move people around like pawns on a chess board. They focus on how to make the most money possible by building and managing these places for old folks to be let out to pasture, but there are no green pastures and no one to care for the little guy without family. They drink martini lunches and screw their secretaries. The CEO of this zillion-dollar company will not even take my calls or answer my emails. 'Tis two in the afternoon on Sunday, so I should not expect to hear anything from BUCHA until the work week begins and that is fine because The Manager has a need to die regardless of what happens. The man is obviously in mental and emotional pain and must be dealt with in a compassionate and swift method. I need to prioritize myself after I get whatever information I can from — admittedly cute — Kevin Vernkowsky.

He has taken me aside in private more than once and flirtatiously said to me 'My door is always open if you need anything.' And I will be damned if that is not the case when I arrive at his office unannounced — as only someone with my stature should be able to do here at Hacienda Mirage. His office is indeed open. He is crammed in a chair protected from all of us oldsters behind his desk and snuggling in front of him sit Cookie Nussbaum and Elmore Fudd. The three of them are having a tête-à-tête about me.

"Good afternoon, Gavina," Vernkowsky says. "I'll be with you in a moment." I think he wants me to leave or sit in the outer waiting room. But I will not depart to be plotted against by these monsters. When I do not budge, he continues, "If this is about your account, I spoke with Mister Adamsdaur."

"What about my account?" I cry. "What is wrong with my account? It gets paid way beyond my control. My people pay your bill."

"Please give us a moment to finish here. You can have a seat in the waiting room."

"Quinn Adamsdaur is her benefactor? I don't believe it," Cookie pipes in with that fake regal tilt of her head.

"That guy's a criminal. He owes me ten thousand dollars," Elmore says.

"How do you two animals know Quinn?" I shout. "They know my Quinn?"

I do indeed need to sit down now. My knees are beginning to buckle and there is cotton candy clouding my eyesight and hindsight. The shock is sending me on my way to my secret place. Kevin squeezes out from behind his desk and grabs a chair from the waiting room and tries to put it up under me. Surprisingly gallant. Now there is hardly any room to move with the four of us in here and ma heid's mince. I collapse beside the chair onto the floor. Fainting, I am.

Elmore

I'm not going to be able to get down to the floor to help Gavina and then get up again, but Kevin is quick to the rescue. He has darted around from behind his desk. He's Sunday casually dressed in polo and khakis. The banded sleeves of his shirt strain around his biceps. His pants could use a little tailoring, but the relaxed fit still works okay for him. And for me.

It's surely not the first time he's had to help an old lady off the floor. But when Gavina doesn't respond he grabs his desk phone and hits one button for what is probably an emergency squad for situations such as this. His very own in-house 9-1-1. I'm learning so much today. Truth be known, I could sit here forever watching Kevin even if he was just silently doing paperwork.

Cookie seems less concerned about her fellow Hacienda Resident than she is about Quinn. I don't know who she's talking to, but she speaks in a controlled tone as if she were conducting a therapy session. Referring to Gavina she says, "She's got to know where Adamsdaur is. Get her awake so she can tell me where to find him."

"I think Kevin here has the situation well in hand," I say. A little support and flattery is bound to get him to like me. If I had my peek-a-boo wig on, I would be flipping my hair back away from my eyes, but I doubt that my now eighty-year-old drag persona, Miss Elmoreof — or any drag queen for that matter — would be his thing. I'm not sure if that part of me will ever come out here at

The Hacienda. But never say never. Stranger things seem to happen around here.

"Quinn is her so-called man-friend? I'm gonna murder the bastard," Cooke says. Her calm face belies her aggressive words as if she's just asserting a fact. She's watching Kevin tuck a pillow — that he makes appear magically from out of nowhere — under Gavina's head. I can see the waistband of his white Calvin Kleins when he bends over. And a slight ass cleft barely peeking.

"Is she alright?" I ask from my make-believe Elmore Throne.

"She's probably faking it," Cookie says.

"Come on, Cookie ... how can you be so cold? What has she done to you?" I ask.

"Nothing, I guess. I just don't like the way she waltzes around here like she reigns over everyone."

Cookie sits back and mulls over what she has just said, like you do when a thought that is hidden inside your head surprises you when it comes out of your mouth.

"Isn't that *your* job?" I tease. She must be able to tell I am trying to lighten the mood because she offers me a self-deprecating smile. I do like a woman who knows herself. Even when she's being somewhat difficult.

Kevin is now sitting on the floor next to Gavina, when a very competent-looking person — not sure if it's a man or a woman — comes in with a defibrillator and props up Gavina's legs onto the chair that I have finally vacated. And before you know it, Gavina's eyes open very wide for just a moment as Rudy appears in the doorway nearly dragging Quinn Adamsdaur a step behind — the two of them handcuffed wrist to wrist. Be still my prison-porn heart.

Quinn

"I got him," Rudy says like a child who's captured a butterfly. As if he expects everyone in the room to be thrilled at the sight of me. This is fast becoming the worst day of my life. And as you can imagine, I've had a lot of bad days from the time I made it in Hollywood at the age of around thirty-five to the current era of me having basically crashed and burned. The funny thing is that things were fairly great during those good years. I had money, a successful film under my belt, and good times with top-notch people who were at the height of their game. But then there was too much partying — cocaine, booze, and girls. A couple of them who joined forces to drag me through court. More things and stuff that only Gavina knows about and has always held over my head to get me to behave. Not just her uncle's death over thirty years ago, but other things and stuff that you don't need to know the facts or details about. Let's just say, I have to walk a thin line not to piss her off.

And I'm weirdly afraid of *Cookie*, too. She was the court-appointed shrink during my sexual harassment lawsuit and she was supposed to help me stop being addicted to sex. Instead, she opened *her own* legs to me. I was vulnerable. She got into my psyche, and I reported her. Look, I've already admitted to you that I've done — should we say *inappropriate* — things but *Cookie* had sex *with a patient* for fuck's sake! Now *that's* just plain fuckin' wrong.

Which brings me to *Elmore,* who decorated my bungalow in Topanga Canyon. Big deal. Not worth the fee. He's a harmless old goat now, who was nevertheless alleged to be some sort of mobster at one time. I need to figure out how to maybe pay him off or let Rudy charm him into giving me seed money for the film. I used to love a challenge, but this thing is becoming awfully complex and causing me to want to drink at three in the afternoon on a Sunday.

Vernkowsky evidently wants an apology. And I still want to shoot my film here. But right now, from the way he's staring at Rudy — like I stare at chicks I want to fuck — there might be a fag angle I didn't count on. Kevin is all googly-eyed at Rudy, my captor.

The nurse who's helping Gavina looks like one of those twenty-something androgenous types who likes to tie men and or women up and spank them with a snappy, black leather whip. I'm distracted and discombobulated by the beast. "Not now," I say to myself. "Get a grip."

So here I am with all of them. And to divert my attention from the dominatrix in the loose-fitting grape nurse's scrubs, I blurt out a hello to the group. "How's tricks?"

"Shut up," Rudy says.

"Just wanted to get the party started," I hear myself say.

"This isn't a party, Mister," the nurse person replies. He/she is all business.

"Shit. Too bad. Nursey here looks like *they* like to party."

"Excuse me, Sir," the nurse says — monotone voice as stern and unruffled as can be. "There's no need to be rude to me or anyone. Back off ... whoever you are. It's people like you who have made people like me suffer for long enough. Don't get me started."

Which is when Rudy slaps me smack across my face. And everyone — except Gavina — spontaneously either shouts 'YES' or 'RIGHT' and claps hands. Not the type of applause I'm looking for.

Cookie

The slap takes me back to over ten years ago. I had a full therapy practice. Not *in spite of* my edgy reputation, but *because* of it. High-profile, successful alpha types *want* to be confronted and challenged. They crave help from someone who is not intimidated by them. Not the true narcissists like Quinn, mind you. But my clients overall, appreciated getting a new perspective from me because I insisted on breaking through to them. And occasionally they misinterpreted my assertive style — and my boundaries may have gotten weak, leaving me vulnerable to the advances of some clients. It was rather fashionable at the time for women over fifty in Hollywood to still consider themselves sexy. I looked good and Quinn Adamsdaur never held back with his compliments and flirtations.

I had no more appointments one day after he was with me, and he wouldn't leave my office. Perhaps I did offer him coffee instead of insisting that he go away. There's a chance that I joined him on the couch usually reserved only for clients. But there's no way in hell that I laid a hand on him before his own hand was making its way up my leg. It should have been one of those things that happens and is forgotten. People move on. Most folks don't want a scene or a scandal. But Quinn was run out of luck and enjoyed his part in seeing me go down. I have memorized the salient part of the report.

> *Respondent has subjected her license to disciplinary action for unprofessional conduct and is convicted for various such*

conduct related to the qualifications, functions and duties of a Licensed LCSW. By Default and Order, license revoked.

Nowadays, I can no longer remember why I go from one room to the next or why I open a cabinet door in my apartment, but I remember that decree perfectly. And I know full well that this is the man who fondled me and then reported me.

Here stands the guy I've been hoping to get even with. He's handcuffed to my Rudy, who has a self-satisfied grin on his face as if he's a tomcat proudly presenting a mouse he's captured. My hands are making useless fists. I've waited for this day. But as fate would have it, my hip arthritis is preventing me from rising out of my chair and I feel claws grip my old bones when Rudy slaps Quinn. I feel like my imaginary hope to see Quinn suffer is being played out before my eyes for real. I watch Quinn's face open in surprise at the slap and seemingly freeze there for me to remember forever.

Elmore grabs and squeezes my hand, and it feels like we're experiencing something important together. Needless to say, we've both piled a whole lot of our own baggage on this man. I can feel a storehouse of anger and then a rush of fear followed by profound sadness. I hear the words *'it's over'* in my head.

'What's over?' I ask myself.

It almost feels as if the words are coming to me through the walls of The Hacienda itself.

Rudy

I step back and drag Quinn with me into the waiting room, so the nurse can help Gavina through the doorway. It looks like the old woman has just come out of a faint and might go right back into another one. I've seen that expression on the faces of people who pass out from a too intense work out at the gym. Once I had a client collapse during a session in her house, and when her husband walked in, I was giving her CPR. That turned into a huge, big, giant scene with a lot of misunderstanding and various interspections. The kind nurse in *this* instance tells us that they are taking Gavina to her room to lie down and rest. It's obvious that Gavina needs to be taken care of and has mixed emotions and feelings about being carted away. She blows a few kisses that I think are meant for Quinn — or maybe me — as they pass.

Then we step back into the still-crowded room that doesn't have much space for the five of us because it's small and jam-packed. Elmore looks normal. Good old Elmore is not mad. He usually has a devil-might-not-care look on his face as if nothing unusual is happening. I guess it takes more than this to really piss him off after all he's been through in his life. And whatever is going on in his mind is tickling him. But he's pointing and shaking a boney finger at Quinn, and he doesn't stop wagging that finger like a church lady scolding a bad boy who's bound to be punished. He's holding onto Cookie with his other hand.

Cookie has not said a word, so I do. "Are you alright?"

She doesn't answer. It's as if she is in her own world thinking about something else and not what's happening and going on in front of her — you know like when there's like a scene playing inside your head and you're there but not really there.

"You look kind of like in shock," I continue. "I brought this guy here to apologize to Kevin and the rest is really none of my business, Cookie."

"*You* are very much my business," Cookie says. Loud and clear.

“I don’t really want to beat Quinn up for you if that’s what you want, Cookie. We’re gonna make a movie together.”

As I say this, I turn to Elmore. When I do, he sits down on the only empty chair, lets his hands fall into his lap, stares at me and says, “This clown’s not making any movie, Rudy Honey. He seems to owe Hacienda some money for some reason, and he’s been delinquent on my invoice forever. Rumor has it that he’s homeless. No one’s seen him for years. My collection agency gave up on him. Why don’t you hold onto him and bring him to my apartment, and we can deal with this the old-fashioned way.”

“That won’t be necessary,” Kevin says. “He’s caused enough trouble. Let me take care of this.”

I wish Kev’s office would clear out so I could be alone with him. He wants to somehow fix all this and for all I know, maybe he can. But together, we could do anything. It’s all I can think about. I should be focusing on what to do for Cookie and Elmore, but did I mention how Kevin’s eyes are like the ocean? I recognize the look on his face as like a kid dead-set on being an adult.

“Let’s let the boys handle this,” Elmore finally says to Cookie, as he wrestles himself out of his chair and offers to help her up and out. It’s like they’ve read my mind, or some invisible force is moving them for me.

Once again, I step aside nudging Quinn toward the waiting room, and we let the two of them pass like an old married couple. Elmore winks at me. Cookie steps right on my foot. On purpose. I know how she can be. And then with her head held high she swings a low pitch of her fist right into Quinn’s groin.

Chapter Eight

Gavina

The nurse lowers me onto my bed with surprisingly strong arms and a genuine kindness that I have only experienced in the care of an occasional health care worker — or during the time when Florence Nightingale would bring me tea with a smile while I transcribed her *Notes on Nursing*. By the way — not that you care — Florence was single just like me, but we never had a sexual relationship if that is what you are thinking because neither of us was that way. Thank you very much. And she seldom wore that stupid rag on her head like you see in old fake drawings.

I seem to be coming in and out of a fog. However, after a while, I sit up and convince the nurse that I am alright.

I am not.

I am mostly thinking about my two suitors bound together into one delicious package of man meat. There they were — Rudy the Conqueror having taken Quinn the Marauder into servitude as his prisoner. Hero linked hand-in-hand with Outlaw. Both lusting after me and receiving my airborne kisses with the delight of masculine pleasure steeped in anticipation. Causing me to swoon, once again as I am apt to do now and then, more and more every day lately.

"Okay, Ms. McVey," Nurse says. "But I'll be back to check on you before dinner. Please just relax for a while. And I suggest not lying down. Perhaps a walk in the garden?"

"I am fine," I say in my most polite manner. "Thank you so much for your assiduousness."

My options are increasing in leaps and bounds. I could live with Quinn, although did I mention that I am beginning to not like Quinn so much anymore? Better yet, I could move in with Rudy. Or I could add myself to The List and be done with it. I guess that is not exactly leaps and bounds but it feels like it because of the electric rush that is shooting through my veins. I sponge myself down with a very hot, wet washrag that feels good against my skin, and I get dressed in my best Sunday orange shift with the large pockets in front because after all, one never knows when one may need a roomy pocket. I pull my stockings up way over my knees so the hem will fall over the elastic bands. No shoes since I am not going anywhere just yet. I am ready to properly greet my two men when they come to my door. One to apologize and the other to declare his love. I sit patiently in my chair, hands floating onto my knees like a lady in waiting, and I gaze out my little window at the endless lush green hills and valleys of my native Scotland rolling to infinity in the late afternoon sun.

I assume the Final Solution supplies I bought online will arrive in the morning and I shall go on my shopping trip on the shuttle to town for the provisions.

Elmore

When we get to my suite, I offer Cookie a drink and she says, "Yes, please. Gin and tonic." She's placing an order, not *asking* if I have the ingredients for her preferred cocktail.

"I can manage that. I'm a vodka man myself."

Here's the deal. If they found out that Rudy was ever in my apartment sporting a friendly erection, the shit would hit the fan. The gossip would get even more intense than I figure it already is regarding me liking men. Around here, a woman in a man's apartment is enough grist for the rumor mill. I've already seen a couple instances of the old guy with the fedora sneaking through the door of two different Independent Living Girls. So, rumors about Cookie and me will spread like Hollywood Herpes if anyone sees her come in here. Of course, as you can imagine, that sort of gossip is fine with me, and I'd guess fine with her. Let them all fan the contradictory speculation. Is he gay? Is he having sex with Cookie? Huh?

"Well, that was something," Cookie says. We both know she's referring to the scene in Kevin's office. "Quinn Adamsdaur. Can you believe it. Our mutual archenemy. Handcuffed and face slapped. Isn't life grand?"

"Indeed. I felt something loosen in my bowels. And it's not diarrhea."

"What?"

"I mean I feel lighter, like a score's been settled. And I didn't even do anything. Rudy did it for us. I love that guy," I say, happy to have company so I can use my gold gilded highball cocktail glasses. True Hollywood Regency Style.

"I know exactly what you mean. I've been imagining running into that asshole, Quinn, for years and there he was like a captured animal, tail between his fat legs. He looks old and fat, doesn't he?"

"Older and fatter anyway. I can't be the pot calling the kettle black. Look at me."

"You look fine."

I serve up the drinks and we sit at my solid wood, mid-century modern table. I've hauled a few of my favorite pieces from my house in Studio City. The Sun Coast Dresser, the planter table with Formica tops, and the curved sectional sofa that has endless stories to tell from the naked bartender soirees back in the day. I had to donate the rest since I've downsized and all.

Neither of us speak for a while. Cookie sighs and sinks comfortably — elbows on the table either holding her up or positioning her for an intimate conversation. I mirror her and we both begin laughing. Here we are sharing another good chuckle.

"Aren't we supposed to be furious and plotting revenge?" I ask.

"I know, right?"

"I used to be someone you had to reckon with. Now, not so much," I say.

"I already heard a rumor in arts and crafts this morning when the other girls were gossiping about you being mafioso. Isn't that a kick in the pants?"

"I don't mind. It's ridiculous. People have been saying that for a long, long time. It makes me seem dangerous."

"What's the story?" she whispers, hoping for something juicy as she leans in conspiratorially.

"I've told the story a million times. Once I was even interviewed for The Village Voice."

"Go on," she sighs, nursing her drink like a lady who's lunched.

I tell her about how I'm from New Jersey but moved to New York in 1966. "I suppose being the *bon vivant* that you are, you've heard of The Stonewall Riot," I say, leaning back with my drink in hand and hearing my voice become more affected. I go on talking, even though to this day the retelling of the story makes me want to weep. "Every drag queen in the city knew of this gay bar that allowed us inside. The guy who eventually interviewed me was arrested around that time — not even in drag— for holding another man's hand as they crossed the street. That's how fucked up things were."

It was over sixty years ago and yet I still choke up when I talk about roaming around the city and feeling all piss and vinegar mixed with fear and shame. A righteous, lost, skinny boy with absolutely no idea who I was or what I was going to do with my life. Only knowing I didn't fit in anywhere until finding my way to Stonewall through a friend I met in junior college. Ricky Wynn.

After telling her about me and Ricky in way too much detail, I go on to explain to Cookie that when the pigs raided Stonewall — as they often did just to harass, rough us up and arrest us — we freaked and started to fight back. Enough was enough. This one gray clay-faced cop said something to me about Judy Garland deserving to die the day before and I hit him over the head with a bottle. Just like that. Well, maybe I was a little drunk. Things got crazy after a few of us did shit like that. An article in the newspaper a day or two later offered a bullshit convoluted story under the headline, *Homo Nest Raided, Queen Bees Are Stinging Mad.*

"Like many New York clubs in the 60's, The Stonewall Inn was owned by mafia. And just like the old telephone game when you whisper in one person's ear around a circle, and at the end of the line things get muddled ... I suppose that's how the whole mobster thing rubbed off on me. I've never minded. I've learned to embrace that lie about me."

"Oh, Elmore ...." All the guile drains from her face and Cookie sighs.

"It's alright," I say.

After retelling that little part of my life before I got to L.A. to build a career for myself, it seems trivial to worry about some guy stiffing me for my design fee.

"Elmore," Cookie says. "You're crying."

She reaches across and takes both my hands into both of hers — two octogenarians reaching across a mid-century tabletop.

Quinn

I've sat in the hot seat often enough. Never actually handcuffed to another man. But here we are and once again I'm face-to-face with Vernkowsky while practically holding hands with Rudy, who I have now seen naked which might be the reason I can so strongly sense the homoeroticism between the two of them while I am just a straight bystander. That feeling of being kicked to the sidelines is brewing in me again, just like it did the last time I was in this shoebox of an office in this godforsaken, last-stop, so-called *rest home.* There's nothing restful about the place. While they're making inviting glances at each other, I'm merely a sucker wasting time. I can't stand feeling like I'm waiting for a cab when I should be in a chauffeured limo.

"First of all, how's your nose?" Rudy asks.

“I’m okay. It’s not broken,” Vernkowsky replies.

“I brought Quinn back here to apologize and maybe find a way to make things right.”

“I was sure taken by surprise. I’ll tell you *that*. He asked to use The Hacienda to make a movie. I said no. And he punched me.”

“That sucks. I’m sorry.”

“You didn’t do it. He did.”

“I’m not apologizing. I just mean I’m sorry that happened.”

I swear I don’t know why I’m even in the room. These two only have eyes for each other. If I don’t speak up, they’ll just go on and on. But then it dawns on me. Rudy is the one who can help me get what I want. I’ll just apologize, sit back, and go with the flow. Not my style but I’m the type of person who respects others and learns and grows and can take a back seat if I have to.

“I’m sorry that I hit you,” I say. They both turn to me as if it’s the first time they realize I’m in the room. “You did not deserve it. I’ll pay for any doctor bills.”

“My God!” Vernkowsky nearly shouts. “There are no doctor bills. It’s all taken care of. The bill you should be concerned about is Gavina McVey’s monthly.”

“What’s that about?” Rudy asks.

“He owes his part of her fees. He’s past due by months.”

“You’ve been paying for her?” Rudy tugs at my arm when he raises his, talking with his hands which by the way is the worst thing an actor can do. I doubt that I'll be able to break him of that habit. Nor assume he could remember his lines without a shitload of help and technical assistance, which costs money.

"Long story," I say. "Not really either of your business really. I helped her out in the beginning. But I stopped ages ago. I'm getting fuckin' sick of hearing and talking about it."

Whatever Gavina has on me makes no difference now and no one would believe anything the old witch says anyway.

"Jesus, you're cruel," Vernkowsky says.

"I just don't see why everything has to be about money. What about art? I'm a filmmaker," I say.

"He wants to put me in his movie," Rudy says, not knowing that he has already lost the job even if I find a way to get the money.

"Can I go take a leak?" I ask. I've had enough of these two. "I have to go to the bathroom. By myself!"

"Let him go," Vernkowsky says.

And so, Rudy whisks out the key and unleashes his half of the cuffs — more anxious to be alone with his boyfriend than deal with me.

"Where's the john?" I ask.

Vernkowsky gives me directions to the Men's Room with all the sudden politeness of a guy who runs an old folks' home. He must have developed a keen sympathy for old men urgently needing to empty their bladder. I dash off like a little boy who doesn't want to wet his pants or wet the bed and embarrass himself and gets humiliated and beaten for not being able to control his little bladder.

"Hate to let him go like that," I hear Rudy say on my way out.

Gavina

I hate it when I faint. I miss all the good stuff. Alone in my room, I can only imagine what went on in that little office after the nurse escorted me out. I am sure that her majesty Cookie yelled and screamed demanding all the attention as if she was the one with a busted nose. As far as she is concerned, she is the only one on the whole planet who matters. The new guy, Elmore, was for certain waving his hands in the air like an old, wrinkled Grimhilde and trying to calm Cookie down, so he could take center stage. Quinn must have busted out of the cuffs and is heading my way to beg me to abandon ship and run away with him. But he has probably left poor Rudy knocked out on the floor with Kevin Vernkowsky frantically trying to revive him with mouth-to-mouth resuscitation. And I had to pass out and end up woozy and all alone in my room, wondering if I can just go off with Quinn while they tear the place down and not knowing if Rudy is okay. 'Tis not really fair that he and I have not had a chance to get to know each other better. I think that if folks got to really know one another they would find out that even if you believe someone is one thing, she may be another.

In the midst of my going over all this in my mind, I look out of my window and see the bulldozer sitting across the parking lot. The thing is mean and yellow and has a bucket in front like a gigantic mouth ready to eat up and level anything in its path.

And to accentuate this sight, there is a knock on my door.

It takes all my energy to get up and open it. 'Tis *not* Quinn or Rudy. 'Tis The Manager. He just stands there as if he has no idea how he got here or why?

"Come in," I say, thinking about how I need to get going on my plan to help him depart.

He comes in but does not sit. I only have one chair and a bed and he is the sort who would not sit unless the lady does, so I sit on my bed. He is like a lost feral cat, matted and confused. Dear Heart.

"I suppose you want to talk about crossing over," I say.

"Drowning, burning at the stake or hanging?" he mutters and then chuckles a bit of a gallows laugh.

"Oh, no," I say, reaching for both his hands and leaning him closer. "It will be much less painful and humane!"

"When?"

"How about I put together the plan and we make arrangements for next week?"

"Next week?"

"Yes. I have a lot going on." There is no need to explain everything about the others and how we might have a full house of people who must go. 'Tis a lot of pressure and I have to figure a lot out. Not just methodology, timing, etc. But also wardrobe and final participants.

"Tuesday," he declares.

"Okay. Yes ... we will try for Tuesday," I agree. It takes him a million years to get up, turn around, and get himself back out the door, but eventually I am alone again and feeling quite agitated and a bit overwhelmed by all there is to figure out before that horrific bulldozer starts coming for all of us.

Cookie

Sipping on my adult beverage — nicely served in a gilded highball cocktail glass — I look around Elmore's apartment and realize it's the mirror image of my own. This gives me a sense of comfort and safety, and since Elmore has confided in me about Stonewall and everything, I feel as though I ought to share something heartfelt with him. It seems Rudy was the one who helped Elmore into Hacienda Mirage and you've probably guessed that he did the same for me once he saw how I lived. He just appeared outside my door one day with a concerned look on his face and said something like, 'Why don't you ever invite me over?' I had to let him in and that was that.

"Sometimes I've acted crazier than you might think," I say to Elmore. "It kept people away, and the older I got the more I never wanted anyone too close. I was on my way to becoming a hoarder."

"A what?"

"I kept things. Still do. Never throw stuff away. When I lived alone, I started to keep piles of things in cardboard boxes from the Self-Storage. They were stacked everywhere. And just as many odds and ends randomly left all over the place. I knew it was more than a mess but having everything around me made me feel safe. Rudy didn't berate me. He sorted stuff out, dragged stuff away and eventually physically drove me here to live. I still think he exaggerated the paperwork, but once they saw my bank statements, I was in."

"Secrets revealed."

"The Hoarder and the Drag Queen. Sounds like a B movie. We ought to pitch it to Quinn."

"Or better yet, forget about him entirely."

"You're right," I say. "Fretting about Quinn Adamsdaur is trivial. I'm getting too old and tired to need revenge."

"You said it. Not me," Elmore says. "If you're like me, you get a tad too vindictive."

Funny isn't it, how someone can throw a dig at you and it's easier to take when they begin with a self-deprecating phrase like *if you're like me* so you don't feel attacked. I let Elmore get away with it and wonder if he has better light or a nicer view here in his apartment than my place.

"I don't like being fucked with. Excuse my French," I say.

"I get that. Me neither. But let's face it ... what's done is done. And anyway, it looks like karma has taken care of Quinn. We're too old and from what I hear from each of us, we need to move on and face that we both belong here. I have osteoarthritis from head to toe and you're literally a mess."

"I still won't make a bed or wipe a sink. I'm a happy *pay-for-services gal* here. Besides, Rudy said he wouldn't visit my apartment if I messed it up. So he only comes occasionally and always on days when I know the housekeepers will have straightened me out. They do so every week."

"We really ought not be drinking."

"I love your glasses. But I don't need a refill."

"Thanks. Me neither."

I reach into my purse and pull out my iPhone. Rudy answers immediately. I put him on speaker, and ask, "What's happening? We're in Elmore's apartment. I think he might have a better north/south exposure. Are you still with Kevin and Quinn? The suspense might kill us both."

"I'm still here with Kevin. Quinn went to the bathroom. Are you two mad? Are you planning my determination?"

When Elmore and I glance at each other, it's clear we are both thinking the same thing. There are times when it's challenging to decipher what Rudy really means to say. So be it.

"It appears that Elmore and I both love you, and don't give a shit about Quinn."

"Wow. The guy's a total dick anyway."

"We know. And he's not worth the trouble."

"I'll come see you in a little while. Just stay put."

"Okay," Elmore says loudly, meeting my eyes. "But take it from the two of us, Quinn is *not* in the men's room taking a whiz."

Rudy

"You're not Elmore Fingerton's *son*," Kevin says, looking at me with the kindest, puppy dog eyes. The Band-Aid on his nose makes him look like a boxer. And you know how I like me an athletic man, even if he was the one who got decked.

"No. I'm a friend," I say.

"Why'd you tell me you were his son?" Kevin looks hurt, as if my lie has disorientated him. "I wonder where I was when Elmore applied or moved in."

"I don't know. We met a nice lady who handled everything."

"Oh. Okay. That's Mrs. Carter, my assistant manager. She's great. She should have introduced me..."

"Sorry. I feel bad. I don't want to piss you off or hurt your feelings," I say. "At least we got to meet now."

Kevin just sits there waiting for me to go on.

"Well ...." I continue. "I'm surely not Elmore's son. But we used to be ... um ... friends with benefits? And now I sort of fool around with him sometimes ... and I know residents here aren't supposed to sex it up behind closed doors for some reason but that's not really what we're doing."

"Old folks could have heart attacks behind locked doors if they get overly excited."

"Well, sorry. Now you know."

He seems happy at this news instead of indignated. And he takes his time thinking about what I said about me and Elmore. I've been around a lot of men in my time, but I don't remember ever wanting to just chill and talk and relax into conversating like I do with Kevin.

“And Cookie Nussbaum?” he asks.

“A friend.”

“With benefits?”

“Uhm. Yup. Old people type of limited benefits.”

“Gavina?”

“Just met her yesterday. Don’t know her. She seems mental.”

“We try not to talk about our residents that way.”

Kevin has either overlooked the sex confessions or doesn’t care. Or approves. Who knows? He is leaning back in his chair and stroking his chin as if he has a beard — which he doesn’t unless a sexy light brown stubble quantifies as a beard.

“She seems a brick shy of a full load,” I say.

“We try not to talk about our residents *that* way either.”

He’s smiling now and all his serious, professionalized ways are falling off him. He’s flirting with me. Believe me, I know when someone is coming on to me. I’m never wrong about that. I’m often not on the spot about a lot of things, but there’s definitively a vibe here.

“I also just met Quinn,” I say, before he can ask.

“Okay,” he says.

“That’s it?”

"To be honest, I have more important things to worry about. My nose will be fine," he says.

"Nice nose, by the way."

"Thanks," he says, as if he either doesn't realize that I'm hitting on him or he's not interested, and I mistook about him which will be the first time that's happened to me, and I may have to rethink my opinion of myself as a perfect read on being cruised.

"That's it?" I ask.

"It feels like I can talk to you," he says.

"Sure. Talk away. I'm a good listener. What's going on?" Back on track, no need to doubt my gaydar.

"My stepfather is an Assisted resident here and he's going downhill fast. I actually have always called him my dad since I never knew my biological father and Grayson came into my life when I was pretty young. He founded and used to manage The Hacienda ... and now I do."

Kevin goes on to tell me that his wife is leaving him! And he doesn't know how to let that poor Gavina woman stay here if Quinn doesn't pay his share. And if he really has not been paying, who has? And he's sorry to bend my ear and doesn't know why he's telling me all this.

"Nothing to be sorry about. That's a ton of stuff to deal with."

"Not your problem."

"No. But maybe I can help."

"He's not coming back, is he?" Kevin asks.

"Who? Quinn?"

"Yeah."

"Nope."

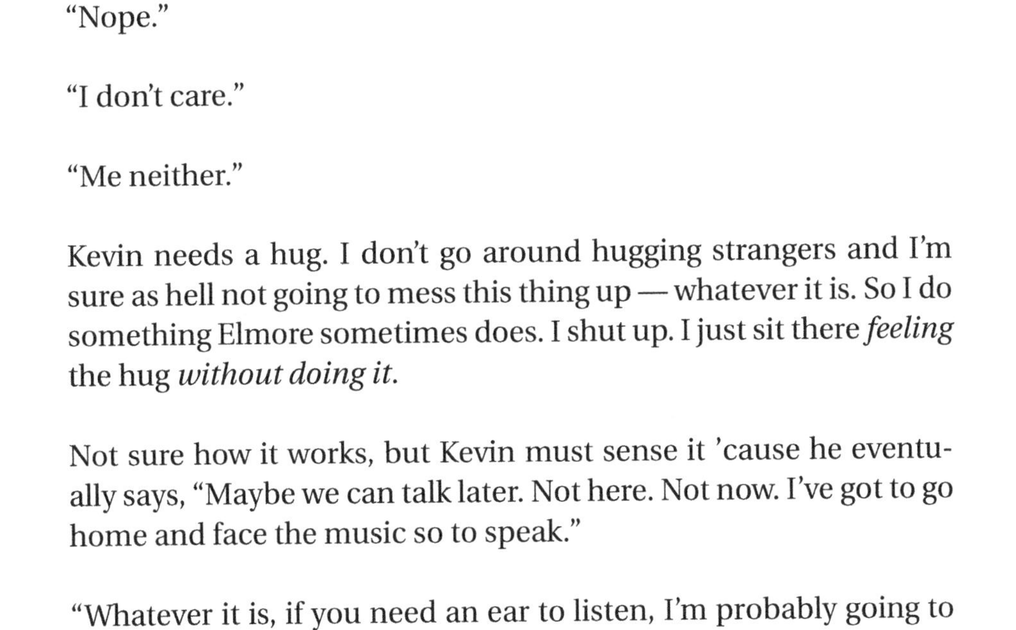

"I don't care."

"Me neither."

Kevin needs a hug. I don't go around hugging strangers and I'm sure as hell not going to mess this thing up — whatever it is. So I do something Elmore sometimes does. I shut up. I just sit there *feeling* the hug *without doing it.*

Not sure how it works, but Kevin must sense it 'cause he eventually says, "Maybe we can talk later. Not here. Not now. I've got to go home and face the music so to speak."

"Whatever it is, if you need an ear to listen, I'm probably going to still be here tomorrow."

"That sounds good actually. Maybe after I go to the gym ..."

"Where do you work out?" I ask. I *knew* this guy worked out.

"Obie's in town," he says. He's blushing and rubbing his bandaged nose like I've been known to do *when a wound starts to itch* — if you get my allegory.

"Then I guess I'll see you in the morning," I say.

It feels like he's teleporting me a hug when I get up to leave. The overhead lights flicker — like they're winking?

Gavina

I have spent most of my life waiting. The Elderly Me sitting here on the bed in my room is still the Five, Ten, Twenty, or Fifty-year-old Me. Anticipating. Waiting for something or someone to change my life and make it a song. My feet barely touch the floor and I have a stooped posture that turns my head down toward my own lap as if I am born of a horrible shame and worthlessness. I could sit here like this for hours. Sometimes I do. I sit and pass the time with at least *half* of myself knowing that whatever it is I wait for will not come. But my other half hopes. The hope feels dusty and crusty by now. It has no life. 'Tis like hardening clay. And just when I think my heart will indeed turn to stone, there is a knock on the door. I hear it but I am not at all sure if it is my imagination or if it is real. I know that sometimes I have these spells when I cannot tell the difference between fact and my own fiction. So it takes me a moment, but when the knocking continues I force myself to stop thinking about The Manager and The List and to open the door. Hoping it is them.

But it is Rudy alone, almost bowing at the waist, Japanese style and with a look of boyhood all over him. Quinn is not with him. Once again, Quinn is breaking me and gone. I feel like a cracked vessel thrown into the river and about to float downstream to an unknown abyss.

"Good afternoon," Rudy says. "I just wanted to check to see if you're okay."

His dark eyes penetrate my soul and I freeze midstream on my way down the deep dark river. 'Tis like when Orpheus fell in love with

Eurydice, who tragically died on their wedding day when she was walking down the aisle and stepped on a poisonous snake and he made his way to the Underworld to convince Hades to release his true love. Hades agreed but only if Orpheus would lead his bride to the world of the living without looking back to make sure she was following him. Poor guy almost made it all the way to the surface before he could not control himself and turned around to see that Eurydice had been following him the whole time. But once he looked at her she was immediately taken back to the land of the dead for eternity. Something like that. I painted a picture of it once I think.

"Would you please come in," I say. "I have to sit down again. I am still feeling a little weak."

He takes my arm and helps me into my chair. And he sits on the bed, right in the groove I have left from my own sitting. I catch my breath. It feels like he is on my own lap. My Rudy.

"I see that Quinn's not here," he says.

"Quinn is not here," I echo. "I do not know where he is." I do not know what else to say. I am glad he is confirming my own observation that he is there alone, and Quinn is indeed no longer chained to his wrist. I can trust my own eyes. Would not that be nice if I always had someone by my side to confirm what I see?

"Do you see a bulldozer outside my window?" I ask. I get to see all of him — head to toe — when he rises from the bed and looks out.

"I do, actually."

My hands clap without me telling them to do so. I feel like a child who has just been properly validated instead of ridiculed and scorned. I applaud weakly with whatever energy is still left in my fragile hands and wrists.

"You do? You see it?'

"Yes, I see a small Bobcat."

"A bobcat? You mean like a leopard or a tiger?"

There goes my heart, madly beating again now in fear of a wild beast.

"No. No. No. Not an animal. A Bobcat excavator for digging. Moving dirt. A machine."

"Oh, thank goodness. You got me frightened as if I was a wildcat's innocent prey for a moment."

With that he turns 'round and sits back on the bed, reaching out for my hand which I automatically offer him. He pats it and lets it go. But the taste of his hand on mine lingers.

"People around here do not believe that they are going to tear the place down, but there you have it. Thank you very much. The heavy machinery has begun to arrive. Where is Quinn?"

"I don't know where Quinn is. And I don't think anyone is going to tear the place down."

"The miscreant has not answered my calls or texts. I do not know where he has been or where he is now. He has left me in the lurch once again like he always does."

"You mean like he's abandoned you?"

"That is what leaving someone in the lurch means. It comes from a sixteenth-century dice game where a lurch meant you were left far behind."

"How do you know that?"

"I read a lot. A whole lot. Always have. I am annoying and nuts but learn-ed. Where is Quinn?"

"I'm pretty sure he's run off ..."

"I scared him off."

"I doubt that. He's in a mess of trouble with a few folks here. Seems he has a suredid history with Cookie, Elmore and now Kevin. And evidentially, *you*."

"I have nowhere to go. Not sure I want to live anymore without him and if my heart does not give out, I am going to put an end to it all. Me and The Manager."

"Not sure what you're talking about. But it doesn't sound copathetic."

"Not sure that's what you mean, but it is indeed a very satisfactory solution."

"Solution to what?"

As I explain the problem to him, he listens like no one else has. His eyes are on mine — moist with desire for me and an understanding about how dire the situation is with The Manager and the others like Cookie and Elmore without family. When he says, 'let me help,' I know I am not alone, and Rudy means to assist me in providing a painless and swift end to the lives that are in danger. But then again, maybe he will take me in, and I will not have to include myself on The List.

Elmore

We have Rudy on speaker again as we huddle around the phone placed on my coffee table book of male bodies — Robert Mapplethorpe's portrait of Arnold Schwarzeneger semi-nude staring at us as if we've pissed him off and he wants some sort of misplaced revenge. Hasta la vista, Baby.

It's late Sunday afternoon, and it took us a while to reach Rudy. We start the call trying to sound like concerned parents rather than jilted lovers. Nevertheless, I'm sure we're failing because my first words already sound punishing.

"Where are you!?" I grumble.

"I'm back at my motel. That's where I am."

"We've been trying to reach you. Did you get our message? It's Cookie and me, Elmore."

"I've got caller I.D."

"Are you leaving town?"

"No. Just going to spend the night, get a morning workout and figure out what to do."

"Why don't you stay at least one more day. Come back to The Hacienda and we'll sort things out," Cookie says. She sounds less judgy than I think I do. She's got her bitch-self under control, while *mine* seems to be freely escaping my lips — like she has for decades on both coasts and occasionally in Europe during the Seventies when I was the proverbial secret boy toy for he who shall remain an unnamed movie star.

"Are you both fighting?" Rudy asks.

"We're not fighting at all," Cookie says. "We're not mad, Rudy."

"But we do have a few things to sort out between the three of us," I say.

"I know," Rudy says.

"We've been talking ... Elmore and me ... and it seems like you're getting some sort of renumeration from both of us," Cookie says.

"*And* money," Rudy says.

"It might be time for you to find your own way," I say.

"Are we breaking up?"

"No. No Rudy. We both love you and want you to be a part of our lives. Forever if you want."

"I need to figure out how to make it totally on my own, huh? Ligiteraly."

"It's time."

I imagine Rudy looking so dear right now as Cookie and I say 'it's time' while exchanging a knowing glance as if we are thinking the same thing about sweet Rudy finally becoming *ligiteral.*

Part 3

Monday

Chapter Nine

Kevin Vernkowsky

There are fewer than the normal number of Monday morning people in the workout area — a large, gutted room in the old brick building that used to be a local bank before Obie took over the space. He was a war veteran and bodybuilder who moved up to San Luis Obispo from Santa Monica to open his own gym years ago. He left the bank's main lobby as an open space and filled it with equipment that echoes the clatter of cast iron and stainless steel hitting the racks and floors. Whatever sounds the brick walls don't absorb clamor like a melody. There's an ancient sign painted on the wall. *Bank on Us.* The letters are fading. There are no showers — only changing rooms. That saves Obie a lot of money and just as much aggravation from leaks, floods, towels, cleaning up after the sloppy men and the occasional embarrassing locker room/ shower jerk off session.

I look at most everything these days with an eye for ROI and all the practicalities of running a family business with its own intriguing history.

When my grandfather died in nineteen eighty-five, my dad did *not* want his cloying mother moving in with us. We were a happy little family, and there was scarcely enough room for my parents and me. I was ten years old and already afraid of my grandmother, who I thought was going to eat me because she often said so as she pinched my cheek. *'I could just eat you up.'*

She grumbled what sounded to little me like nonsense and wore clothes that smelled like moth balls although I didn't know what the odor was at the time. I just knew that something didn't feel — shall we say *normal*? As I grew older, I learned that without her husband around, she was becoming more and more confused, had trouble moving around, and clearly needed personal care that no adult child would be comfortable providing themself — even if the old parent was an okay person. The only alternative was a nursing home. Yet, she wasn't *that* sick. She was just a bit delusional and sometimes seemed unnecessarily angry. There were no decent places at the time like what we now call modern Independent or Assisted living for vulnerable folks who needed help or had no family to take care of them.

"I found a jewel of a place," I remember Dad saying. An imposing and yet gentle man, he talked as though you better listen — not because of any threat, but because it all sounded so important and fascinating coming from him. He'd go on and on over the dinner table. Mom and I would listen intently even though some of it was over our heads.

He called it '*a house with a soul.*' Perfect for him to convert into an old folks' home.

He said that for any building to have a soul, it has to be built by well-meaning people with as much wood as possible. As I got a bit older, the house became his focus and he talked about it as if he was a professor of mission architecture. I learned what I could about arched corridors, curved gables, wide eaves, and sloping tile roofs. The place was nestled on a ten-acre site in the hills, and groundbreaking for the original 1920's structure was respectful and blessed by Native American Chumash elders.

He spoke of the original site as if he had actually been at the groundbreaking event himself, ten years before he was even born. Over sixty years prior to it becoming The Hacienda of today. According to local archives, there was chanting and singing. Dancing. Feathers and drums. Warm coastal breezes. The sweet smell of earth being moved to begin building what would become the home of the Idlor Family — Montgomery Idlor, a retired sea captain and Smithsonian researcher, his wife and four children.

The great room had vaulted ceilings and a stunning fireplace highlighting an oversized dining room. In total, nine-thousand square feet of living space, including six bedrooms in the main house each with a private bath. There was a separate oversized master suite. The deal was cinched for Dad by the beautiful garden with its variety of fruit trees including citrus, plums, apples, and pears.

He bought the place and turned it into a group home for the elderly. The Hacienda Mirage Rest Home. A jewel of a place indeed that feels to me like an extension of my dad and a part of me.

I don't want to sell.

But there is a tempting offer from Billingsby Ultra Care International to buy us out and clear up this Independent, Assisted, Long-Term Nursing differential. Plus, there's this sudden Gavina drama and the good-bye note that Melba left me this morning after a night of mutual tears, all leaving me uncharacteristically confused and overwhelmed. I could really use a friend.

And like so many coincidences that come out of being part of The Hacienda, it turns out that Rudy and I go to the same gym, another landmark building that I enter now carrying more emotional weight than any dumbbells will challenge me with.

I spot him doing hundred-pound bench presses. We're both wearing nearly identical gym shorts and tank tops. His white. Mine blue.

I don't have to tell you how good he looks. And how confused my excitement makes me feel.

"Looks like you might need some spotting," I say, as I approach him lying on the bench.

"Yeah, that would be good," he says. Both of us start the conversation without even saying hello as though we've known each other forever.

"What rep are you on?"

"I'm just on two. Going for ten."

"Okay," I say, getting in position above him and watching for when he might need my help. I keep my hands off the bar and my eyes on Rudy as he approaches *eight.*

"You can help me out on these last two," he groans, as the bar stops moving.

"I think I should return the bar to the rack," I say. And when he nods I do just that.

"I was doing ten, but it was my third rep this morning. So, thanks," he says. "Your nose okay?"

"Yeah. I'm fine."

"I usually don't ask for help. But you seem to know what you're doing."

"Right. Not as strong as you, but I *am* a regular here. I figure as long as I keep coming, I'm doing pretty well. It's about consistency and following through for me — more than bulking up or looking good."

"I'm bulking up and *need* to look good," he says, blushing with either embarrassment or satisfaction. Hard to tell which.

"I didn't mean to insult you."

"No insult taken. I'm a personal trainer and actor and have to try to look a certain way."

Wiping his hands on a towel, Rudy sits on the bench looking up at me. Neither of us says anything for the longest time.

"What's the story on The Hacienda, anyway," Rudy breaks into my musings as if he is reading my mind. He seems truly interested and acts like he has all the time in the world.

"The original Hacienda opened in 1985 ..." I say, wondering if I'm about to talk too much, but going ahead anyway. "... and besides accommodating my grandmother, it housed six old people and two old couples. All of them long gone now of course. It didn't take long for Dad to realize that if it was going to be a thriving business, he would have to fix it up and manage it himself. So he put all of his restaurant experience as the owner of Padre's Bar & Grill to good use and turned the place into a quick success. Am I talking too much? Sometimes when I'm nervous I talk too much. I've been told I'm boring."

"Hell. No. Who says you're boring? No. You're a good talker. I mean you talk good. Go on ahead."

He seems like he really does want me to go on, so I find myself telling him that about ten years ago when I was living in Los Angeles,

Dad was eighty and needed help managing things. Help from someone he trusted. That was me. And by the time I was forty, I became the manager of the place. Lock stock and barrel.

"One of the few independently owned elderly facilities of its kind, accommodating forty residents in the expanded space. A place with a great reputation, especially among the Los Angeles film crowd who loves the mysterious synchronicity rumors that came with the original so-called haunted property, and which stick to this day."

"It does have kinda a vibe. Not bad but ... inneresting," Rudy says.

"Yeah. Well, in addition to the Hacienda's reputation, I inherited the task of managing the fact that since the beginning, Dad didn't want to discriminate against any old person needing or wanting residency. Everyone was housed in one messy pile of aging humanity. And there was no differentiating the neurotic from the psychotic or demented. Independents and Assisted were all blended and integrated."

"You mean like all eating together and stuff?" Rudy asks.

"Yeah. Right." He's looking at me like it's reading time at the library and he's hearing a great story that he wants to really understand. I go on talking about how Dad truly gave up the reins and guided me into becoming the boss.

"But now that his Alzheimer's is getting the best of him he's no help at all. For nearly a year or so, all that the dad I love so much talks about is wanting to die. That is, if and when he talks at all."

"He seems like a good guy. Old..." Rudy says.

"He's old indeed. And you know, these people like Gavina, Elmore and Cookie are in the final chapters of their lives and my dad is near the end. They're harboring old resentments, trauma, challenges, and unmet goals — while I'm still gathering such things into my own baggage. They're either going to let go of their issues or die angry. All I know is I'm not a therapist or a priest. And I myself am just trying to cope with my expectations and the surprises of life yet to come — or already on my doorstep."

"Hell. I think I know what you mean. What do you mean?"

Rudy looks attentive but confused. Endearing. Curious. Sexy.

"You're saying the old folks are in a different stage of life, right?" Rudy goes on with eyes wide open.

"Exactly."

"I could listen to you talk forever. Sorry. Sounds corny."

"Not at all."

"Can I ask what's with your wife? She lives with you here or L.A. or what?"

"She's been spending more time *there* lately. She comes back here now and then, although I'm not sure she's ever coming back."

"What happened?"

"Can we talk about it over breakfast? Someplace private?"

"Sure. Let's get out of here. Tell you what ... I'll go shower and change at the motel and meet you at Padre's Bar & Grill. Are they open for breakfast?"

"No ... but it's not very private for me there anyway. I'll go home and change ... and meet you at SLO Café for breakfast."

"Okay, I know the place. On Second Street. Right?"

"That's it."

"That's where I captured Quinn the Face Puncher."

"Where is he?"

"Don't know. Gavina says she doesn't know how to reach him. Doesn't answer his phone or text."

"Gavina knows how to use a smartphone?"

"I think so. She's a smart cookie."

Gavina

I am inside the shuttle waiting for it to transport me from The Hacienda into town so I can do my shopping. I am the first on-board which is fine with me because it is quiet and there are no voices bothering me. The shuttle is always parked right here atop the gravel driveway, with its doors wide open to admit the fresh air. The stepstool is in place and Jacko, the driver, is leaning against the outside of the van puffing on a cancer-causing cigar as if he were Winston Churchill himself. Although Winston would never smoke one of those cheap, awful smelling Fiddlestones. As you may have guessed, Churchill and I met through our mutual, rather stuck-up friend, Frederick Lindemann. I was Freddy's housekeeper, and he was Winston's scientific advisor.

Which reminds me, speaking of science, I might as well tell you the whole truth about Hacienda Mirage and the column I wrote for the L.A.Times about four years ago when I had been here for about six. That means I have been here for about ten in case you need help with the math.

The original building now only houses studio apartments and The Manager's quarters. The fancy bedroom units were added to the main house. So that newer part of the facility does not talk. But the segments that have any of the *original* wood have plenty to say to inspire me, lecture me, or just annoyingly cry and moan. The floor whispers with sighs of pain whenever I pace in my room or step outside my door into the narrow hall onto the covered floorboards. *Watch where you're stepping, Missy.* Shushing sounds that scold me to speak more softly. *Shush. Shhhhh. Shhhhh. Quiet!* The remaining old wood shingles threaten me with warnings about Quinn — and now — admonitions about the others. *Be careful there, Gavina. You're all alone in the end.* And yet, sometimes this old house takes care of me, is helpful, and points me in the right direction.

When what was left of the original paint on the windowsill began to talk *about the link between people who enter The Hacienda,* I decided to write about it. I anonymously sent the article to the L.A.Times in my charitable attempt to help those who might not know about these things. The term *Good Samaritan* comes from the parable in the Book of Luke telling of a resident of Samaria who stopped to help a man who had been injured and robbed, while others passed him by. That's how I am. Thank you very much.

They printed my article, but *I did not* write the stupid headline. Some grandstanding junior journalist got it all wrong. And Quinn tried to make it the anchor of a film that never saw the light of day, while The Manager got a kick out of it, and researchers to this day continue to study it. Here is what was left after the rest of the article was cut and made into more of a blurb than a full-on story.

The Old Folks Haunted at SLO's Hacienda Mirage
by Anon

> *Here is what the voices in the walls are telling me as a resident of The Hacienda Mirage Rest Home. You do not need to know who I am. Everyone on this planet is separated by only six other people. There are six links between us and everyone else. The President of the United States, a gondolier in Venice, just fill in the names. I am bound, you are bound, to everyone on this planet by a trail of six people. You are one link from everyone you know, two away from everyone they know, and so on. This fact debunks the false belief that there is no such thing as a coincidence.*

Coincidentally as I am thinking about this, onto the van struggle Butters and Twigs — sans wheelchair and walker which Jacko probably stashed in the back of the van — followed by Cookie and Elmore. The doors close and the shuttle departs with the five of us. The two women begin an animated discussion in the seat behind me and seem to be able to hear every word the other is saying. Most of the conversation is nonsense about global warming, some new alleged virus, cancer research, and it all quickly becomes empty noise to my ears. Whenever I catch them in their I Cannot Hear You lie, it makes me very angry. I do not like feeling very angry and I know full well that allowing people like Butters and Twigs to bother you is a waste of human time and energy. I guess that since no one ever does the right thing — and most people are basically selfish, stupid, and lazy — you are wasting your fast-depleting energy that you should be saving for the fleeting positive feelings of joy.

I do not always practice what I preach.

When Cookie and Elmore sit in front of me and begin giggling like children, I can feel my rage champing on the bit. My tongue wants to scream for them to shut up and my fists open and close. My teeth want to bite them on their necks. But then I remember I am a lady.

“Did you find your friend, Whatshisname?” Cookie says, as she tilts to face me. The woman cannot keep her big mouth shut even though I have done absolutely nothing to invite her to speak to me.

“Quinn,” Elmore says, all proud of himself for remembering his name. He is now turning his head toward me, too.

“Are the two of you some kind of perverted lovers now?” I spit. Who knows how freaks like them bond together?

“Friends,” Elmore says.

“Just friends,” Cookie repeats. “Is that okay with you, Gavina?”

“My Uncle Ian was my friend. Quinn was my friend. Ian’s dead for decades and Quinn was evidently not nice to either of you.”

“Well ... that is correct. Good of you to notice,” Cookie says. She looks surprised. Probably at the fact that I can weave words into coherent sentences without even using Scottish slang.

“I have told you before, Cookie. I’ve been in America for over forty years. And I may be crazy, but not stupid. I have read more top shelf books than there are in the entire Hacienda library.”

That shuts her up.

Elmore

When we stop at the main square near the old Mission, Gavina is the first one off the van and — being the most spry among us — she hurries off down the street. From the little I really know of her, I'm pretty certain she's got lots of experience in the art of dashing away from all sorts of situations. She reminds me of myself when I was a kid in New York, dashing down the street to get away from whomever was harassing or threatening my then pretty face.

I'm only on this excursion today because Cookie invited me to join her on her *makeup run* as she called it. And she offered to help me buy new shirts that she says would be more suitable for a gentleman of my age, rather than the spiffy T-shirts I seem to live in. It's a funny thing about T-shirts, isn't it? Certain ones are impossible to part with. Like the one with the totally frayed neck that I bought in the Caribbean with Chico before he dumped me for a Speedo-wearing doctor from Texas. Or the shirt that reads *Be Yourself* — that I've had for centuries and is the softest one. Or that Silence=Death shirt that was torn while lying in protest in front of the White House during the March on Washington in 1993.

"Let's just walk. We can browse and I'll show you my favorite place for cosmetics. Maybe you can find some moisturizer for yourself," Cookie says.

"Do I need moisturizing?"

"Darling ... when was the last time you cleansed and oiled that puss of yours?"

"You mean *my face*? Or ..."

"Shut up."

"No. *You* shut up."

"I said it first, you're a fool."

"I know you are, but what am I?"

"Just walk."

Cookie has a list of the items she knows she wants and carefully inspects the packaging to be sure everything is what she calls 'co-pacetic.' Then she samples a few things without any intention of purchasing them. I'm glad she passes on any more Elsy Louder perfume as she uses too much already, and I know I will eventually have to tell her so. She asks the nice young salesclerk for her opinion on some nail polish and then ignores the girl's pick. Do we dismiss young people when we grow old as much as they dismiss us?

I feel like I'm eighteen years old watching Aunt Bea shoplift lipstick while I distract the saleslady at Bloomingdale's cosmetic counter just by being there and looking as odd as I must have looked.

After cosmetics, Cookie and I stroll through town toward the men's store. We step aside to let a woman with a stroller pass us. A skateboarder zooms nearly knocking us over. We carefully walk around some dog shit and amble along the flowery walkways. We're by far the oldest people on the street. Even sixty-year-old folks circle around us on their way. And every man, woman and child looks healthy and robust in comparison to us. I've felt like an outsider for most of my life and now I have one more reason to feel different, since ninety percent of the population is younger than Cookie and me — doing their best to render us invisible and inconsequential. Just by being.

Nevertheless, we proceed to the Gents of Today men's store — a surprisingly chic little shop with casual clothing lining the walls and counters. Nothing dressy. No pushy salespeople. No hip-hop retail music. Nevertheless I hate shopping. I'm sure my utter disgust in going into stores to try on clothes stems from my Aunt Bea days and the times in New York when I hated feeling on display — even when I was *dressed down* so as not to attract attention.

I'm only here to humor my new friend, although I'll have to set her straight ASAP about not mothering me, suggesting moisturizers, or selecting wardrobe. But she's on a roll right now. And like a momma with a helpless son, Cookie picks out two shirts and I select two and she follows me into the dressing room.

"You don't want to see this," I say.

"See what?"

"Me without my shirt. No one but Rudy has seen me without a shirt since my melanoma surgery."

"Oh, for goodness sake, Elmore. Try the shirts on."

"No."

"No? What is wrong with you?"

"I don't like the way it turned out. I have scars and bumps where they shouldn't be."

"Rudy doesn't mind?"

"Rudy is basically a good guy. In case you're deaf and blind and haven't noticed."

"Try the ones I picked out first. Then yours. I'll tell you which ones look the best."

She's now holding three shirts in her lap and handing me a shirt she chose. The grin on her face is that of a woman who is proud and sure of herself. I take it from her and turn away to hide, but then realize that she can see my back *and* my front in the mirror. After the fourth shirt, she says,

"You know which two look the best, don't you?"

"Yes, Mother."

"Now be a good boy and go pay for these and call us an Uber. No need to ride back in that tacky old shopping van."

"Let's go to a movie instead," I say.

"Oh, that's a great idea. Let's play hooky."

Rudy

I had plenty to think about after the gym while I got ready to meet Kevin at the SLO Café. Truth be spoken, maybe *too much* to digest and calculate through my brain. Most of it made sense and helps me understand things. But it's the way he spoke to me that turned me on. Like, with such *R-E-S-P-E-C-T.*

From the minute I walk through the door hummin' along with Aretha Franklin singin' in my head, The SLO Café looks completely different than when I was here with Quinn. Then, I didn't notice the bright tablecloths and cheery waitstaff in checkered shirts. I missed observating the funky, old, wooden Home Sweet Home type signs and flower baskets and chicken statues like the ones grannies supposedly have scattered all over their houses. My abuela only had a bunch of crosses and Jesus pictures. No cute plastic bunny statues smiling at you from the wooden shelves.

Yesterday, I sat here with Quinn on bar stools at a high top. This morning, I join Kevin in a corner booth against the wall. Everything feels different. And for the first time in my life, I feel totally gay. When I sit and the waitress immediately shows up at our table, I don't even take notice. She could be a hot, Cal-Poly co-ed or a mature J.Lo type. I can't tell you which. I order a cup of coffee without looking at her. Kevin is already drinking his java.

"Where were we?" he asks.

"I was bench pressing. You were spotting me. You mentioned your wife leaving and I told you I was an actor."

"Okay. Well. We're jumping right in, aren't we?"

Kevin stops talking and looks like he's going over what to say like I sometimes do, so I save him by doing the talking.

"As it turned out, our man Quinn was at Padre's last night, and I was having dinner at a table and this girl ... this woman ... comes over to me and sits down, asking me to rescue her from the creep. I didn't know it was Quinn until much later. But she was nice, and we realized that we did this Kibbles and Bits spot together which we had a laugh about and then she left, and I went to sleep in my motel ... by myself!"

"Slow down."

"Nothing happened."

I look down and see Kevin's hand is now patting the top of mine, transmitting something like *there, there ... it's all right ... I believe you.* When I put my other hand on his patting one, he pulls his fingers out from under me and both his hands disappear under the table like scared white mice.

The waitress person is back to take our breakfast order. When I see that she is indeed the cute university type, I feel nothing sexual-wise toward her and once again focus on Kev. Mind you, I am only now calling him Kev in my brain, not out loud to him or anyone else. Yet.

"I don't know why I'm here," Kev says. "I should be at work."

"Aren't you the boss? You can get there whenever you want," I say.

"Well ... I suppose that's true. I've got a lot on my mind, Rudy. Don't want to bother you with it. You've evidently got your own issues to iron out with Dr. Nussbaum and Mr. Fingerton. I don't really care much about Quinn or Gavina today."

"Me neither. Just chill. You're here because you want to be here," I say.

Sometimes you're somewhere with someone and you're not sure exactly why but something somewhere inside of you wants to be exactly where you are even though you feel like you're there by some sort of magic and you didn't drive your own car there to randyvoo with that other person or you're in their bed and can't remember how you got there.

"Melba is leaving me. It's been leading up to this. She told me yesterday."

"That sucks," I say, wondering if that's the right responding in this set of circumstantials.

"Not sure if it sucks or not," he says.

"Okay. Not sure if that sucks or not?"

"Correct. I'm unhappy but confused. I'm sitting here with you, instead of following after her to L.A. or trying to talk her out of it ... or I don't know."

"Why?"

"Why what?"

"Why is your wife leaving you?"

"I just met you."

"Okay, listen Kevin ... you have got to chill. Who else do you have to talk to?"

"No one. I work among old people. Most of them delightful. Some of them quirky. A few completely nuts ... and all I do is work and work because my stepdad slash dad left the business to me. But it's all become way too much with him basically out of the picture because of his Alzheimer's."

"So wait a minute. Is your dad the guy they call The Manager?"

"Yes."

"Shit, Man. *That* sucks. But you need to know that Gavina McVey plans to ...."

"Plans to what?" His hand is all alone back on the table now, and I stare at the very white indentation and tan line that goes 'round his naked ring finger.

"Gavina told me she plans to help The Manager *put an end to it all.* Her words, not mine."

Gavina

Having done not only my Master Plan research but also my MapQuest walking route, I know just how to get directly from the van stop to Mel's Auto Parts only minutes from my bank and the post office box and down the street from the art gallery. I already phoned Mel's and I know they have what I need.

I prefer to call it *engine coolant.* Does that not sound nicer than ethylene glycol? It has no smell or color and is sweet tasting, so it is perfect for my purposes when added to the proper beverage. In the Nineties when I tried it using Vodka on Quinn to punish him for murdering my uncle and absconding with the money from the sale of Ian's house, I did not add enough coolant, so Quinn was sick but not eliminated. This time, I will be sure to add at least 100ml to the drinks if I have to serve Elmore and Cookie. We shall see. On the other hand, since The Manager lives in the largest apartment and has a kitchen, I am going to make him some homemade sausages with what I figure is about thirty times higher amounts of non-GMO, gluten-free, vegan sodium nitrate than allowed by law.

I love the taste of the auto parts store with all its tools, fluids, rubber hoses, and assortment of accessories all deliciously mingling with the overwhelming aroma of car tires and gasoline — reminiscent of Uncle Ian's old garage in the back of his house where he kept his not-so-secret stash of booze so he could get tanked up and rubbered. I did not mind it one bit because he was sloppy but sweet with me and when I was out there talking with him, Quinn would sometimes come out to the garage and mumble 'hello' while checking on Ian.

So, I am enjoying myself roaming the aisles when all of a sudden, I do not actually know where I am or why I am where I am at.

I assume that if I ramble around a bit, I will come to my senses like I usually do when this sort of thing happens. 'Tis like a suspension of time where you float along mindlessly — and I must say, painlessly — looking at your surroundings but not understanding what you are seeing. Shelves of auto supplies can become just a veiled corridor to nowhere. I do not know how long it is before a pimpled-skinned boy — freakishly tall for his age — asks if he can help me find something.

"This place smells like an old garage," I say, still thinking about Scotland.

"Makes sense," the boy/man says.

"Is it a garage?"

"No, Ma'am. Store."

"Store?"

"Mel's Auto Parts. You're in a store. Are you lost?"

"No. No. I am looking for some anti-freeze," I say, not knowing where that insight comes from.

"My grandmother forgets where she is sometimes," he says.

"I am not your grandmother."

"I know, but you sort of remind me of her. Although she would have no use for anti-freeze. I can tell you that!"

"'Tis for my car."

"You live up in the mountains?" He is leaning against an empty shelf now. Not doing his job if he works here. Chatting with the customers instead of doing what he is paid to do. Or do they pay kids now for customer service? I doubt that. Most kids are rude, even if they are working. The girls at the doctor's office are downright dismissive and never take their eyes off their computer screens even when they talk to me about my meds or lab results. Last time I was carted off to the hospital, the unfriendly techgirl doing my stress test did not look at me when she robotically mumbled, 'Not great. Lots of plaque and some blockage.'

"The mountains?" I ask.

"It gets cold up in the mountains. That why you need anti-freeze?"

"Just point me in the right direction, Young Man."

"Aisle Twelve."

"Got it. Goodbye."

These days I do not know if walking is good for me or too stressful, but after purchasing what I need, I leave Mel's and head toward the post office. I had rushed from the van, but now I am doing more of a stroll, feeling lucid and happily knowing full-well that I am going to pick up my meat preservatives from the PO. Box. The sidewalk is lined with lovely colorful flowers. I pick a few to carry with me for good luck and I step gingerly over some dog poop so as not to mess my slippers. The brick buildings are fronted with old Ficus trees that form a canopy covering parts of Guera Street. I hear the eerie call of loons in the distance. I remember where I am and start to write a poem in my head about this moment. If it turns out good, I will add it to my private collection of written verse.

Life at both ends
The smell of waste and flowers
The cry of the loon and the tortures of the heart ...

To my delight, my package is in my postal box, and it fits nicely in the auto parts bag, so I am on my way back to the van if I do not get lost and have to become one of the Assisted, who I am sure never do walkabouts alone without a staff person. Except for The Manager who seems to roam around at will like I am doing right now.

Cookie

Today is a good back-hip-and-energy day, perhaps triggered by seeing that fiend Quinn get slapped. And being in town, I feel free. I like it very much. I love it. So instead of calling an Uber to take us back, Elmore and I keep on strolling. We could become runaways. I don't want to ever go back there.

The worst thing that ever happened to me was when they took away my driver's license. Don't get me wrong. Needing to move out of my condo into The Hacienda because of the so-called hoarding was bad. Living alone was difficult the older I got. Losing my professional license was awful. But not being able to drive legally was the worst blow to my possibly false belief that I was an independent, self-sufficient, still-active spicy person.

I bought my sweet condo in West Hollywood in 1990. I decorated it myself. No need for a fancy designer like Elmore — who I just learned by digging around online was indeed quite the bigshot with that huge walk-in studio on Robertson Boulevard under the name of Elite EL Design! Anyway, I furnished my place with art I had acquired on my travels and bought furniture retail at Gilda Home Furnishings — the place on Sunset with the anxiety-riddled brothers Donny and Ronny. Don't ask how I know them. You can guess.

At first my home was a showplace. I entertained colleagues, acquaintances, and occasional acquaintances of acquaintances, all of whom started to bring me little presents instead of wine. Each hostess gift was a delight. Throws and pillows, glassware, cheese boards, salt and pepper shakers and more earthenware than you'd find at a fully stocked ceramics store. I suppose my guests pitied me for not being married and thought they'd make it up by bringing me traditional bridal shower knickknacks. I kept them all and not only that, I also never put anything away or gave anything away. I bought bookcases and shelves to display things. When the shelves got overloaded, I stopped entertaining. I may have stopped having so-called friends. But I continued shopping for myself. Clothes, magazines, books, and all sorts of stuff I just had to have from thrift shops and the Dollar Store. Mostly bargains as well as some things I could ill afford. By the time my career was over, and Rudy first saw my place, you could hardly walk from room to room. Might as well admit it. If you can't admit stuff to yourself, how are you going to have a chance in hell to fix it or even change it? And don't tell Gavina about any of this, or go playing high-and-mighty with me. Look around where *you* live and see the mess *you* make.

It's his fault. The whole thing started with Quinn. I dismissed my instincts about his being not only a narcissist but a sociopath—and a vindictive one at that. I treated him even though he frightened me. I let him have his way with me, which means he made me break every rule. Then of course, he was the one who ended my therapy practice and released my own demon — the part of me that held on for dear life and couldn't give anything away or clean anything up. The part of me that Rudy discovered and helped me manage with the sale of my condo — for four-times what I paid — and by suggesting The Hacienda Mirage, a place he said was famous for helping people like me. I assumed at the time that *people like me* meant *special* in the true sense of the word and not in the special difficult-needs category.

And then. Then I failed both my vision and my driving test. And I became dependent on others.

"Let's not go back," I say to Elmore, as we casually walk through the enchanting town.

"I suppose if we don't take the van, we could stop for a cup of coffee or better yet, an ice cream sundae. But we ought to tell someone that we're not riding back in the shuttle van." He pulls out his cell phone.

"Just say that we'll get back on our own. They don't have to know our every move."

As I watch him place the call to the central Hacienda number, I assume one of the welcome ladies will answer and probably get the message wrong. But I don't care. Hopefully Elmore will help me come up with a plan for us to create our *very own truly independent living* instead of being trapped in Independent Living in an Insane Asylum.

Chapter Ten

Kevin

When Dad started The Hacienda, he used to drive up to eight people into town in his big old Buick Roadmaster Station Wagon. But then again, there were only around ten seniors living at The Hacienda at the time, so it was doable. Our shuttle van now holds twice as many, but there are usually no more than ten out of our forty residents each week. My accountant says he's not sure we can keep up all of payroll unless Jacko does more than maintenance, driving and gardening. He wants Nurse Hemmings to do more admin. He'd like me to cut the food staff. Or he thinks I should grab the offer from Billingsby to buy me out.

Rudy is looking at me across the SLO Café lunch table with his big brown eyes inviting me to spill my guts. Words that carry my feelings usually get caught in my throat but I push through, saying, "I guess if I sold The Hacienda, I could move to L.A. with Melba and find some sort of job at one of the elder care places near wherever we settle."

"You have an offer from someone to buy you out?"

"One of the big corporations that do the whole Independent and Assisted thing. They have a lot more resources. But it's like a chain ... and my father would *not* approve."

"It's a cozy place right now," Rudy says.

"I hate the idea of giving it up and I'm not willing to leave my dad."

"Then don't."

"I'm a mess," I say, rubbing the Band-Aid.

"Leave your nose alone. It'll heal better left alone."

"Yes, Sir."

"Don't call me sir. I'm not much older than you."

"Sorry."

"Just teasing you, Kevin. Relax. Do you ever chill?"

That, coming from Rudy, stops me. I think about the question. And then while unsuccessfully fidgeting to avoid his eyes, I say, "As much as I mostly love my job caring for these old folks ... being with you and having an adult conversation is refreshing. You know what I mean? Our residents are surely adults, but they're in their final chapters and their thoughts and feelings are decades further along than mine. Whereas you seem to be struggling with some of the same things I am. Job, money, and relationships for example. Right?"

"I guess so. I wouldn't say struggling, but I really need to become more independent and settle down. And I don't have much of a meaningful social life."

"Me neither," I say, looking around the café to see if I know anyone. As if I'm a criminal.

"Did you say you might sell *and* chase after your wife to L.A.?

"Maybe."

"Maybe not," Rudy says, with a penetrating grin that could melt steel.

There's no reason for me to feel guilty about being with him. Yet contriteness is my constant companion. Sometimes, no matter how hard you try, others still need or want more. Or you make yourself feel at fault for having a cup of coffee when you should be working. But I go on telling Rudy about Melba, who has her own part-time career as a molecular biologist and who has no real interest in building a life in San Luis Obispo.

"She has wanted me to sell The Hacienda and move to L.A. She's been blaming my devotion to The Hacienda on our not having kids and on me not being able to '*deliver the goods.*' And I'm the one who dragged her from L. A. to begin with once Dad started getting ill and I had to take over."

Now I can't seem to stop talking. He's still listening as if I was telling the most interesting story you can imagine, instead of the gory details of my life.

I tell Rudy about how Melba and I met at an Overeaters Anonymous Meeting when I was working in Los Angeles. "I sat next to a beautiful girl who admittedly looked like she could lose a few pounds, just like me. We got to talking about our eating habits. She had just devoured an entire cake, which motivated her to get to the meeting. I came from McDonald's where I had ordered a burger and fries after finishing lunch ten minutes before. We began to go to meetings together and then I found out that I had to move back to San Luis Obispo. I proposed. She said yes and we agreed to both get on a serious diet and exercise program and she said she would marry me if I would vow to as she put it, 'stop ogling men' and give her a baby."

I owe her.

I should have said yes to Quinn if he was really going to make a legit film here. Rudy said that Quinn offered him a part playing a character *based on me!* I don't know what that means to me because I just met him. And Melba's definitely *not* the type of woman who would put up with me sneaking around with another man. She's already accused me of being unfaithful, even though I've *never* cheated on her. I've honored the promise I made with her that I never would explore my sexuality if she moved to SLO.

"Just take it slow," Rudy says. "Let me help you sort it all out."

"I've got to go," I say, in my usual not very chilled tone.

"Okay. No problem," he says, as we both stand and equally split the bill. I head to the door like a kid who's stolen a candy bar. And when we're leaving, we see Cookie and Elmore walk by. They're arm in arm, seemingly helping one another stay upright without losing any of their shopping bags. They look like one of those all-too-rare, still-in-love, long-married couples.

It makes me miss my mother — who died right before Dad's diagnosis and luckily didn't have to watch him drift away. She often took my dad's arm when they both were alive and healthy. I think she did it not so much out of love or need for help walking, but more as some sort of attempt to hold onto him on the rare occasions when he was with her and not working. It was my job, early on, to keep Mother company and take care of her as best I could while Dad was growing The Hacienda. Mom had a lot of emotional needs that always seemed more intense and urgent than any of mine.

"Well, well, well," Elmore says. "Look who's palling around with who."

"Hi, Folks," I say, once I get my bearings. "Heading back to the shuttle?"

"Shuttle. Schmuttle. We're going to go see a movie and have lunch," Cookie says – head held high.

"Kevin and I ran into each other at the gym ..." Rudy says, as if we've been caught making out.

"You don't need our permission," Elmore says. "I was just surprised to see you both. Surprised and delighted. You're a beautiful sight for sore old eyes."

"I think Elmore's right. You two deserve each other," Cookie says.

"We're just having coffee and a chat," I say.

"Well, go on then. On your way. Back to work!" Elmore says, as he tugs Cookie away down the street.

Rudy

I tell Kev I'll stay in town another night and spend the rest of my day trying to find Quinn who evidentially really hurt both Cookie and Elmore and we all know he punched Kev. And if you want my opinion, Gavina deserves better — even if she is a bit weird. I think Kev was okay when I used that word. 'We're all a little weird, aren't we?' he said before heading back to The Hacienda after agreeing that I would catch up with him over dinner at a place he suggested that's on the ocean at Avila Beach. Sounds pretty romantical, doesn't it?

I'm not sure how to find Quinn, but maybe a walk through town will help me figure out how to go about it. It's a beautiful day to clear up your head. I like to just walk sometimes without having to monitor my heartbeat for a good cardio workout. There're all sorts of interesting hippies, students, tourists, and businesspeople. The shops have neat stuff in their windows. Even the head shop has an artsy look with neat glass pipes and funky T-shirts. There are yellow and blue flowers growing along the edge of the sidewalk and luckily, I've stuck a few in-case-I-gotta-sneeze napkins from the restaurant into my pocket, so I use them to scoop up and throw away some dog poop from the sidewalk. There's a ton of brightly decorated waste bins all over this town, reminiscing me of Mister Roger's Neighborhood of Make-Believe.

I googled this Quinn Adamsdaur guy last night. And the dude actually did do what they call a *break-away hit film that became a cult classic.* The film's budget was only $750,000 and ended up getting over double that at the box office. Not bad for a first-time director back over twenty years ago. So where is he? Maybe he's more down-and-out than we think. He could be homeless. Or suicidational. Or he might have just run away. I hate it when people disappear, and you never know what ended up happening to them. Even nowadays, with sociable media and all, you can usually find out something on just about everyone. I found some info about an ex-client of mine who wanted to become an Olympian and had a Facebook profile showing her with two kids and a curvy mom bod. And I tracked down a guy I liked a lot in high school, who ghosted me when I tried to reach him. But I cannot find zip about Quinn after 2010. You're probably thinking I didn't try very hard because of me not being able to concentrate on anything for too long before I get antsy and lose my patience and need to move on. I'm telling you though, I really tried last night. I didn't find any way to see Adamsdaur's *actual movie,* but I did fall asleep to *Brokeback Mountain* which I was watching for the fourth time.

I'm now passing by an IMAX movie theater showing *Nomadland,* which I know is a film about living in a van which is my worstest nightmare. But I see Elmore and Cookie going into the theater and I'm thinking I don't know what's up with the two of them but at least they're relatively safe inside. Although it's 'spose to be a depressing movie. And I hate for them to be disdressed and all. I've been through each of their disdresses a few times.

Like the time I was helping poor-but-rich Cookie go through her things so she could move out of her condo. I was holding up one of her very red dish towels and she'd moaned, "You never know when you might need things like that."

"But it's old and ragged," I said.

"So am I."

"No you're not. You just need some help ..."

"You're taking away all my things," she said, as I put useless stuff into one of the many boxes I was taking to Goodwill. Piles of newspapers, books and magazines were next.

"It's just a pile of magazines," I said.

"They're trade publications. *Psychology Today* and *The Networker*."

"You're retired."

"I need to keep up."

"But these are all old magazines. This one is dated 1980."

"It's historic. It's my life. My career. Being a therapist was everything. My whole identity. The only thing that gave me intimate contact with people."

"You can go to a library," I said.

"My friend, Tasha gave me that," Cookie said when I put an unopened set of napkins and placemats in one of the Goodwill boxes.

She was sitting on the floor in a new-found space, her arms wrapped around her knees like a disrested little girl.

"I don't have many friends. Tasha was always friendly," she said.

"Tell me about her," I said, trying to divest her attention and itching to get the place cleaned out.

"I don't know much about her. She lived down the hall. Died in a car accident."

"I thought you said she was your friend."

"Well, I don't know. It's just silly napkins. I don't know what's happened to me. I hold onto things and then the things morph from friendly reminders to my captors. They possess you. You have no power over them. I get it ... even though I have a hard time stopping it."

That's when I saw Cookie cry for the first time. Actual tears and sobs. I watched, not knowing what to do. I was pretty sure it was not sex that she wanted. So I just gave her a long hug and watched her wipe her face with — you guessed it — one of the red dishtowels.

"You're holding on to the past," I said. "You can't stop time." I'm not sure what that meant or what part of my brain it came from, but I remember her face lighting up as if she was consuming what I said.

And then there's Elmore.

The worst I've seen him was when his best friend Carl was in the final stages of dying from AIDS. I didn't know Carl very well at all. But he didn't recognize Elmore when we went to visit him in the hospital. At least they let us in. Carl could hardly see or talk or move. I get choked up remembering how Elmore just sat there, holding Carl's hand, and talking about the great times they had together. And they weren't even fuck buddies. Just friends.

I can still hear Elmore whispering. The only sound in the room. He was talking about the time they used to go to Numbers on Sunset Boulevard and pretend they were hookers. He talked about one time when some cute old guy picked them up, hoping for a three-way and they asked if he could take them to an ATM because they had run out of cash. And he threw them out of the car.

"It was on Sunset, but the upscale part," Elmore had said. "We laughed ourselves silly. And the time we dressed up on Halloween and did Santa Monica Boulevard with Richie and Rob as the moo-moo girls. Took pictures and competed to see how many photos we could each get with the hottest guys. Before you and Rob started to get sick ... and I didn't. I always loved you, Carl. You stood by me when I began my business, which is picking up and is going to be a big success because of you — behind the scenes — encouraging me on."

I did then the same thing I did later with Cookie because what else can you do when someone you care about is crying, but hold them tight?

And I'm all choked up now when I look up from my downtown SLO bench and see Gavina — of all people — standing there in front of me. Like some sort of magic or something.

Gavina

I am carrying Mel's Auto Parts bag in one hand and wondering what to do with my other hand since it is just hanging there at the end of my arm feeling left out. When I stop walking, I find myself standing in front of the most beautiful man I have ever seen sitting on a bench with his head bent low just like I do when I am in the garden sometimes after a particularly hard morning trying to connect or communicate with the other old women in the dorm. I am not sure I know him, but he knows me.

"Gavina!" he says, looking up at me.

"Hello," I reply.

'Tis good to be polite even if you are not certain who you are talking to. I sometimes forget this but when met with such a wonderous face as his, I know I have to be on my best behavior if I expect him to like me.

"Are you lost?" he asks.

"Hello," I say again because I am not sure if I am lost but what I do know is I have secrets in the bag that I am carrying.

"Would you like to sit down?"

"Yes," I say, as he scoots over to make room for me on the bench. 'Tis a nice bench and one that suddenly reminds me of a garden. Then I remember. Quinn ... and how he nearly fell off the bench where I sometimes feed the poor homeless kitties. Then I remember The Hacienda.

"Give it a minute," he says. "Take your time."

"You are not Quinn," I finally say.

"Nope. I'm Rudy. We met on Saturday. Yesterday you told me about your plan ..."

"I did?"

"You did."

"I should not have done that. 'Tis private. 'Tis important."

"Okay. Well, we've got to talk about it. It doesn't sound like a good idea to me."

"Rudy?"

"Yes. I'm a friend of Elmore and Cookie," he says.

The two of them I remember! Take it from this old woman, you do not just remember the good things only. You remember scary things and people who might harm you or whom already have. Am I right?

"Cookie. She's a monster. So rude. So stuck up," I say.

"Cookie can be difficult."

"Who is this Elmore guy?" I ask.

"He's an old friend of mine. As is Cookie."

"We are all old."

"I mean I've known them both for a long time."

"Hence ... *old* friends."

"Hence?"

I do not think he knows what I mean because he has an inquisitive look on his face. But he is not being unkind. He is trying to have a conversation with me. It makes me feel less lonely and suddenly less confused. Funny how that works. Aha! This is the man I fell in love with days ago. And here I am falling in love with him all over again. 'Tis fine. It would be all right with me if I forgot and then got the thrill of meeting him over and over again. Suddenly I know what is in my bag.

"I have got to get back to the van," I say.

"Do you know where Quinn is?" Rudy asks.

"Still not answering my calls. Do you want his number? I do not like him anymore."

"Yes. I'll take his number."

Quinn never once in his life sat and talked with me like this. He always talked about his self. We call that a staisgte in Scotland. Stuck up. Rudy takes my phone and does some fancy thing to capture Quinn's phone number onto his own phone. I do not know how to do that. Nor do I really care to learn. I just like sitting here with him and wish I could stay.

"So many people just disappear, don't they?" I say, as I watch passersby.

"One minute you're hanging out with them and the next they've moved cross country and you never hear from them again. I was just thinking about that," Rudy says.

"They just disappear," I say. "Cannot even find them on the internet. Gone. All you can do is wonder. Most all you can ever do is wonder. Sometimes all you can do is ponder or try to forget them."

"Whatcha got there in the auto parts bag?" Rudy asks.

"Are you friend or foe?" I reply, hoping he is not going to grab it from me and create a scene because if he does, I will scratch his deep brown eyes out of his perfectly shaped skull.

"Friend."

"Okay, then. I have some supplies to help The Manager cross over to the other side."

"Oh. The Plan!"

"Yup. Someone has to help the poor old guy. He is a dear and needs help."

"Tell you what ... why don't you just sit and relax here, and I'll get my car and drive you back to The Hacienda myself and we can figure this all out."

Elmore

My new friend Cookie and I emerge from the movie theater onto the streets of San Luis Obispo both feeling the need for a shower — knowing exactly what the other is thinking and feeling about *Nomadland* with Frances McDormand losing her job and converting a van to live in and travel cross country by herself. The idea of the dusty road, dirty old rattrap vehicle and lack of toilet has pretty much freaked us both out. No toilet. Can you imagine? But I gotta say, if you weed out the horror of living like that and focus on the warm human relationships that are formed in the film, it doesn't feel so disgusting at all. I mean don't get me wrong. It's not for me. I like my own private shitter and clean sheets. I wouldn't be living at The Hacienda if I was able to live like a pig.

"Is there such a thing as a *Glamping* Nomad?" Cookie asks me. "I'd need a glamourous RV with beds, kitchen, and a proper potty to say the least. Maybe a living room and roll-out awning with one of those big fake lawn rugs."

"AstroTurf," I say.

"Whatever."

"And a handsome driver."

"For sure."

"We could buy such a vehicle and ask Rudy to drive us around until infinity."

"Rudy at the wheel. Can you imagine?"

"Yes. Actually, I can picture it quite clearly. It's called a motorhome. Far from a van. Probably costs at least fifty thousand dollars or more," I say.

"I could chip in twenty-five," Cookie says, smiling like she's just robbed a bank.

"Me, too. Hey ... speaking of vans, we're going to miss our ride back to The Hacienda."

"Screw that. That's why God invented Uber."

I love this woman.

After a slow stroll past the precious little shops, we agree that neither of us want to walk any more. I admit my back is bothering me and Cookie tells me her bad hip is needing a rest and she's craving a juicy cheeseburger. So we duck into Padre's Bar & Grill for lunch. According to Cookie this old bar and restaurant was a major hang out for perverted priests and naughty nuns back in the day when the clergy got away with God Knows What. Of course, that only makes me excited about the place. If it's one thing I truly miss as I look back in time, it's discovering those seedy, magical places where you never knew who you might leave with or what might happen. The Hangry Cat swiftly went from a gay paradise to bridal-shower watering hole. It closed entirely about a year ago and is now a mega hair salon. What used to be The Eagle and Spike Bath House is now a mammoth sporting goods store with bungee jumping harnesses replacing the suggestive leather ones, and soccer balls, volleyballs, and basketballs taking the place of — well you get the picture.

"We *could* buy an RV, but for now let's go apartment hunting," Cookie says, as if it's the second greatest idea of all time. We both move our shopping bags onto the top of the table so we don't forget them. Our purchases hit with a muffled clapping sound.

"So what should we do about Quinn?" I ask.

"I don't know or really care. I might have his number in my phone from the time he was seeing me. Maybe it's still the same."

"I'll bet I have one, too," I say, as we both pull out our phones.

"He really *did* direct a pretty popular movie," Cookie says.

"What was it called? Maybe I know it. My friend Carl and I used to *love* cult classics."

"*Scottish Mistress.* Who do you think inspired him to make that stupid movie?"

"He directed *Scottish Mistress*? It's about Gavina?"

"From what I know it's *inspired* by her not *about* her. I never saw it. I just think she had something to do with it. No one ever made a movie about me."

"I love that movie."

"You know it?"

"I've seen it a thousand times. Carl and I used to dress up — free-balling under our kilts — for watch parties."

"How wonderful. Sorry I didn't know you then."

"Men only. You wouldn't have been invited, Honey."

"Shut up ..."

"No ... *you* shut up."

We're each holding our phones out for one another to see. Cookie has the same number for Quinn as the one I have.

"Same number," I say. "Let's call. I'll put it on speaker."

Sorry.
You Have Reached a Number
That Has Been Disconnected
or Is No Longer in Service

"Oh well," Cookie shrugs her shoulders and grins as if to say *that settles that.* "Let's go see that remodeled Three-Bedroom on Banal Street."

Rudy

I'm pretty sure Elmore and Cookie are okay. But I shouldn't have left Gavina sitting there while I went to get my car. She was gone by the time I drove up. Maybe she reminded me of my mother, who I learned to leave alone and eventually stopped trying to help. Not that I knew *how* to help her when I was a little kid, but I did *want* to. Now that I'm older and more wiser and all, I know you can't help someone who doesn't want to help themselves. I've had clients who want me to train them, but they don't want to work out without me when I'm not there and they have to do it alone by themselves. Or they eat between workouts. I mean *eat*! They don't admit it or tell me the truth about eating too much or what they're eating but I can tell. I have an intuitional sex sense about stuff like that.

I drive around for a while wondering if I should just let other people take care of their own shit and me take care of mine. I've spent plenty of time the past couple days dealing with these people and maybe it's time I just focus on me for tonight.

So I head back to the motel.

Alone in my room, I'm thinking *I might be going on a real dinner date tonight.* The last time I went on a date was in 2010. New Years.

We were to meet at The Pacific Dining Car restaurant — a dark, sexy place where a lot of lovers met for clamdestined dinners. He was a bi-married man who was about to finally leave his wife, after dating me for about six months on the DL. Well, not a lot of *dating*, but we did go to this particular place sometimes because it was far from his home in the San Fernando Valley. And lucky for us, his wife was stuck back East in a snowstorm or something. I was so into this man. This was going to be *it* for me. He wasn't the type to correct me or condrasend to me. He was smart and didn't have to prove it. Oh, and did I mention, he was hot? I was right on time for our nine o'clock reservations, but by nine-fifteen he was still not there. There were just cell phones then. None of the fancy smart ones like now. I had my flip phone on the table, as I waited for him. I had been saving up, so I was going to be able to pay my own way. It was important to me that we set up an equal-type relationship for the new year when he would get divorced. I wanted him to know that I could support my part of whatever living arrangements would be best. I had finished my second glass of wine and had ordered a third. I nearly downed it in one gulp after he called and told me that his wife had come home after all, and we were through. That was the last alcoholic drink I've ever had.

"I can't do this anymore," he said. "I'm staying with her. She's pregnant."

"How unoriginal," I said.

Needlessly to say, I'm more than a little nerve racking now about my dinner by the sea with Kev. It feels way too much like that other thing, so I crawl under the covers to take a nap after leaving Kev a voice message when he doesn't pick up.

Gavina is heading back to the van.
I just ran into her downtown and she seems loopy.

Please be aware and careful about what I told you
about her and your dad.
See you soon for dinner.

Kevin

The phone is ringing, and messages are going to voicemail. The afternoon sun is beating down on the building as if it was summer instead of February. And Monday is always a busy day here. Jacko is in my office — wringing his bucket hat as if it were a wet beach towel — and he's looking down at his boots, like a child about to be sternly punished. I've never seen him like this. And I've never even had a harsh word with the man, so I know I'm not to blame for his being nervous but nevertheless it breaks my heart.

"They weren't in the van, so I called ... and Stella told me they would get back themselves. But I think she got it wrong."

"Stella?"

"The lady at the front desk who answered the phone. She said I could come on back without them because they called."

"Who called?" I ask.

"I figured it was the missing three riders. The funny Gavina lady, Doctor Nussbaum and the new gentleman. I never leave town without the people who I came with but Stella said it was okay."

"It's okay, Jacko. Sit down and let's figure this out together. I'll get Stella in here."

"Okay," he says, while I summon Stella, who has evidently completed her shift and is in her room.

"What is it?" I ask Jacko who is still fidgeting with his hat. He's a short man looking small in his seat. He's got to be around sixty by now, as he's been here since the beginning. He was the gardener here when dad originally bought the house. And he claims his family goes back to the Chumash. Hunters, gatherers, and fishermen who lived in big, dome houses made of willow branches.

"Don't tell your father about this mix-up."

"It's okay, Jacko. We'll sort it all out."

"How *is* Grayson?"

"I haven't seen him today. But to be honest, he's not doing so well. Lately he just wants to die."

"I don't blame him," Jacko says. "He was always a man of dignity. He's not himself anymore. And he's ninety years old."

"Are you saying that ninety years is enough?"

"Not that. I always respected your father. He was always good to me."

"I know. You're right. What can I do?"

"There's nothing you can do ... but The Hacienda will direct things for the best."

"You're one of the last hold-outs that trust in the soul of this place."

"It's always done right by me."

"Well, okay. I don't know."

"I do."

Jacko wants to reminisce about the good old days when my dad would take him out for a beer or slip him some extra cash. He tells me about how proud of me Dad always was and how he hoped I would take over the business. And all the time Jacko talks, I keep thinking about my tragic P&L statement and the Billingsby offer. If I do it, they would have to agree to keep Jacko on and make sure everyone was properly settled or relocated. I know they would weed the Assisted out from the Independents.

Stella arrives looking insulted and upset.

"Did I do something incorrectly? Is there something wrong?" she asks.

"No. No. No. Please sit," I say. "I really appreciate all the volunteer time that you spend at the front desk. We just want to find out about three of our residents who did not come back on the shuttle."

"Oh. Cookie and her new friend Elmore called and left a message on voicemail that they would Uber back."

"I see. And Gavina McVey?"

"Ugh. Her. Hasn't she moved out yet? I hear that Meadowbrook Nursing Home has an excellent psychiatric department."

"She wasn't on the ride back either," Jacko says.

"Well, she's probably with the other two. They're not here. I checked. Can I go now? I feel like I've been called into the principal's office. I didn't appreciate it then and I don't like it now."

After Jacko and Stella retreat from my office, I feel like I'm the grown-up around here. Calling people into my office. Listening to everyone's problems. Everyone else's thoughts and feelings. My office suddenly seems suffocating. I should go ahead and have Elmore help me tear down a wall and maybe eliminate the waiting room or something. I need more breathing room.

When I walk out into the hall to go for a visit with my Dad, I walk with thoughts about how I'm going to have to bring in round-the-clock care for him now. It's very expensive and another reason for me to be considering taking the Billingsby money and moving him into a proper facility. But for today, he's basically in my care. And have I mentioned that I love the man? He's been the greatest dad a guy could hope for.

I've become more and more slow on my feet when I'm on my way to him as his illness progresses. I'm in no hurry to get to his apartment right now. He's gone from asking the same questions over and over, to being uncharacteristically angry, to hardly speaking. And he needs assistance dressing and using the john since he can't control his bladder very well. He often doesn't know who I am.

But then again, neither do I.

When my phone rings outside Dad's door, I see it's from Billingsby so I don't answer. After I let it go to voicemail, I listen to my first message. It's from Melba and it crushes me.

Hey, Kevin. Hope you're okay.
I know it looks like I ran out on you, and I supposed
I did.

I'm going to stay in L.A. for now.
Might come visit your dad in a couple of weeks. Hope he's not in too much pain.
You know how much I love that man.
Please take care of yourself. Call if you want. There's no reason we can't talk.

As fate would have it, the second message is from Rudy. He mentions Gavina, but the most uplifting thing he says is 'see you soon for dinner.'

His voice cuts through the mess of it all.

I have sort of a date tonight. I don't see how I can go — what with Gavina missing and having to deal with her delusions about demolition and her plan of helping my dad die.

Chapter Eleven

Gavina

I only see him from behind at first. As grubby as he usually was, I loved my Uncle Ian and I feel that affection for him now. Naturally, I have to follow him as he comes out of SLO Liquors. I do not know what SLO means but it might be a clue as to where I am. Uncle Ian looks pretty much the same as he did on his worst days — wearing that long, filthy coat hanging off his skinny body. Dirty sneakers and the smell of alcohol trailing behind him like vapor from a bad muffler on a Sixty-Three Ford. I dare not speak to him or call out his name because I know he will run. I would not be able to dash after him, so I walk carefully at a distance remembering to look inconspicuous while tracking him — like Dick Tracy taught me regarding using your wits on city streets. Ian does not look back, so we go along for about twenty minutes before he turns into a sad dilapidated building. There are shopping carts, old bicycles, and all manner of bags and boxes along the side and back where he enters, and I follow him up moaning stairs and into a small apartment no larger than my studio at The Hacienda but with unfinished nearly rotten wood paneling and no closet. And when he stops and sits down with his legs crossed on a large cardboard, I can no longer contain my excitement.

"Ian. Ian. Uncle. How are you? You don't look so good."

"Not your Uncle Ian, Lady."

"Ian. Are you drunk?"

"Not your Uncle Ian, Lady."

"Do not be rude, Ian. Can you not see how happy I am to see you?"

"Not your Uncle Ian, Lady."

"May I join you?" I ask, and without waiting for an answer I place my shopping bag down and Ian immediately grabs it and rummages through it.

"Give that back," I say.

"What the fuck?" he says. "What's all this stuff for? Looks like you're a car mechanic or a short order cook. This stuff is lethal."

"Of course, it is lethal. *That* is the point. Some folks just want to end it all and meet their maker."

"I could go for that," he says. "Except I don't ever want to see my wicked mother's face and *she's* the one who made me. There's no God made me."

"Of course, there is a God. It is whatever you think it is. But it is."

"You planning to crash here?" he asks.

"I think not. Not too sure of much right now."

"Got any booze?"

"Ian, stop it."

"Again ... not your Uncle Ian, Lady. Why don't you take a load off and lay down for a while? You look tired. An afternoon nap might do you good."

Just the mention of resting suddenly seems delightful so I go ahead and recline on another flattened cardboard bed across from his and rest my muddled head on the stained but fluffy pillow, feeling myself drift off aboard a Scottish gray cloud. Cookie Nussbaum and Elmore ride there with me in my dream as if we are all heading toward the same destination.

Cookie

I'd prepared a list of possible apartments for Elmore and me from my rather sketchy smartphone search. But we weren't too sure about what we would actually see once we visited the listings. And indeed, although not far from the movie theater downtown, the first place we looked at was awful and ugly in every conceivable way. Two flights and thirty-two steps up and no elevator. It took us forever to get up there and heaven only knows why we bothered to put ourselves through the feat except possibly to prove to ourselves that our stair-climbing days are over.

So, Fifteen-Seventy-Five Banal Street put a huge dent in our plan to find our own place within our budget.

After wasting all that time, while on the way to our next viewing, I remember noticing a woman on the sidewalk who looked a lot like Gavina.

"Was that our Gavina I saw earlier ... following that homeless looking character?"

"Where?" Elmore asked.

"Across, over there," I said.

"It couldn't have been because she's got to be back on the shuttle by now."

"Right. My eyesight ain't what it used to be."

Now, Elmore motions for us to sit on one of the low brick walls along the walkway. A couple very cute squirrels run off, insulted that we took up their space. I'm impressed with myself for enjoying them and seeing the critters as cute instead of nasty. That might be as mellowed-out as I'll ever become.

"We ... and by we, I mean *you* ... should be nicer to her," Elmore says.

"Who? Why?"

"Come on, Cookie. Who does Gavina remind you of? You're a therapist for Christ's sake. It's not hard to see that you overreact to her."

"She takes up too much space."

"Not enough room for *you* in other words."

"Don't be a bitch."

"It just seems like you're used to being seen and treated as special. And she sure doesn't do that."

"I feel a lot like I did with Judy Hickson in high school. What ... sixty-five years ago? Are you happy now Mister Freud?"

"Tell me about this Judy bitch," Elmore says.

"Can you guess what started my problem with Judy?" I ask Elmore.

The vivid thought of her wipes out my mellow moment as I hear the squirrels dashing about in the branches.

“A guy!” Elmore says, as one of the squirrels returns for possible crumbs.

“Andrew Quarterback.”

“That was his name?”

“That’s what everyone called him. Right out of teen-heart-throb central casting. And we were dating. He asked me to the junior prom.”

Here’s where you would expect the person hearing this tragic story to either interrupt with questions, comments, judgments, or unwelcomed sympathy. But Elmore sits quietly waiting for me to continue — his hands on the wall helping to support him on either side of his body and a tender look of empathy on his face as if he’s remembering something of his own.

“I was the editor of the school newspaper, and she was a reporter, so technically I was sort-of her boss. But she ignored my suggestions and always went around me to the advisor. This girl was not as cute as me. I dressed better and was a whole lot smarter. Anyway ... I don’t think Andrew knew that I was Jewish. In those days, Jews and Gentiles were not encouraged to date each other.”

Still quiet, Elmore nods. I’m really liking this Elmore character more and more, when after another pause, he says, “And this Medusa outed your Jewish butt and he broke up with you.”

“And she took over the paper the next semester. I didn’t even try to stay on as editor.”

"And ..." Elmore coaxes.

"I began to establish my reputation as *an easy girl.* Easy make-out. Willing to go to second and maybe sometimes third base."

"And ..." Elmore is elbowing me.

"Well ... okay ...." I say.

"Take your time."

"My mother began hating me more than she did already. I could never live up to her requirements for me. I was not the daughter she wanted. She made that clear and then once I began sexually acting out, she could go at me with both barrels."

"And you blame *Judy* Whatshername for all that."

"I suppose."

"And you *blame Quinn* for losing your license and forcing you into retirement."

"That's enough," I say. "I'm not ready to be analyzed while sitting on a public wall plotting to run away from home like I did when I was a senior in high school. Besides, that damn squirrel is staring at us."

"Okay."

"Okay. And if we're going to do this living together thing eventually, after we really get to know one another ... let's look at *single level houses* and up our budget."

"No apartment or motorhome?"

"No. I think that ship has sailed."

"Right. We need more of a Golden Girls set up."

"They were supposed to be pushing sixty in that show, not eighty."

"Eighty is the new sixty."

"Tell my hip joints that."

"Let's Uber back. I'll summon a carriage," Elmore says.

So there we are. Two teenagers in our eighties waiting for a ride to take us back to our new-found home. We both know full-well that we are on our last leg. And I can't tell you how annoyed I am when I see stuff online or read anything about people in their nineties still doing marathons or yoga or whatever else makes them appear to be so much younger than they are. I just read that Mick Jagger is doing a tour where he travels with his own cardiologist so he can push himself to Mother Nature's limits, resisting the horrifying truth of his natural diminished capacity. I want to live on my own, but I'm scared. I'm not giving up the idea mind you, but I'll need Rudy's cooperation and some serious household help. Maybe a live-in caregiver who can provide whatever nursing we'll need as we near the finish line. Terrifying. Horrifying. Can you imagine — me without the admiration, adulation, validation, and compensation that I have enjoyed most of my life?

"I'm scared, too," Elmore says.

"I didn't say anything about being scared," I reply. "Was I thinking out loud? Hell! I hope not."

"You didn't have to *say* anything," Elmore declares. "Let's go...."

Elmore

The grey car pulls up to the curb where we're now standing. These guys are quick and it's better than a cab because once you're on your way, everything is paid for automatically.

"Are you our ride?" I ask, through the open window on the passenger side of the Uber car.

"Yep. Good afternoon, Folks. Come on in," the smiling driver says, as I open the back door of her car and climb in first. That's an elder man's way of being polite, so the lady doesn't have to scoot over. Cookie gets in next and sits close, since my scooting distance is not impressive.

"Where to?"

"The Hacienda Mirage," I say.

"Doesn't your app tell her where we're going?" Cookie asks me.

"Not sure I put that info in," I say.

"No problem," the driver says, as she pulls away from the curb. "I know where that is. Been around here forever. You can put your packages up here if you need more room."

I hand the shopping bags over, and she places them on the front seat next to her.

"So ... about our plan ... what are we afraid of?" I ask Cookie, as she makes more room for herself by adding her purse to the stash up front.

"Aside from needing to get to know each other better. What if we run out of money? Or end up with health issues that a private caregiver can't handle?"

I listen to her list of concerns. And they all make sense. Interesting that I share her fears, but she hasn't mentioned my main one. Pain. I'm more afraid of surgery, recovery — or lack of — and at the top of the list — dementia. No one has ever been able to convince me that forgetting who you are and what you've done is manageable for the victim. And that's what you are. A victim. A zombie. I am most scared of losing my mind or being in constant pain.

By the time we are at least ten minutes from town, I realize that the scenery is unfamiliar. And just as I do, Cookie asks, "Where the hell are we going, Miss?"

"Why don't you two just shut up going on and on about getting old. You're depressing me," the driver says. Her messy hair is piled high and also falling around the back of her head so we can't see her face. I feel my heart quicken.

"Did you just tell us to shut up?" Cookie says, leaning toward the driver just close enough so that she can nudge Cookie right back against our seat before taking a sudden turn that tosses us around even more.

"I hate old people," the driver says, still not turned around. "I'm gonna let you out. People like you should have expired by now. You're just takin' up space."

"Let us out where?" Cookie screams. Her voice is a mix of anger and terror. She's indignant but leans into me as she speaks. "You can't do that. I'll have you know..."

"I'm gonna slap your mouth before I let you out. Never shut up, do you?"

"Just go ahead and stop the car," Cookie shouts. "You're not going to slap anyone."

"You know what, Lady. I have a nice little pistol right up here in my glove compartment and I can just as easily shoot you. No one's around."

As far as I'm concerned, anyone who threatens you with a gun is someone you don't want to mess with.

I'm hot and sweaty all over and now I want to get out of the car. The driver is mad, more at the world than she could be at us two. The descending darkness outside cools the air that is streaming in through the open window of the passenger seat. Of course, Cookie demands her purse back and the driver just laughs. She stops the car and orders me to hand over my wallet and phone. You can bet I do.

Then she darts the car forward just enough to slam on the brakes. She does this quick start and stop another time. This startles Cookie enough so that at the next full stop we hurry out as fast as we can — me coaxing Cookie from behind and the car then darting off before I'm totally out of the vehicle.

When it stops again — still in our view — I catch my breath and hold Cookie's sweaty hand.

Chapter Twelve

Kevin

Dad's apartment is in the old part of the house, overlooking the garden. He isn't looking at me. He's gazing out the window, like he often does.

"I know the garden needs to be worked on," I say. "In spite of my money issues with The Hacienda and the need for so many upgrades, I'm having the garden relandscaped. I already hired a landscape architect to spruce things up. They're going to start prepping the land."

Sometimes I talk to him as if he were still the best friend he came to be as I grew into adulthood. Nowadays — thinking that maybe he's listening and understanding — I talk quietly to him. I don't expect advice. I don't *want* any advice. I've recently learned that just airing out my thoughts and feelings helps me in some mysterious way. The closer I get to accepting that he's not here for me, the more I feel he is. I know that's strange, but it's true. I'm sure that after he dies, regardless of what I decide about this place, I'll visit the Hacienda Garden where his ashes will be discretely scattered. And I'll still talk to him.

"I'm supposed to have dinner with Rudy tonight," I say. "I think you saw him in the dining room during the Gavina drama on Saturday. He's very nice, and awfully good looking. Something strange and interesting is going on with us. With me. Primal. Comfortable in a way that I've never felt with Melba."

Did Dad just nod?

"I don't see how I can go to this dinner with Rudy, though. Gavina is missing and she's having delusions about demolition. She's spreading a rumor that The Hacienda is being torn down! And I hear that she's planning of all things ... to help you die."

Another nod?

"That is not going to happen, Dad. I will not let that happen."

He looks puzzled. It seems like he's thinking. Wanting to speak.

"And Cookie and Elmore are still not back in their apartments," I continue.

I imagine he's somehow digesting what I'm saying. I know that the right thing is to cancel Rudy and find The Missing Three. And I always do the right thing, don't I?

"I always have to do the right thing," I say out loud.

"Kevin," he says. Loud and clear.

He says my name. And it seems like he wants to go on but he clearly isn't able.

As he searches for the words — or I imagine them myself — I can almost hear him say, 'Doing the right thing is often doing *what someone else wants you to do. Or not to do!*'

So for a change, I am going to do just what my gut tells me to do. I will make sure that Jacko stands guard, and no one gets to Dad. He'll be safe until I get back here. I can tell it's a test-my-own-wings kind of moment. The floor is springy beneath my feet and doesn't make its usual creaking sounds. I'm leaving the nest.

On my way out, I close the thick oak door and pause to run my fingers along its varnished grain in what feels like a harmonious and conclusive good-bye.

Grayson Previn – The Manager

Kevin,
I heard you earlier tonite. I do not know when we will be able to speak a proper good-bye but since I am mildly lucid at the moment and tomorrow I very well may leave I am writing you this lengthy maybe jumbled note to tell you how very much I love you and am proud of you and appreciate you but also to give you some instructions regarding life and The Hacienda that are outside of the ledger books so I will write until I run out of steam because this is certainly my last hurrah and I do not seem to be able to speak to you directly.

I am going to seal this letter and leave it with Jacko for you along with some other important notes that I cannot remember if I gave you or not before I lost my mind. I trust he will get it all to you when the time is right!

I feel evening sinking into the bones of The Hacienda and anchoring its tired timber further into its footings and the walls tugging at the studs and ceiling joists and the mortar aching with age and the renovated sections wrenching on both sides yearning to pull it apart so new materials can be installed and The Hacienda Mirage can expand further I do not know what this structure was before it was a tree but when it was just a tree it had to take care of a lot of grumpy beetles and other insects birds and the like and it just stood there and could not relocate so it learned as it grew very tall to get along and maybe even help those creatures that depended on it as it breathes what we exhale and we need what the tree exhales all beings part of a vast web of inter-connections and dependencies as things come into and go out of existence because of conditions caused by other things.

There is a place called The Vision Rooming House for example who comes from the same land as The Hacienda so they have known each other in part from when they were forest. As soon as the pines became dominant in their stand they drastically changed the environment beneath them especially decreasing the amount of light reaching the ground and a much greater use of soil water by the trees and the combination of these and other factors made it impossible for most of the pines to reproduce and grow in their own shade so other species that could tolerate those conditions began to grow under them and set the stage for the next step in succession as hardwood developed and eventually replaced them so first fell the trees to make the lumber for The Vision and then for what was to become The Mirage.

'Tis the cycle of life.

Dwellings not only talk to those who live or visit within their walls and are willing and able to listen they also talk to each other and certainly to me more and more each day now. The Hacienda is with all who come here in spirit as its mother a wise old oak used to say before she was felled and taken off to become lumber.

They will find their way home wherever that is for each of them.

The floors rattle to get me to pay attention the only way now to get me to listen. Years ago it took no effort at all but it seems that just like with the original owner Montgomery Idlor the older I get the harder it is to get through to me yet unlike the Idlor Family members I still hear what these walls are saying and am grateful for whatever help I am receiving to be able to write to you like this even though I am not sure I am making sense.

Gavina is out so she may not be bothered by The Hacienda's musings and Cookie and Elmore live in the new section so even if they were here they would not hear the nudging of the rafters and let us face it you are not here because you my dear have gone to your dinner date and although you might think that I am old fashioned about sex and gender and the like I am thrilled for you and what I hope is a new found love and not just the kind of messy sex I have seen enough of that around here with these old folks bed hopping as if there is no such thing as STDs. I kept trying to tell them. Now I can hardly speak. I do not know why or how I can write this unless it is not me doing the writing.

No one but me and Gavina seem to listen although I think if I could spend a bit more time with the others they might possibly see the light not just about sex but about everything! About life. And about death. About how algae from the ocean floor becomes plants that become trees that can become wood to build houses and it is okay that before and after all that there is the unknown.

About the adventure and awe provided by infinity.

About Karma.

With a little more time I know they will learn their life lessons and I will pass painlessly.

I am hearing The Vision Rooming House which is no hardwood mansion turned old folks' home since it is not one of those buildings that you would rightly say has good bones. The aging of wood unlike that of some cheese or wine does not make it better nor does it improve the strength in its hundred year old joists and frail rafters except for the drop in moisture content everything else works to weaken it because it has been exposed to fungi insects heat especially on its west and south-facing roof and It turned a dull grey decades ago and lost its pleasant scent thanks to mold and mildew soon The Vision will be torn down to make room for a big trendy hippy condo building with ground level shops and extra parking and you will make some money because I own the property but I suppose when you are mostly pine and a little maple from the start you only live for so long and when your time is up that is that and you have to accept yourself and what you are made of and go from there.

The Vision was once a decent little building in the early nineteen hundreds with small but cute studios perfect for nurturing communal living for students artists and writers when it was known as the vision rooming house and those who lived there had life changing experiences many of which are still echoed in books movies and prayer meetings. Sometimes if they got really old and were decent folk they might come to The Hacienda where I would take them in.

Lately I imagine people sneak in the back door of what once was a shared kitchen and is now a stripped-bare open area where they lumber up the broken stairs and claim their space mostly one per studio when they are not sharing booze or drugs or stories of their lost lives and they all now shit and pee in the only bathroom with a toilet that used to flush sometimes but as disturbed criminal drunk or high as these residents were they were still human beings in need.

Which brings me to some housekeeping if these walls allow me to keep writing this here.

I think you know to keep Jacko employed. He has not only been a loyal worker but a friend and he is a pretty good judge of character and a man of few words so do not think he is just useful for tasks and chores but go to him if you need anything out of the ordinary.

And you should know that Melba came to me a short while ago when I was doing so much better and asked me if I thought you liked men and I told her that everyone deserves to be happy and stuff like that so she is going to be okay and anyway let her go.

Oh, and one more thing the original Idlor House portion of The Hacienda sometimes communicates and makes stuff happen but only in a good way do not ever give it up in any way and you shall be fine.

DAD (and The Hacienda Mirage)

Chapter Thirteen

Gavina

Just because I am basically alone lying on a cardboard box in some catawampus old boarding house does not mean that I cannot, do not, or will not hear The Hacienda. Its old floorboards and lath-and-plaster walls have been yakking at me for years. And by now, I can very well hear some of whatever it is trying to say. Most of it is a beckoning for me to come home and to flee this place so I can get on with helping The Manager depart this life.

"You've been asleep for a while," I hear a man say through the fog of my awakening. "They call me Farris the Juggler. Used to be with Cirque' back in the day."

He seems like a perfectly nice gentleman, who has graciously offered me a place to rest and is now extending a chocolate power bar swathed and unopened in its original shiny foil wrapper.

"Do not mind if I do," I say to the gentleman who I now see is *not actually* my dead Uncle Ian but could very well be Ian being channeled by this hobo. I will listen carefully since Ian's wisdom was washed away from booze but might be accessible through my soon-to-be lover — a man living on the top floor of a two-story ramshackle building.

"Nap's done you good," The Juggler says. "You look fresh as a rose ..."

"Are you flirting with an old woman?"

"Not older than me, Miss. Right age for me. I like your all-red outfit."

"In Scotland, people used to paint their doors red to show they have paid off their mortgage. Out of the red, you know. I myself never had a house or a mortgage. Thank you very much. But I like to think of red as passion. I am nothing if not a passionate woman."

He writes in a little notebook as if he cannot keep up with his thoughts. The man needs a laptop. Probably does not type though.

"You're quite well dressed for a vagrant," he says, without looking up.

"I prefer *person without housing,*" I reply. "Your lamp smells of kerosene."

"That's 'cause that's what it is, M'lady."

"You should use olive oil."

"You some sort of a cook? We could've used a creative cook around here. Someone who could make up healthy shit from foodbank crap. What's the anti-freeze for?" he asks.

"You have been in my bag?"

"Yes, Ma'am. Never know what you might be able to use."

"Do not call me Ma'am. You were just flirting with me, I thought. And open the neck of your shirt there, so I can see."

"See what?"

"Never you mind," I say.

I can only marry a man with chest hair. And try as I might, I am never sure what constitutes enough fur. So in a way — what with my being away from The Hacienda — I am on my own, as I look around the tiny room and think about how I lived on the streets for a short bit and how I am now way too old to ever do it again and I am wondering how I can keep this new relationship going because as you might have guessed, The Juggler is now displaying a good amount of chest hair.

"Where ya going? Or where ya coming from?" he asks.

"I thought you were someone else. I followed you," I say. "Sometimes I lose my way. I live at The Hacienda Mirage. You know the place?"

"Yup. I stayed there years ago. Nice place. Too spooky for me."

"Spooky?"

"They had me locked up in one of the old lobotomy rooms."

"What in heaven's name are you talking about?"

"They didn't do it there, but the head-docs used to drill a pair of holes in the skull and push a thingamabob into the brain."

"They never did that kind of horror at The Hacienda. I would have heard about it."

"I din't say *they did it*. I said I had a room where they used to do it a hundred years ago. Anywho ... I felt too confined there."

"You are a weird fellow. You make stuff up."

The Juggler takes another notebook out of a back-pack — a nice haversack. He writes something down with a fancy pen."

"It's a Montblanc," he says, noticing I am staring as he continues writing. "Got it from a professor of mine back when I was at Northwest."

"I am not sure what you are saying."

"Good pen. Good school."

"Still not getting it."

"Never mind. I just got a great idea for my next mini-series. Have to write things down before I forget," he says, now taking off his overcoat.

As you know, The Juggler is wearing an open neck old flannel shirt. I see now that it is remarkably solid red. A true Monday color. His hair is surprisingly thick for a man of his advanced years. His skin is wrinkled and pale. But he is so dignified and dashing. Like Sean Connery. Maybe he *is* Sean Connery. But Sean just died did he not? He was at least ninety years old. I was twenty last time I went out on a date with him. I have dated most of the James Bond 007 actors. Sean and I liked to go skinny dipping. We went to the movies sometimes to see *Dr. No*. Whenever his close-ups came onto the screen, he'd mouth the words out loud. '*World domination that same old dream.*'

"Did you just say something about world domination?" The Juggler asks.

"Did I say that out loud?"

"I do that all the time," he says. "The folks I crash with are used to it. But new people just hightail away or try to snuggle up close to me, depending on what I'm mumbling."

"You are not mumbling, Darling."

"You know you can't stay here. Giggles and I are the last to leave. They're tearing the place down tomorrow. It's made it into the local news! Maybe ya read about it. So we're each movin' on."

"Who is Giggles?"

"She's sort of my house mate. Crazy as a bed bug the girl is, but she's like the clever daughter I never had. Got no family. Neither of us. She poses as an Uber driver sometimes if she can find a car to borrow."

"You mean steal."

Cookie

Well, that's what happens when you trust a man to do things. Elmore didn't check on the car or the driver and here we are at sunset, lost and alone on a dusty road — me without my purse or any of our purchases.

"Give me your phone. I'll call The Hacienda," I say.

"She got my phone and wallet, too." Elmore says.

"You gave them to her. You just got into some random car that wasn't even an Uber."

"Get off my case. What was I supposed to do?"

I'm telling you my nerves are shot by now. I'm not a big fan of depending on anyone else to do the right thing. We're stranded.

"Calm down. We're fine. She didn't hurt us," Elmore says.

"Don't tell me to calm down. Don't *ever* tell a woman to calm down. *You're* the one who got us into this mess."

"Really, Cookie? And we're supposed to live together ... with you blaming me for anything that goes wrong?"

"*I* would have checked the car description and the name and photo of the driver."

"Well good for you."

"I'm not sure exactly where we are, but we can't be all that far from town," I say.

So this is the way it would be. I move out of a substandard old folks' home with Elmore into a substandard house for just him and me, only to be plagued by yet another dumbass who can't figure out how to get from Point A to Point B. No thank you. People are idiots. If you think you can count on any one of them to do any one thing right, you're kidding yourself. People are stupid and lazy. And now I'm living in and among the elderly, most of whom turn out like Elmore who put us in the car of a heartless, spineless criminal who robs old people of their shopping bags and their purses. A woman no less! What's this world coming to?

"We're lucky she didn't hurt us," Elmore points out again. Does every person over seventy repeat themselves?

"There's a directional sign *Idlor Farm and Feed – One Mile.* Let's go," I say. "We can walk that way."

"Not sure I can do that. I banged my leg on the door when she ordered us out of the car."

Sure enough, there's a blotch of blood where the leg of his trousers is torn. So now what?

"I'll give it a try," he says. "Let's just see how far we get."

He reaches out his hand suggesting that I help him along. I'm supposed to be his nursemaid now?

Elmore

Poor Cookie. The old gal is scared out of her wits. I don't really blame her because that was one hell of a ride we ended up on. It's not the first time I've been in that kind of danger, but when I was younger it was less upsetting. My resilience was more impressive and recovery time was a lot quicker. My leg hurts but it's just a little gash and a couple stitches will take care of it. It's clear that the less I say right now the better.

We begin our walk — Cookie still unsettled by the realization that things no longer roll off her back. This is not a woman who's used to being frightened easily. Not only that, but a gal without her purse is like a mountaineer who's lost their sunscreen, compass, and repair knife — along with whatever mysterious essentials are in their pack.

The thing that is shaking *me* right now is the ambushed nature of what's happened. I was innocently riding along with my friend, planning an exciting adventure as I often have in my life. I felt childlike and hopeful. And then out of the blue comes an assault. The first time I remember feeling this way was when my father ambushed me on a Saturday morning when I was down in the basement of our modest little New Jersey house. I was playing with my Lincoln Logs, building a house with a roof that just kept falling down. Happy that the little orange pieces were finally fitting together, I heard his footsteps and his booming voice calling me as he often did before a beating. "Where's my little sissy?"

Cookie has the same look on her face that I must have had on that day well over seventy years ago.

"Are you okay?" I ask, letting go of her arm and stopping to catch my breath and check my wound under a huge oak tree with a couple of its very large branches having fallen horizontally to provide a natural place to sit.

"I'm fine. Jacko will probably come to take us home if we can find a phone."

"Home?"

"Let's be grownups, Elmore. I hate to say it, but The Hacienda is our home now. At least we can feel safe there until we become Assisted or have to go into a true 24/7 nursing home."

"What about our big adventure? What about the Golden Girls?"

"I don't know. That whole ride with that woman got me upset. I suppose I took it out on you."

"Um ... yeah."

"Did you see her face?" Cookie asks.

"No ... not really. I couldn't identify her unless maybe if I heard her voice again."

"She's probably driven out of reach and will be in another state by the time we can report her."

And then Cookie starts crying. I'm sure it's been a while since she's done so.

"Where did all the time go? I was a busy, successful woman who could do a million things at once ... juggle appointments and projects ... have plenty of adventures ... and now I can't comfortably walk a mile or deal with a purse snatcher."

"A purse snatcher? She said she had a gun, Cookie!"

"I know," she says, wiping the tears from her cheeks. "It's not that. I just don't know who I am anymore. I don't know *what* I am. I used to keep busy enough and do well enough so that I could avoid hearing the voice in my head freaking me out."

"We'll get you some new mascara," I say, as if she was a child. "We'll get you a new purse."

That makes her smile.

I know exactly how she feels. I suppose that's part of the reason why I worked so hard all my life, too. And why doing drag was so good for me. Not only did I get to liberate my feminine side, but I got to be someone other than myself — something bigger than myself — and be appreciated with applause and dollar bills. Sometimes even ten or twenty-dollar bills handed to me just for being fabulous.

"If we stay at The Hacienda, we're gonna have to be more tolerant and find things to do for fun and keep our minds occupied ... with more than just feeling sorry for ourselves while we wait for the inevitable," I say.

That makes Cookie crumble.

Rudy

I'm worried about Elmore and Cookie. Neither of them are answering their phones. But as the sun falls into the ocean from behind some fluffy gray clouds, I'm thinkin' about how some people say there's always a silvery lining surrounding what might feel like a gloomy day. The bright edge around one bunny-shaped cloud is sidetracking me as I near the Avila Beach Grill. Driving through the green and suntanned mountains, I'm not sure if I should feel hopeful or sad. It seems that when I build up my hopes, I'm usually disappointed.

I think Kev wanted to meet outside of town and a while away from The Hacienda so no one would see or bother us. So maybe he'll be less sick at ease. That would be good. But what if he has bad news about us or something? Then again, there is no *us* so what am I spinning about? The guy is married and no matter what, the rules of the road always say don't mess with a married man if you want a real relationship. And even if he's breaking up with Melba, you shouldn't be with someone on the remound. At least he doesn't have kids. Parents should never leave their kids.

I'm a little early for our seven o'clock reservation, but I sit at our table, and it looks like we didn't need a reservation anyway since the place is small, dark, and nearly empty. Not that you don't need to make reservations just 'cause a place is small or dark, I guess.

I order a club soda from a hot — but young and very gay — guy with a man bun and torn jeans. You know what I mean by *very gay*, even though I know I shouldn't talk or think that way as if I'm better because I can pass as straight. Sorry.

I realized when I was leaving the motel that I only have tight shirts with me because both Cookie and Elmore prefer that. But I don't want to do anything to freak out Kev, so I leave my hoody on and zip it up. I like this place. There's boat stuff on the walls, like anchors and rope. The tables are shellacted with shiny tops that are sort of sticky but remind me of fun times and spilled beer before I got sober. There are hamburgers, chicken, and salad on the menu, so I don't have to be anxious by a fancy choice of food like Elmore or Cookie always used to flavor in the places they would take me out to eat.

Kevin's there right on time. I'm relieved to see that he has a shirt on that is as tight as the one I'm hiding under my hoody.

"I see that Marty brought you a drink," Kevin says.

"It's club soda. I don't drink the hard stuff," I say.

"Me neither. Just a glass or sometimes two of wine."

"You must come here a lot," I say.

"Not a lot. Occasionally."

"You come here to see Marty?" I ask, smiling. I've been told that *a knowing smile* will get you close to people if you're being silly — as long as they don't read it as a smirk which is like a smug, stuck-up, judgy grin.

"It's quiet here, and yes ... if no one's around I chat with him. He's a nice kid."

"He's chicken to you and me."

"Chicken?"

"You don't know what that means?"

"Not really."

"He's at lease twenty years younger than us."

"So?"

"So, you ought to flirt with men your own age," I say to the man in the shirt that is happily stretched across his chest as he sits at my table in this romantical place. His face is now as red as the painted wooden lobster hanging on the wall.

"Maybe I shouldn't say this. We just met. But ..."

"Go on. Looks like you need to spill some guts," I say.

"I'm a gay virgin, Rudy. I've never cheated on Melba and never even been with another man ... or woman for that matter. And I've never seen Marty anywhere except *here* a few times. *Maybe* he's why I like it here. But I don't really know because as of this week, I am one baffled and bewildered man."

"You mean like confused?"

"Very."

"That's okay. I don't mean to push you or make you feel not comfortable."

"You make me feel *horny*, Rudy. I know the feeling, but it usually passes ... or I rationalize it."

"Why do you need to ration it?"

"When I feel this way, I typically just figure ... oh, I'm envious of some man's body or he's more handsome than me and I wish I was better looking ... or ... maybe that guy in an ad or movie has an easier time with women since I have never felt truly relaxed with Melba or any other woman."

"Uh huh." That's all I can mutter as Marty brings a glass of white wine, which Kev didn't even need to order. He doesn't come here a lot? Marty knows what Kev wants. And as he sets the glass down on the table — before turning away without speaking — he gives us a *knowing glance* that I read as maybe approval?

"What's it like being bi-sexual? I'm intrigued," Kev asks. The dimness of the room makes it feel like we are in our own little world where nothing we say or no one around can perpetrate our safe private space. Nothing fancy about what's going on in and around here. I can say whatever I want.

"For me ... it's more like ... I don't mind having sex with women ... especially if they uhm ..."

"Pay you?"

"Hell. That sounds not nice. It's odd to hear it put that way. Straightforwarded like that."

"Sorry," he says, looking right into my eyes as if he'd just smacked me, which he didn't. He was just being honest. It's sexy. I like it.

"I suppose in some way it's true. Don't love hearing it, but I don't think I have sex with women who are not clients or renumbercate me in some form or another. And frankly I need the money. I know I should find another line of work and make an honest living. Maybe as a physical therapist or start my own fitness business. I don't know."

"Never been married?"

"God, no."

"Ever been in a relationship ... long term with a woman?

"I've never been in what I think you mean by a long-term real relationship *with anyone,* Kevin."

"Would you ever want to be?"

"God, yes!"

Chapter Fourteen

Quinn

I've been — shall we say — *passed-out drunk,* but I didn't disappear on purpose. It just happens sometimes that I go incommunicado. People do that. I'm not the first. Don't tell me that you never flaked on anyone or ghosted someone and left them wondering. The thing is, I've been with a wild woman having sex on the floor in what is probably some kind of safe house where the worst traits of yourself show up and make you overlook your surroundings. She's probably in the john right now taking a leak, so let me catch you up on what's been going on for me since yesterday — before I pass out again. Not that anyone cares. Someone could be laying in a blackout or sick as a dog and people just walk or drive on by while they continued to listen to their audio book or latest kiddie rock Billie Eilish song.

So there I was on a cloudy Sunday afternoon — handcuffs dangling from one arm. I think it was yesterday, but it seems like forever ago. I stood for a while on The Hacienda's dusty gravel road — a man alone on the planet. I could have been on Mars with its cold desert the color of blood.

And then as if I was waking from a nightmare, I begin hurrying away from The Hacienda.

I used to run four miles a day thirty years ago, but now a usual walk for me has been to go from my tiny apartment to the car and back again. That is, before I was evicted. You read that right. *Evicted.* Or

I'd stroll the aisles of the grocery store to buy whatever I could afford at the time. Occasionally, I'd stop by the one and only remaining video store in my neighborhood, now called Vintage Disks, where they have old vinyl records and DVDs. They carry three copies of *Scottish Mistress* and I'd get a little mood boost and validation if even one was rented out. I'd smoke a cigarette outside the door on my way in and out, hoping to run into someone who might be an old movie buff with tons of money, wanting to invest into a sure-to-be big hit Hollywood Independent film. Has not happened.

It's all over for me if this new film isn't funded. It's my last hope. I know I've run out of steam. The well has run dry. I have no money and no new ideas. I wrote the script for *Old Folks* about two years ago with every ounce of creative juice left in me. True confessions. Happy now?

I was out of breath when I reached the motel last night. I climbed inside my car and took off. And no, I did not check out because when you do that, they expect you to pay!

I had to get those cuffs off me, so I began looking for a dive bar on the outskirts of town, thinking maybe there's someone who knows how to jimmy the lock if I find the right place. And for once, after striking out in the first joint I was in luck with the dark and dingy Magic Tavern — a true hole-in-the-wall. Christmas tree bulbs strung along the ceiling, half of them burned out. Floor so sticky that it took me forever to mosey up to the bar with its barnwood ledge rubbed raw by too many elbows over too much time.

The place was nearly empty. One bum in the only actual booth. But his head was on his arms, folded onto the table. Near me on one of the four uncomfortable wooden bar stools sat a woman *not at all* like the pretty girl who turned me down on Saturday night. Probably a lesbo. But this one was young and very friendly.

“Hi,” she said before I could order a drink.

“Hello, Darling,” I replied, even though I sounded like a desperate Gavina. But it was enough to somehow ignite her toward the stool right next to me.

I’ve hidden my hand under the bar, yet she asked, “Trouble?”

“You could say that.”

“I love a little trouble.”

“How much for a shot of whisky?” I asked the old woman behind the bar.

“A buck for the basic.”

“Great. Line up three for me. And one for the lady.”

“I’m Giggles,” the girl announced.

Surprisingly she smelled clean but otherwise looked homeless. Considering my actual situation, the fact that she was coming on to me made my blood race to places that had been limp for far too long.

“Quinn,” I said, all smiles and charm.

“Thanks,” she motioned to the barmaid pouring the shots. Then to me, “Bitch took my shot glass away after I couldn’t pay for no more.”

“I’ve plenty of cash. Probably enough for as many as we want. I’m fucking loaded here.”

"My kinda guy. What's with the cuffs? Some sort of fetish?"

"No fetish. Bad karma. Long story. Looking for someone to help me out of them."

"Do you think this hairdo is just for looks?"

"Wait. What?"

"I don't have my hair piled up like this with bobby pins for no good reason. If you're me, you never know when you might want to jimmy a lock."

Obviously, my luck was taking a turn for the better. Handcuffs came off and she invited me over to her place.

Turns out to be *this* true shithole.

Now, I'm in very dark room. There's no light getting past the newspapers that cover the windows. This is not the first time I've come out of a blackout not knowing where I am. But *it is* the first time I wake on a dirty floor, on a flattened refrigerator box, in an empty room, all alone, naked. My clothes are scattered, and I crawl around like an animal, looking for my missing phone. I'm not sure if I'm still drunk, hung over, drugged out or some combination of all that. There's a cheap little alarm clock next to the cardboard box with a curious bunch of unopened packs of batteries. 'Stolen,' I think. The cracked screen reads *Monday 8:00 p.m.*

Feeling a little more clear-headed, I get dressed and look for a john. The bathroom is disgusting, and the building looks like it's about to fall down or be torn down — which reminds me of fuckin' good-for-nothing Gavina and her plea to come live with me. If she only knew that *I* was the homeless one. No longer able to pee like a real man, I squirt a bit over and over and try to wash my hands but there's no water and the toilet won't flush. After searching for my things back in the room again, I trek down the stairs and out the back door, looking for my car but don't see it anywhere which is when I remember that I drove that girl here and fooled around with her until I must have gone down for the count. She's gone and so is my car. My pockets are empty. No cash. No wallet.

The air is muggy and stale. I feel gross and clammy. Is this how it's going to end for me? What a shame. Alone in the middle of nowhere California, where dreams are made and then die from starvation.

And then I hear footsteps. The man behind me is big. He's wearing the coat of the homeless, ready in case winter lasts all year. Shaggy hair. Beard. And he's grinning ear to ear.

"Evening, Brother," he says, as he walks up to pat me on the back. "Name?"

"Yours or mine?" I ask, frightened of the guy and wondering if I'm staring into my own bleak future.

"I'm Farris," he declares like he's on a stage. "Washed up professional juggler and sometime writer for television."

"Quinn," I say. "Washed up professional filmmaker."

"No kiddin.' Whatcha doin' standing here?"

"She stole everything *including* my car..."

"Who?"

"The girl I slept with last night up there."

"Up there in the Vision House?"

"Whatever."

"That would be Giggles. I'm off to try and find her myself. She's a squirrely one. Loves to steal things and harass people. But we were going to take off *together* today. She could have changed her mind. Let's go find her."

He nudges me along down the street and continues blabbing in my ear.

"Where we going?" I ask.

"Let's start with a drink. You smell like you could use one and I know I can. I have a few bucks I borrowed from a lady I happened to meet this afternoon myself. She's napping. I'm leaving town."

"You sound like a thief yourself."

"Takes one to know one."

"I'm not a thief."

"But you're a crook, aren't you?"

"I'm a writer."

"Same thing."

Giggles is not in the Magic Tavern. There's a new bartender from the night before. He's my age and looks as down-and-out as his patrons. When he shuffles over to ask what we want, The Juggler orders a shot for each of us as if he knows the price is a dollar. And I begin to cry. It's a strange feeling that takes over my entire body. I'm glad it's happening here in this nowhere bar with these no-count people. It takes a while for me to stop. Shoulders stooped and bobbing forward like a lost boat in a storm.

"Holy shit, Brother. What's this all about?"

"I'm not your brother," I correct him. The guy's an imbecile. I wipe my eyes with a flimsy bar napkin that must come from a pack of one hundred from the Dollar Store.

"Hell, Man. I'm just trying to be friendly. Us writers need to stick together. You ought to go on the road with me. We can compare notes. Read each other's stuff."

"I do not need to read your stuff. I need to make my new movie. I need to direct."

"You write and direct for money?"

"I used to. I need to do it again."

"I don't write for money. I did a bunch of spec scripts when I was younger and later on I partnered with a great lady who might have ended up selling one or more of the better, later ones ... but I don't care. I gave up all the rights. I don't care. I write 'cause it's fun."

"Fun? Are you fucking kidding me? What do you mean *fun*?" This clown is so annoying, I might punch him. I learned long ago that you do what you do in order to make enough dough to do what you want to do which is make money and if you don't, *you're* the imbecile.

The drinks arrive and we both down the shots as if we had done this together a thousand times. I hate the place. I hate the smell and the damn Christmas bulbs and the dusty bottles of booze lining the back of the stupid bar. I hate this Juggler asshole, who goes on and on and on about the joys of writing just to write. To do his art because it puts him *in the groove*. How happy he is only when he's lost in creating. He talks and talks about traveling with the circus and how he met Giggles and has felt like a father or an uncle to her even though she doesn't deserve it. It's getting dark outside and we've each downed three-dollars-worth of cheap booze. I've spent the past twenty-four hours in the company of derelict morons.

"She's sure not here. I'm gone," he finally says. "On the road again solo."

"What am I going to do?" I mutter more into my empty shot glass than to him.

"You got someone to call?"

"No. Well ... maybe." I'm thinking about Gavina. She could help me. I have absolutely no idea how.

"Hey, Ralphy. Can my stuck-up friend here use your phone?"

When the bartender flat out refuses me a phone, The Juggler stands to leave and says, "Go on back up to the house. I've got a couple burner phones hidden in my room. Number 7 up the stairs. Good luck. Thanks for nothing, Ralphy. See you around, Mister."

Gavina

Carefully hoisting myself from off the floor, I am up to pee. I have never appreciated sleeping in a bed as much as I do after this nap without one. My body aches. I am in an empty old flop house. And the hairy old man is gone. He was not my Uncle Ian. Rather, he was someone who called himself The Juggler, I believe. He was very interesting looking. I will remember his face. I would like to paint him sometime, so I shall store his image in my brain. Good news is I am surrounded by lots of weathered old wood. Panels about to fall off the walls. Perfect for me to use one by one.

I am not sure that the hairy Juggler man did not touch me at all. He took my purse, but my phone is still tucked into my bra. There's a very dark pale in the air encircling me.

'Tis usual now that I am an old hen for it to take me a while to stretch my limbs before shuffling along to the john. I cannot remember if or when my body and my mind *both* worked well in concert. Maybe never. It might very well be time for me to become an Assisted. And just as I am perusing that thought, I have another illusion. I imagine seeing Quinn coming into the room. The sight of him sets me reeling once again as I am losing my mind and seeing things. I feel very dizzy and down I go.

Quinn is sitting next to me when I wake up. He has a wild look in his eyes. We are alone in The Juggler's room. In Victorian days they would say that I swoon. And I guess I do. I was doing so much better when I first got to The Hacienda. Of course, I was younger. But nowadays, I do get bewildered, and I do tend to keel over like a rag doll. The light dims and then goes to black and I hope that is how the final end will come for me.

"Hi there," he says.

"Are you a ghost?" I ask.

"Not a ghost. It's me."

"What are you doing here?"

"Came here with a friend last night. But she turned out to be a crook. Stole all my stuff. Ran off in *my car*. I guess I'm pretty tanked-up again now."

Quinn is sitting on the floor, legs flat out in front of him as he rummages through my bag of lethal goodies and looking like a desperate ghoul.

Look, you know I hate violence. If I want to make someone pay their dues, I humanely poison them. I do not like to see folks suffer, even if they deserve it. I don't think I want to hurt Quinn. My plan about the Manager and the rest of us adult orphans is not about hurting anyone. 'Tis a benevolent means to escort our way out of a sticky situation.

"I'm done," Quinn mumbles. The universe is trying to tell me something."

"Not sure it is the universe. It could be the woodwork ... but drink up," I say. There is salty water in my eyes, and I feel a storm of colors swirling inside of me. Gray, blue and then beige.

"I've done you wrong," he slurs.

"Yes. Thank you very much. That is true."

I begin walking toward the stairway. My feet are carrying me out of this place determined to take me home to The Hacienda. I am shaking from exhaustion and fear. I want to go home.

"God speed," Quinn says. "See you around."

"Are you going to use that stuff?" I ask, referring to the bag of poisons that I must leave with him and replace, rather than wrestle them from him. "You look desperate."

"I helped end your Uncle Ian's life. He asked me to do it. I gave him antifreeze like the one in this bag," he says, clutching the sack close to his chest.

"You killed my uncle."

"I didn't kill him. I helped him die. He left me the house. I knew he would."

"Go ahead, Quinn. Do yourself a favor," I say, thinking about my promise to The Manager — who I have nothing to gain from helping him to die. He was always kind and good to me. But staring at the shell of the man that once was Quinn, my heart freezes not only because of the drunk, drugged-out, and downright mean person sitting on the floor in this derelict old building, but also from the fear of what happened to me today. My skin is thin, and my nerves are shot. I itch all over.

I leave the bag with Quinn — tuck under my arm some wood panels that have released themselves from the wall — and once outside, I reach into my blouse for my phone to call Kevin.

Kevin

Since Rudy is away from the table, I should probably answer my phone even though it's an unknown caller. On his way back from the john, Rudy has stopped to talk to Marty at the bar. I watch them like a jealous lover. An old neon cigarette sign is lighting up Rudy's face making him look like a ruddy Marlboro Man. I'd like another glass of wine, but Rudy doesn't drink so I'm not about to fumble my way out of what might turn into something important if I get up my nerve and stop tapping my foot and cracking my knuckles. I feel like a teenager. But not the teen I was — who was supposed to be lovesick over Jessica Norden or Rebecca Nunes but who instead was shy and felt mostly nothing but dread when I was around those girls.

Now, here I am finishing dinner with a man who wants a real relationship and is clearly coming on to me. And so far, I've been way too nervous to lead or follow the conversation in that direction. We've talked about physical fitness, health, diet, and other safe topics such as career and family, or lack of such. I choked up when I told him about my Dad, Grayson Previn, and his history creating The Hacienda and how his days are numbered. I talked about him not insisting I take his last name when he finally married my mother, so I could avoid being mocked. Kevin Previn. And he talked about hating to be called Rudolpho, especially with his father's last name, Schneider, that didn't fit with Rudy's full first name. He told me about his grandmother raising him after his mother was deported and that his father went to Mexico to find her and then vanished. I've got to remember never to do anything that would make Rudy feel abandoned like that, although I don't know why I'm getting so ahead of myself here.

He's now coming back to the table and sits staring at me just when I accept the call. I hear the voice say, "It's Gavina."

"Ms. McVey. Gavina. How'd you get my number? Are you alright?" I nod to Rudy and switch to speaker so he can listen in.

"The Manager gave me your number awhile back. And no. I am not alright. I am lost and it is very, very dark."

"Where are you?"

"Not sure."

"Are you outside or inside?"

"I am outdoors. Near a run-down old building near town."

"Are there any street signs or places of business?"

"Idlor and Priest. Come for me. Please. I am frightened."

"I'll come get you. Are you alone?"

"I think I see Cookie and Elmore. Or I might be having one of my visions."

Rudy

Okay, so Gavina and maybe Cookie and Elmore are lost. I don't want to count my ducks until they're in a row, but this gives me a chance to continue my night out with Kev, even if it's on a rescue mission. I won't have sex with him. I don't want to ruin this by freaking Kev out before we have a chance to get to know each other for real. It'll be hard for me not to make it into something fleshly since I get so turned on, but I will not be nonappropriate. We'll be like Batman and Robin going to the rescue. The Dynamic Duo.

"Where is she again?" I ask.

"Somewhere near the feed store, I think. I'll show you where to go. Just follow me."

Okay, so he's gonna be Batman. I thought he was Robin. But what can I do? I guess I have to go along with this recasting against type.

"Relax Kev," I say. "We'll get her. Or them."

"She said she *thinks* she's with Cookie and Elmore. How can that be? She either is or she isn't."

"Well, they were in town today and didn't seem to want to take the shuttle back."

Marty is at the table as we get up to leave. "Looks like you're out of here. Anxious to go?"

"A bit of an emergency," Kev says to Marty who's grinning like he's thinking we're going off to hook up and I don't have time to set him straight even though it's none of his business, but I don't want him to be assuming the wrong thing because that would make him an ass out of you and me.

Walking out to our cars, Kev continues the conversating.

"If I call the police, they'll say I have to wait twenty-four hours before they can do anything. And they'll remind me that it's not unusual for one of our residents to go missing for a day."

"Not just residents. Looks like that Quinn guy has gone missing, too," I say.

"I don't really care about him right now. It's fine with me if I never see or hear from that man again. Ever."

"I know. Me neither. Not to change the subject, but speaking of missing ... have you heard from your wife?" I ask this as we get to my car, and he stands next to my door. I can't help myself from asking even though it's one of those times when I realize too late that I'm putting my shoe in my mouth.

"You're asking me about her *now*? Really?"

"Right. Sorry. Poor timing."

I get in the car and roll down the window. He's resting his shaking hand on the ledge. I reach over and rest my hand on his. My hand stays there for a moment, and we snatch each other's eyes, as they say. And then I look away and start the car. He watches my hand leave his as if it was a bird out of a cage flying away from home.

"Poor timing. Sorry," I say again, looking forward — ready to drive once he leads the way. But he keeps talking.

"My wife wants to stay in L.A. She's getting a promotion at work which means full time and she's being friendly on the phone, but I don't think she'll stay with me ... and I'm not sure she should ... or if I want her to ... and I think she might be seeing someone else."

I don't have a cue about what to reply, so I just sit quietly molting over what he has told me and then I say, "Let's go find our lost old-timers."

Cookie

It's getting late and Elmore and I have not said a word for quite a while. His leg hurts. My everything hurts. And I'm still frightened by what happened with the wild Uber chick and the alleged gun. I figure I'll try to make it to a phone and let Elmore wait here. Then the thought of him sitting alone in the dark makes me want to sob but I've had plenty of boo-hooing already. Don't need any more tears. And then I think I see Gavina walking toward us. Of all the bizarre things that come from being at The Hacienda, here *she* comes like out of a dream. Or nightmare.

"Is that you?" she murmurs.

"It's us. You're not seeing things," I say, noticing my sarcasm and how it might sound. Of course, Elmore tries to stand and reach out to her. He's right about me being rude to this woman, so I then say, "It's good to see you, Gavina. What's going on, Dear? What are the wooden boards for?"

"Never you mind," Gavina says.

"Sit," she says to Elmore while looking at me looking up at her. *I* have *not* gotten up.

"What's going on?" Elmore asks, as he stops trying to stand.

"I find myself a bit lost. And a bit confused. And quite a bit upset."

"We were robbed!" I say, almost absent-mindedly. "I'm lost and upset myself."

And after a remarkable silence, she laughs. She chuckles as if she has just heard the most marvelous joke. It's a deep, genuine sound. Elmore joins her. And it seems as though rather than laughing at me, or mocking me in any way, they're enjoying the relief that only a good laugh can bring. Before I know it, I'm giggling with them, and we sound like hyenas in the night. When we hear a coyote howl in the distance, we laugh some more.

"Kevin is on his way," Gavina finally says.

"What do you mean?" Elmore asks.

"I called him to come get me. I told him I thought I saw you. I was in an awful old house down the road. I left Quinn there. Do not tell anyone. They are tearing down the place tomorrow and they might not find him if we are lucky."

"Tearing down that place, too!" I say.

"So I am told."

"Everything is being leveled to the ground, Gavina?"

"Maybe I got my premonitions mixed up. I do not know."

Grateful that Kevin might indeed be on his way, I nevertheless roll my eyes. I swear it's a spontaneous, unconscious reaction to my gal Gavina coming to the rescue with another one of her Grimms' Fairy Tales.

"May I please borrow your phone?" I ask her.

She hands it to me without a fuss.

"Please have a seat, M'Lady," Elmore says, motioning to the large tree limb where we've been perched waiting to be rescued.

When I call Rudy, he answers immediately and says, "We're on our way. Are you okay?"

"Who's *we*? Are you with Kevin the Magnificent?"

"You sound like you're in pretty good spirits, Cookie. Where are you? And yes, Kev and I are on the way to find Gavina."

"Kev? So now it's Kev is it?"

"Cookie, are you with Elmore?"

"Not just Elmore, my love. All three of us are sitting in the dark on a fallen oak not far from a farm supply store called something like Idlor Feed or something."

"Be there in less than fifteen. This is freaky," Rudy declares.

"Yes, Rudy. Freaky indeed. Bye. Thanks."

"Is Rudy your boyfriend?" Gavina asks neither of us in particular. But we both answer in unison.

"No."

"I thought he was your boyfriend," Gavina says, as if she's talking to herself.

"We have both known Rudy for a long time. And up until now, he was a friend with benefits to both of us. Do you know what that means, Dear?" I ask sympathetically.

Yes. It means you are friends who fuck each other. I was not born yesteryear, Miss Cookie. Thank you very much."

Elmore

The crazy shit that's about to go down between Cookie and Gavina brings me back to the old days. And I vowed then not to be that way or even be around it. I'll be damned if I'll put up with that stuff now. You cannot imagine the depth and noise of the cat fights of some of the drag queens who I knew in New York. I once saw a girl rip the wig off another and light a match to it. What a stink! Most of it was verbal, but brutal. I, myself, got the '*you think you're so damn prettier than us*' shade all the time. The amount of right-out insult that was thrown, especially among the young Black and Latino girls was monumental. "I don't have to tell you you're ugly because you know you're ugly." I guess insulting each other was a way to get it all out of the way, said and done, before someone on the outside harassed or attacked us.

"She started it," Gavina says.

"I didn't do anything," Cookie says.

"You always snub me or mock me."

"Everyone knows you're crazy."

"I know I am a bit off. But you are down-right *mean*!"

"You are beyond nuts."

"See ... *that* is mean. I can say keech about *myself,* but *you* cannot. Everyone knows that ..."

"Okay, so you're not always *totally* nuts ..."

"There you go again. *You are the one* who is the eejit."

"I have issues. I'm not delusional or psychotic."

"Oh, you are so much better than me."

When I can't take it anymore, I say, "Listen, you two. I have a great idea. Why don't you try to get along."

"Humpfh!" They both make the same sound.

"And find something to tend to my poor leg wound."

They're sitting now on either side of me and look at me as if they've both just realized I'm injured. Then, Gavina takes her scarf from around her neck and ties it around my calf. And Cookie squeezes my arm and rubs my back. The three of us sitting like bumps on a log.

"We're hardly The Three Musketeers," I say.

"You like historical novels?" Gavina asks.

"Not really," I say.

"The original Three Musketeers was written around 1800 ..." Cookie says.

"Eighteen forty-four to be exact," Gavina says.

"French. Right?" Cookie asks.

"Yup. Alexandre Dumas," Gavina says.

"I prefer more current literary fiction," Cookie says.

"Me, too," Gavina says.

"Like who?" Cookie asks.

They both continue talking to each other discussing shared favorite authors, and I begin to feel the muscles in my neck relax.

Gavina

By the time Kevin's car pulls up and then Rudy behind him, we have determined that Merryleigh Benoot is one of both Cookie and my favorite contemporary authors and we have each read *Lost Dingo* twice. I am just about to relate the story of how I am Merryleigh's first cousin once-removed and was Best Maid at her wedding, when we see the boys arrive and dash from their vehicles.

"What happened? Is your leg bleeding? Kevin asks Elmore.

"Are you all alright? You look alright," Rudy says.

We three just sit there as if we are glued to this make-shift bench, generously provided by the big old tree that has amputated its own limb because all of its tissue was not properly circulating. Oaks know how to let go when they have to in order to survive!

"I found Quinn," I say.

"We were robbed," Cookie says.

"I hurt my leg, but I don't think it's too serious," Elmore says.

The two gorgeous men just stand there looking at us — legs swinging — as if we are helpless, whiny wee ones whose feet barely touch the ground.

"We should not be allowed out anymore," I say. "Can we go home?"

"Of course, we'll take you home," Kevin says. He acts and sounds so much like The Manager when he was younger that it makes me shiver. But it also makes me feel safe. Grayson Previn was always kind to me from the moment I arrived at The Hacienda years ago. We would chat and compare tales. I called him The Manager. He liked that. He would talk mostly about the Native Americas, and his love of the garden and the soul of the very walls of the house he was converting and expanding into The Hacienda.

Don't tell anyone, but one day back then I had the door to my apartment ajar and the window open as I was hoping the air would circulate enough to manage the fumes from the oil paint. Grayson saw it as in invitation. My closet doors were also open and stuffed with my primitive artwork. He knew I liked to paint and draw, and he soon provided me with the materials I needed. Of course, this was long before there was an actual arts and crafts room. That special day I was working on what eventually became the very well-known *Woman and Bitchdog* — a polyptych depicting a huge, fat dog being walked by a small woman in very high heels. Don't ask me where the image came from. Like all my artwork it just appeared through my mindless brush strokes. And I *had* to paint. It was the only way to stop the voices inside my head telling me how horrible I was and how awful a life I had. But when my paintings were being created — or should I say *channeled* — the internal chatter stopped and I felt fine.

Grayson was the first person who saw my paintings and he insisted on driving me to the art gallery in town. The owner was looking for a way to make a name for herself, rather than move down to Los Angeles to try her luck as a dealer. She was so kind and careful with me that over time I showed her some more.

"Divine," she'd say each time. "These are simply divine."

And as I just told you, they were *indeed* divinely inspired.

She took ten works and sold them within a month or two. She not only split the money 50/50, but she also opened a bank account for me. After selling the first ten, she took some more to New York City for what she called a Western Outsider Art Show. Then more and more people saw paintings signed *McVey.* Prices rose. The money was deposited, and Grayson helped me invest. Till this day my secret has been kept by The Manager, who can no longer manage anything, let alone my money. Maybe I will turn things over to Kevin to do whatever he thinks best. 'Tis quite a very big pile of money by now, I guess. I do not care.

"What do you mean about finding Quinn? Where is he?" Rudy interrupts my musings.

"Does it really matter? We're done with him," Cookie says. "Gavina tells us that she followed a man she thought was her Uncle Ian ... who was killed by Quinn forty years ago in Scotland ... and she was in an old building bathed in shadows that will be torn down in the morning with Quinn alone and dead inside by suicide."

That shuts everyone up. They all look back and forth at each other with a bewildered — and I must say skeptical — look that I have become quite used to by now coming at me from a lot of folks over the course of my lifetime.

Rudy

Seamless teamwork — me and Kev. That's what it is. He drives off with the girls. Cookie and Gavina wave at me like little kids as they're zipped away by Kevin. And I'm happily alone with good ol' Elmore who we all agreed needs to have his leg checked out at the nearest hospital. He's sitting in the passenger's seat pressing on his wound.

"It'll stop the bleeding," he says. "I'm alright. Been through worse cuts."

"I know, El. I remember when you fell off that wall on New Years Eve. I took you to the ER then and here we are on our way again. Different circomestandings."

"I remember everyone in costumes then, waiting to be taken care of."

"Remember that guy in the leather jock and harness with the spiked hair?"

"Will never forget. He was drunk and hitting on you like he was in a dark bar backroom instead of a bright emergency room."

"He was pretty aggressive. Not like some people ..."

Of course, I'm thinking about Kevin and glad to be able to talk to Elmore, who isn't showing off an ounce of jealousy or judgementalness about my obvious hots for Kev. Elmore knows me well.

"Like what people, pray tell?" he jokes, as he rests his arm on the back of my seat and pats my head with the hand that is not pressing on the scarf.

"You know," I say.

"Listen, Rudy. When I saw you with Kevin my heart began pounding like a son-of-a-bitch. I'm delighted. It's high time you found someone."

"I know. And become more independent. Right?"

"I wasn't going to say that. But ... yes."

"Kevin's getting a divorce I think."

"Kevin's getting a divorce you *hope*!"

"He's never been gay."

"You mean he's never *admitted* or fully realized he's gay. He's *always* been gay. Don't you think?"

"Just like I've always been bi?"

"Yes, Rudy. But that doesn't mean you can't decide to give up women if you find the love of your life."

"I can easily give up the V."

"Don't be crude."

"Since when. You and I have always been as crude as we can be."

"I know, but I'm old now and more refined."

"What do you mean?" I ask, as Elmore's voice gets very loud.

"Never mind. Look. Look over there. That looks like the place Gavina described!"

It's as if the little old building has a spotlight on it although it's clearly the light of the moon as the clouds move away. There's yellow keep-out tape all around the doors and windows. There're two bulldozers sitting on what once might have been a front lawn. I'm remembering what Cookie said about Quinn being left alone to die, so I pull over and stop.

"I'm goin' in," I say. "Should I go in?"

"I'll wait right here," Elmore answers back.

It's like I know my way even though I've never seen this place before in my entire whole life, but the damn thing is pulling me in through the only unblocked back door and up a flight of stairs. Not sidekick Robin anymore, I'm full-on Batman. Guess that makes me reversatile.

"Hello," I shout. "Anyone here? Hello?"

No sound except my footsteps. It is vey spooky. I feel as though the creaky floor might give way. I can't really see anything much except empty space. I make my way down a hall when I hear what is either a moan of a person or the floorboards giving way. And then, there he is. Quinn Adamsdaur lying in one of the rooms, face up — both the walls and him moaning in pain. I host him over my shoulder and go down the stairs and out into the night.

"Well, look at you!" Elmore says, with his window down. "Whatcha doin?"

"Reach around and open the back door, will ya?"

He does so and I dump a sick, but still breathing Quinn onto the backseat. He's swearing like a motherfucker and then he passes out.

Part 4

Tuesday

Chapter Fifteen

Elmore

The ER doctor at the hospital last night was a cheerful, plump woman who reminded me of Pudge Pie — a drag queen whose shtick was to do hilarious stand-up about food and body image. She'd lip sync to songs like Millie Small's *My Boy Lollipop* and Gertrude Lawrence's *A Cup of Coffee, A Sandwich and You.* Google it. I'll wait. When Pudge wasn't performing, she went to beer busts in her natural rather manly, low-key way, and you'd never guess what his nighttime gig was. But both personas were that of a smart, kind, and clever person who made you feel happy.

The doctor cleaned up, stitched, and bandaged my leg after sending Quinn up to the third floor to get his stomach pumped or whatever.

"Typical overdose. Poor Dear," she said, referring to Quinn. "Badly in need of rehab, I'd say."

"Can someone call us before you release him?" Rudy asked.

"He won't be going anywhere soon," she said, as she finished working on my leg. I didn't feel a thing and I secretly wished she could lidocaine my whole body.

"Maybe we can figure something out for him," Rudy continued.

"Is he the boyfriend of one of you?" she asked.

"God no!" we both replied.

We didn't get back to my apartment until around one in the morning, and I talked Rudy into sleeping over on my sofa bed. Thankfully no hint of hanky-panky. It was a relief to not have to make my desire and my body work like it used to. I'm done with all that as of now. Time to admit wild sex shall be no more — now nestled in my memories as entertainment as long as my remembrances last.

Rudy's ringtone — a rap from the early Two Thousand's *Party Like a Rock Star* — woke me up. We used to get a laugh out of that song years ago. Now it would be totally obnoxious and annoying if it came from anyone but Rudy.

After I struggle through my morning routine in the bathroom, I shuffle my way into the kitchen and ask about the call. Rudy's making coffee. He's splendidly attired in beige boxer briefs that leave little to the imagination. As if I haven't seen it all before.

"Seems like Quinn was not only drunk and high, but he also indigested a little antifreeze," Rudy tells me. "It could have killed him if he drank any more than he did, so we evidently might have saved his life."

"Where'd the fool get antifreeze?" I ask.

"I have no idea. The guy is clearly over the edge."

"Sorry. As much as a jerk as he is, I doubt he deserves to die."

"I don't know. The person who called me said maybe we can get him into rehab or something ..."

The knock on the door could be Kevin. He probably wants to check up on me and find out how my leg is doing.

“Well answer it,” I say.

“I’m not dressed. I don’t want to discombobulate him.”

“Okay, I’ll answer it,” I say, opening the door before Rudy can grab his clothes and make a dash to the bathroom.

“Elmore, are you okay?” Kevin says, straining to see Rudy disappear into the john. “Am I interrupting something?”

“No. No. You are not interrupting anything. No. Rudy slept on my couch. We got back here very late. Lots to tell you. Come on in. We just got up. Missed breakfast, I’m sure.”

I’m like little miss Cupid here. My heart is pounding like an anxious parent hoping that things go well with my middle-aged, still single son and his delightful, perfect-for-him boyfriend even though I know they’re not boyfriends. Yet.

“Want some coffee?”

“Sure,” Kevin says, as he comes in and sits on the unmade sofa bed as if he had slept there himself.

“You didn’t interrupt a thing. Rudy and I have a lot to tell you,” I said, wondering if I was repeating myself.

“Your place looks nice. You’re a retired interior designer, right?”

“Correct. I want to freshen up the dining room and whatever else you let me do.”

"That sounds nice. You're right about it. The Hacienda could use an update. I'll tell you what ... let me review our budget. I'm preoccupied about my father at the moment."

"Cookie would be happy to help me. And I still have a lot of contacts, suppliers, etc. I tried to tell The Manager about it."

"He's not well."

"Names confused me. He's your dad, isn't he?" I ask, as Rudy emerges from the bathroom, fully dressed except for shoes and socks.

"Yes. He's my dad. Stepfather ... married my mother but didn't change my name. Kevin Previn would not work. No. Nope. I'm not sure how long he has," Kevin says. He looks like pent-up sorrow is about to spill as he sees Rudy come out of the bathroom and rush over to sit with him on the sofa. Kevin dissolves into Rudy's strong arms as if they're in one of my favorite romance novels.

Quinn

Rudy Whatshisname and his ancient friend with money — money that I'll never see — brought me here to this hospital last night. How they found my sorry ass is a mystery to me. They've done me no favor! The fat woman ER doctor wants to send me to fucking rehab. I am not doing that! I'm past the point of rehabilitation, let alone usefulness for anything or anyone. When I look around me, all I see is shit. I literally see a haze of feces-colored thickness surrounding my peripheral vision. I'm in a bed that feels so hot and I'm so sweaty that I might already be dead and gone to hell. But I'm untethered. No tubes, no intravenous, no straight jacket. Not even tightly tucked bedsheets holding me down. Just because I failed to off myself last night with Gavina's mysterious poisons, doesn't mean that if I put my mind to it, I can't finish the job. And the idiot nurses — who you'd expect to be cloying after me and making sure I was okay — are not around. Not a one. The nausea undulates throughout my insides begging me to throw up or explode out my ass. I do neither as I stumble down off the bed and look to see if the coast is clear. Before you know it, I'm out of the hospital staggering into the crisp foggy daylight and I begin stumbling step-by-step into the soupy mist. Fade to black.

Cookie

Trying to recover from yesterday's drama in San Luis *Abysmal*, I'm dumfounded as I stand eating my breakfast alone in my apartment in front of the three paintings that are still resting on the floor against the wall — instead of properly hung. My hoarding is much better now but I am still disorganized. I dreamt about these paintings, and I've been ruminating all morning. I'm staring at the triptych of a tree, a house, and a man — painted on three pieces of wood. It's primitive art. Purchased by me beyond my budget in 2015 at Badam & Brocks for a total of ten thousand dollars, which was a bargain according to the gallery owner who lived in my building. Each panel was spaced carefully three inches apart over the sofa in my office. When I had an office. Now ready for hanging as soon as I get my shit together. I may have had a bit too much to drink back then at the exhibit of outlier art. But I loved these pieces the moment I saw them. My neighbor was a salesperson there at the time.

"Not only is this a steal, but if you ask around, you'll hear a lot about this artist. These pieces are a great investment. I can put them on hold if you want to do some research," she said conspiratorially, as I drank another glass of the complimentary champagne.

"There's something eerie but beautiful about them," I said. I felt dizzy with emotion emanating from that artwork. All sorts of feelings that nearly caused me to faint. But mostly joy.

"Eerie but beautiful, right? I know," my friend said. "And it really helps these artists to make some money. Most of them live hand to mouth."

"What do you know about the artist?"

"Absolutely positively nothing. Not sure if it's a he or a she or where he or she is or was."

"It could be the champagne talking, but the tree has so many layers of green and different other colors of paint peeking through that it looks alive. As they say ... these speak to me."

"I know. Right."

The exterior view of the house is outlined against the wood and brushed on so that the walls are bare exposing the wood, but everything else is vibrantly painted. There's a lush garden. And the disproportionately large man in the third panel is done in the same colors and style as the other two. He's standing with his hands in his pockets in profile, like someone who's looking at it all with pride. The whole thing could have been done by a child. I bought them on the spot and as it turned out, a couple of my clients had indeed already acquired *'a McVey'* — an evidently well-known self-taught artist.

Gavina

There have been more people knocking on my door over the past four days than over the preceding four years. I do not know if I could get used to having so many people around. Especially when I am doing an alla prima painting on one of the weathered wood panels from The Juggler's spook house. Quinn has turned out to be someone I dread more than love. Rudy and Kevin are cute, but so into each other that there is no room for me. I do not mind them though. Elmore is mostly a gentleman. And then there is Doctor Cookie Nussbaum, who is standing outside my door as I crack it open, while I am careful not to unhinge the chain lock. When I was hiding from the Nazis with — smart but not actually all that cute — Anne Frank, helping her write her diary, we lived in constant fear that there would be a door knocked down and we would be carted off.

"It smells like oil paint in there," Cookie says. Not *hello*. Not *how are you*.

"I am sort of busy right now," I say, as my paintbrush whines with an insistence that it finish expressing its blues rather than allow me to put it down and reenter what some of you might call 'the real world.'

"Sorry to interrupt," Cookie says.

"Are you okay?" I ask, emerging from my dream of a bear hugging a man while floating amongst the sky and clouds. I do not know why I am painting this. I just render what I feel.

"I'm alright," she says.

"That was quite a night last night, huh?" I can be polite even if she isn't.

"Are you going to invite me in?" she boldly asks. "I come in peace."

"Shall we go out to the garden?" I ask. "I will meet you there in a minute."

There is no way that this woman is going to pass though my door. Not until she proves herself to me. I do not know how she can do that. Zebras do not change their spots and people might be polite once in a while or you may find you have something in common, but you still have to be careful not to give yourself away on a hope or a promise. So I quickly depart my wooden canvas and change out of my painting smock into a nice wrap-around dressing gown and I go outside.

"Your last name's McVey isn't it?" she says to me.

She is sitting on the very bench where I was with Quinn the Terrible just a few days ago when I thought I loved him and wanted to live with him. Now I do not know what to do. The horrible bulldozer is still sitting there baring its teeth. And I have lost all my poisons — stolen by my dead uncle yesterday at that decaying old hideout. The Manager will not be around much anymore no matter what. And I begin to cry. I cannot stop the sadness, and suddenly I very badly want to talk to Kevin, not Cookie.

"What do you want?" I manage to ask.

"You're *McVey* aren't you?"

"What do you mean?"

"You sign your paintings with your last name ... don't you?" she says, as if it is a fact not a question.

In the Wizard of Oz the curtain is pulled back and the true less-than-magic power of the mighty Wiz is revealed. No matter how much money The Manager may have helped me to stash away, I did not want anyone knowing me. I still do not. I do not paint for money or fame. I do it to ward off the monster that has always been after me — just to quiet Baisd Bheulach, the shapeshifting demon in my head.

"I own ... and I *love* your paintings! I had three of them hanging in my office in Beverly Hills and they're now waiting to be put up *again* ... here. Maybe you can help me properly install them."

Cookie is nearly squealing like a teenage who has met one of the Beatles or Jon Bon Jovi. Or more apropos, Frida Kahlo her colorful self — if Cookie even would know who that is.

"I feel like I'm meeting Georgia O"Keeffe or Frida Kahlo," she chirps. "More apropos, Banksy!"

This woman is driving me rocket. Besides making me crazy she is also blowing my mind. Or reading it? Has she even noticed my tears?

"No one knows who Banksy really is, do they? But he must have somehow made a fortune," she goes on. And after a while when I do not answer, she says, "Oh. Oh my. Are you crying? I'm sorry. I can keep your secret. I promise I won't tell anyone if you don't want me to."

And then the bitch hugs me. *And* against all rules of survival, I let her.

Kevin

From the window in my father's apartment, I can see Cookie and Gavina sitting on a bench in the garden. It's a bench we'll keep in place because my father made it himself early in The Hacienda's history — with the help of Jacko. The women look ironically angelic in the daylight. It makes me wonder if we might want a nice sculpture out there as part of the redesign. Something my dad would like. The thought fractures me. But even though I've asked Rudy to come with me — instead of holding me like he did before — he sits quietly in a corner of my father's bedroom where the old man lies mumbling in bed.

Earlier, when Rudy hugged me in Elmore's apartment, it felt comforting at first and I dissolved into his arms like a child. We hardly moved. But when I began to get a hard-on, I panicked and said that I had to go. I ran from the fire in me as if the room was burning, and Rudy followed. We left Elmore there to catch up on some sleep and have the nurse come to change his bandage before lunch. Anyway, Elmore was beginning to feel too much like a surrogate father way too soon for me to process.

It felt like my actual father was calling to me.

"The landscaping company is due to start work soon, after everything is prepped," I say, sitting by Dad's bedside.

I know Rudy is listening but I'm not sure if I'm talking to him or my dad, who is taking long gaps between shallow breaths. He looks peaceful enough and the house doctor will be here any minute to relieve me of having to be with Dad during the crush of the inevitable.

"I've decided not to sell," I mumble. "I'll figure out a way to keep The Hacienda going."

Rudy is my ally — this man I've only known for a few days. I can picture him being here and working with me always, managing things like recreational and exercise activities for residents. We have no one qualified to do that. It would be perfect for him.

I know Dad is leaving The Hacienda to me along with some money. Maybe I'll raise the rents. Everything will work out.

"We'll be alright. Don't you worry," I say.

"I'm gonna take a walk. Maybe check out the lunchroom," Rudy says. "You alright?"

"Yeah. I'm good. I'll meet you there in a while. I can have lunch with you."

"Right. Good. I thought you didn't eat with the residents."

"Times change," I say.

I can't stop myself from walking toward him and reaching my arms around his neck. I pause and look him in the eye, nudging him closer. And right then — in front of my dying father and the sound of the bulldozer starting up in the garden and a strange rattling of windows — I find myself kissing Rudy on the mouth.

He lingers in the kiss and then grins but doesn't say anything and turns to leave me alone with my father.

I turn slowly, and mindfully walk toward the bed. I kiss Dad's cheek.

Then I open the door for the doctor who enters, head bowed, along with Jacko. They shuffle their feet making too much noise. But I'm pretty sure anything that they do might annoy me on my way out.

"He wanted me to give you this," Jacko says, as he presses a key into my hand. "It's time. I put his latest note up in the safe just today. He said you'd understand. 3-6-85. Right. Left. Right."

When I was a little kid, my father used to call it The Reading Room — through a locked door opened by a key on his ring of many. We'd ascend the stairs with a reverence as if the attic of the old house was sacred, high above the rest of the original building. Its cathedral ceiling buttressed above and coming into full view as we reached the landing. Rafters extending to form the eaves that still give the house its distinct exterior.

Behind the remnants of an old mahogany headboard from what must have been a poster bed, we'd sit on the floor and Dad would read to me. Mostly he read from books about indigenous people, botany, architecture, or some other boring non-fiction topic. To tell the truth, I learned very little but enjoyed the sound of his voice and the adventure that came with visiting our private space alone together.

We did this a number of times from the beginning of The Hacienda when I was little, until I reached my early teens when — as I suppose is normal — I lost interest. And he must have moved on to other things.

The key from Jacko feels heavy in my hand now as I unlock and open the attic door and continue repeating the combination in my head 3-6-85 — the date The Hacienda became Dad's life's work. Standard issue cobwebs and dust make my eyes sting and kickstart my allergies.

The wall safe is hidden behind some boards that look like they were meant for some sort of construction many years ago. I'm going to have to have a termite inspection. Leave it to me to have a totally inappropriate practical thought.

The dial turns easily as if it's been used recently. I suppose by Jacko.

There are mementos that seem to be willing to wait for my attention. But two envelopes marked with my name stand out. The first envelope has a long, handwritten letter in it. It's almost illegible.

> I heard you earlier tonite. I do not know when we will be able to speak a proper good-bye but since I am mildly lucid at the moment and tomorrow I very well may leave I am writing you this lengthy maybe jumbled note to tell you how very much I love you am proud of you and appreciate you....

After reading the whole thing, I carefully fold it back up and put it into the envelope and the envelope into my pocket. I stare up at the attic's peak through the dusty light. I take the note out of my pocket. I read it over again. I sit quietly for a while. I know that I will need time to figure out and digest all that it says.

The second envelope reveals a note dated simply *2018.* I assume Dad wrote it a year ago and had Jacko climb the stairs to the wall safe.

> If a man who calls himself Farris the Juggler ever shows up tell him that all the money from his tv series is being invested in the joint account he and I opened for him (Bank of America #2-99677-F) before he ran off. It was his twelfth attempt to get something sold and it hit big just this year and wherever he is, I doubt he knows about it. I helped make the deal happen. He was a very odd duck who came to us through the magic of The Vision Rooming House in its heyday. He left on New Years Eve 2013 and I am legally named as his beneficiary and you are named as my sole heir. All the legal information is in the safe. If he ever does show up after I am gone just tell him you have used what's left of his money for The Hacienda as I hope you do but please be kind and take him in if need be.
>
> Then there is the case of Gavina McVey a gifted artist who I befriended and looked after soon after her arrival because her psychiatrist was a dear friend of mine who died sometime before Gavina came to us and his widow encouraged me to take her in.

I have invested all of her money also at Bank of America #4-10567-M. I am named as her beneficiary and you are named as my sole heir and she will most likely out-live us all and never cared one bit about the money she earned from the success of her art. There is a lot of it. $$$$ I used some of it to keep the records straight by entering her payments in the file to show that she has paid her share of rent here but she is under the sadly mistaken belief that a man named Quinn has been paying her bill even though she has actually been paying for herself with her own money through me. I have also given her a little monthly allowance from her account. I think when I am gone you will have to take this over. The only problem besides her being kooky is that her identity as an outside artist is a secret and you cannot let on that I told you so you shall have to coax it out of her.

Dad

I don't know anything about this juggler guy, but the Gavina payment thing makes sense to me now, since Dad hasn't been able to pay or enter the payment lately like he's evidently done over the years.

Chapter Sixteen

Rudy

I'm not sure if the hug and the kiss are reactions to his father dying or some indicationing that Kev is really into me. Right now it doesn't matter because I am overloaded with emotional and brain activity and I don't know why I think that a stroll followed by lunch in the cafeteria would help or be an especially good idea but I'm standing here anyway, looking for anyone I know. A couple of ladies who were sitting with Gavina and Cookie the last time I was in here come over to greet me. One of them is in a wheelchair and the other on a walker. Both dressed all in black. One of them is skinny and the other, not so much. The thin woman leans one hand on her walker and extends the other.

"We saw you the other day, looking for Gavina. Are you alright? You look rattled. I'm Virginia Stern and this is my sister, Doctor Evinston."

"Call me Evelynn," her sister says.

"You guys are doctors?" I ask.

"Well, yes. I'm the retired head of the Stanford Department of English. She's PhD Biology. Retired. Obviously."

"I'm Rudy. I guess I'm looking for Cookie and Gavina."

"Oh, we don't eat with either of them anymore. It was no fun. But they're right over there just sitting down at The Manager's table," Evelyn says. "Such a sad day."

"You know about him?"

"We're quite friendly with the house physician. He told us today was the day. Sounds like Grayson passed in relative peace."

"How's Kevin?" Virginia asks.

"He's okay. He's pretty upset. Why are you asking me about Kevin?"

"News travels fast around here, Rudy."

"Very fast. Like high school gossip," Evelyn says, as I thank them and walk over to The Manager's table.

"Nice gals. So smart," I say, motioning to the sisters.

Cookie and Gavina don't respond. They look at each other as if I said something surprising or strange or like someone died. I only *think* this, I don't say it out loud. I'm not an animal. I didn't know Kev's dad obviously, but he was evidentially well-liked. Loved even. By a lot of people. Sometimes I think stupid things are funny, but I know not to say them out loud when the timing might be off. I learned that after my poor timing with Kev and me asking him out loud about Melba at the wrong time.

"Have a seat," Gavina says. "We're having salads for lunch. There's a salad bar. They've put up more Plexiglass because people breathe all over the food and spread the flu."

"Never mind that," Cookie says, as Elmore makes his way to the table.

"I thought it was bad before, but all this Lucite makes it look even worse in here," Elmore says, after sitting.

"I think Kevin will let you do your thing in here," I say.

"You mean me beautifying things. Good. I'm ready. How's his father?"

"I think that The Manager passed away about an hour ago," I announce. It's a fact. What else am I supposed to say?

Gavina starts crying. Loudly. When everyone in the room looks our way, I realize *everyone* knows but these three.

"Where's Kevin?" Gavina shouts.

"He said he'd come for lunch," I say. "He could be in his office. Or he might have left and gone on home."

"Don't you say anything," Gavina commands Cookie — right at her, like a red-faced threat about who knows what.

Then the four of us sit there in complete silence until I tell Elmore I'm going to get him and me a salad. He says that's okay, and the two women continue eating small bites while deep in some thinking of their own. When I get back to the table for six, Kev is there and there's one very empty chair.

I sit and take Kevin's hand right on top of the table and before you know it, Gavina takes his other hand. And then Cookie – of all people – takes Gavina's hand along with Elmore's, and Elmore grabs mine, until everyone is holding hands on the tabletop.

Gavina says, "I think I need to move over to Assisted."

Elmore

The idea of creating your own family is not new. Those of us without family or who've been abused, neglected, or abandoned from our biological kin have been forming close ties with people of our own choosing forever. I've surely done it myself over the years. Rudy for example has become like family to me, which is one of the reasons that we have to stop having any kind of sexual thing. And like a good father, I need to help him leave the nest. I think Cookie feels the same way. But that doesn't mean we don't want him around. She and I are like a warped set of surrogate parents. She's like a sister to me, who I squabble with but mostly love having around. Kevin's like a soon-to-be son-in-law and Gavina — bless her little heart — is akin to that crazy but colorful what we used to call old-maid aunt who is always at Thanksgiving dinner.

"This is nice," I say quietly. "I don't mean it's nice that The Manager has passed. Although I hope he ended up going peacefully."

"He was ready to die," Gavina says. She has an interesting look of resolve on her face as she stares unmovingly at Kevin — still hand-in-hand.

"It's nice ... that all of you can be here for me like this. I think of The Hacienda as family, and we're going to stick together," Kevin says.

"No tear-down?" Cookie asks without sarcasm but more like a final statement to end an ongoing debate on a positive note.

"Nope." Kevin says, also encouragingly. "I plan to continue to run this place, and Gavina ... if you want to move over to Assisted, we can make that happen. You'll still be able to share meals and visit with us ... no problem. Why don't we discuss the details in my office ... you and I in a couple of days? And you can help me plan the memorial after the funeral."

"That would be my privilege," Gavina says, hand over her heart.

With that, all clasped hands unfold. And while I look around the dining room and imagine what it will look like when Cookie and I do some necessary upgrades, there's a rumbling — startling at first until those of us at The Manager's table collectively realize that it's the sound of chairs rubbing against the awful carpeting — as the residents all stand in what appears to be silent prayer of some sort. Then two distinguished looking women dressed all in black — one on a walker and the other in a wheelchair —say something like, "Rest in peace, Grayson Previn." They have to repeat it loudly over a bizarre amount of whispering. "Rest in peace, Grayson Previn."

Kevin stands and faces the chorus of elderly and staff. It's weirdly bright in the room, as if the sunshine is successfully fighting its way past the drapes to illuminate the wood grain beneath the painted walls. He bows self-consciously and brings his hands together in what I think of as a universal sign of peaceful prayer or in this case a heartfelt *thank you.* No one moves so everyone is freeze-frame except for the man who drives the shuttle, I think his name is Jack or Jacko, as he walks toward us, twisting his hat like a soaked dish towel. He's heading straight toward Kevin as if he instinctively knows his way around all the tables as he navigates the standing residents and staff. When he gets to our table, he extends his hand out as if to shake Kevin's. But Kevin immediately wraps his arms around the guy, and they stand together in that bear hug for quite a while.

Six Months Later

Epilogue

Gavina

A bunch of us Assisted Folks amble into the garden for Grayson's Memorial/Celebration of Life thing — leaning on walkers and riding wheelchairs. Nurse Hemmings and two of the latest come-and-go willful assistants are with us. They will inevitably quit and leave for greener pastures or unemployment. We are an insignificant little pack of dark-clothed hags along with two old geezers trundling along the newly laid, elder-safe, resin-bound gravel, and I assure you no one is going fast enough to kick up any residual dust.

I borrowed the black dress I am all togged up in from Virginia, one of the sisters who share an Assisted Apartment right next door to mine. As you know, I do not own anything black. And yes, thank you very much, it is the thin sister who let me borrow her dress which is admittedly a tad tight on me. I still sometimes call her Twigs when I cannot remember her actual name. Turns out her fat sister, Evelyn aka Butters cannot join us today because she has just had a hip replacement and knee surgery and cannot get herself out of bed, even though Rudy has been trying to at least get her up and into her wheelchair. She's not as nice as Virginia anyway.

Evelyn and I share the same psychiatrist, Doctor Edelstein, who comes to see both of us on First Fridays and check up on our meds and our so-called *false beliefs* about things and stuff. He has got us both on admittedly wonderful what he calls 'new generation' meds.

I have slightly bonded with Virginia because we have attended every one of Rudy's Stretch-and-Go classes in the newly upgraded recreational activities room, which I have to admit has a very uplifting ambiance thanks to *Elmore's Touch*.

So, I am all in black now, except for the yellow scarf that I am wearing in honor of Quinn, who of course never received a proper funeral or anything. No one around here ever speaks of him even though it was Doctor Cookie who searched and found the police report about the John Doe discovered on the side of a road, left like a goat who wandered in front of some hit-and-run driver on the very day that Grayson passed in February. I am going to use this occasion as a way to silently respect the dead even if in Quinn's case, he was not the most admirable person to say the least.

Kevin has promised the memorial event will be brief and refreshments will be served after the program in the newly redesigned dining room, even though the roman shades have not been installed yet and we will be sitting in the old chairs waiting for Elmore's new cushier ones to arrive.

Spectators, if that is the proper term, since we are no longer full-time mourners, are already sitting in rows of chairs in the garden facing the oak tree that is meant to be planted along with Grayson's ashes in the huge hole that has already been dug by Jacko. It was his idea. And as he assured us during one of our Celebration Planning Meetings — a small amount of human ashes mixed into the soil or spread on the surface of the planting area will not harm the memorial oak. It shall grow tall. Worry naught.

Jacko stands equal in height to the hardy sapling as it already sits upright in the earth's cavity waiting for dirt to be shoveled. That forethought must be one of Johnny-on-the-Spot Kevin's in order to save time and move things along. That Kevin Vernkowsky is the angel who has taken over for his father in every way, including managing my monetary and still secret business affairs.

As agreed upon by the Celebration Committee there is a large shovel with a polished oak handle resting on the ground. Jacko is wearing a scarf with a Chumash design that was given to him by his grandmother on his eighteenth birthday, in that she believed that the number eighteen was sacred or something. I remember watching his Chumash Grandma creating the basket — when she herself was eighteen years of age —with the design that inspired the scarf. I very much enjoyed helping her twining and coiling the pattern in red and black with white sumac and golden tan for background, while we consumed and tripped out on dangerous Datura Plants. By the way, I keep these sorts of precious memories to myself these days. I write them for you but no longer share them out loud with anyone except my shrink.

I have been given a seat of honor along with Kevin, Rudy, Elmore, and Cookie — who are already seated and silent, while listening to Dimitri from the liquor store play some rather haunting music on an ancient looking bouzouki. He is wearing long pants and a white shirt, not one of his usual skimpy outfits. Cookie and Elmore found out that he is attending the SLO Conservatory of Music. They paid for him, along with the potted petunias that will be planted by the bench nearest to the house.

Kevin's ex-wife is in the second row with her new boyfriend, fiancé, husband? Her hand is on her belly. It looks to me like she's either fat or with child, but regardless, they both seem happy. Kevin tells me that she and his father were close, so bygones seem to be bygones.

"Welcome," Kevin says as he stands and joins Jacko. I am sure he is not much of a public speaker and am of course proven right when he hems and haws his first few words. "Welcome to the celebration ... uhm ... or memorial if you wish ... for my beloved father, Grayson Previn."

"Here. Here," Cookie inappropriately says way too loudly and then gives me the stink-eye when I shush her. Ever since I helped her hang the three paintings that she claims were painted by me, although I do not remember doing so, we have enjoyed a truce that allows us to both be civil to one another, although I am sure she talks indignities about me behind my back as much as I trash her when she is not around.

"Some of you knew my dad more than others ... not to say you are older ... I mean, Jacko and I knew him the longest of course ... but uhm, no matter how close he was to you ... I'm sure he touched your lives in some meaningful way or another."

Rudy is leaning forward in his chair, and you can just see that he wants to jump up and give his boyfriend/boss a hug. But instead, he rocks back and forth into his seat as if he has to go pee in the cludgie.

"Anyway," Kevin continues, "some of you know that we had Grayson's actual funeral a few days after he died with only his immediate family ... which meant not many people. But today, we are honoring him by planting this tree in the garden he loved. Now to be known as Grayson Garden. There's a carved wooded plaque on the bench over there."

He points and then looks at Rudy for reassurance.

"I'm certain that Dad would approve of the new landscaping and the added benches. Thank you, Elmore and Cookie, who most of you know help me and Mrs. Carter in their positions as our new Resident Ambassadors. I'll turn it over now to Jacko...."

Taking his cue, Jacko lifts a couple of branches of dried white sage from under his chair. He strikes a match, ignites the sacred herb and blows out the flames allowing it to smolder and smoke. It has a pleasant smell and will help carry prayers up to God. The audience watches as if they are seeing some sort of live-action miracle. Those of us in the front row are smiling ear to ear, including Mrs. Carter who has taken it upon herself to carefully move her chair closer up so she can inhale the magic. The Widow Carter and Nurse Hemmings seem to be very close these days. Mrs. Carter has been quite busy and they say gets paid well. And the nurse? Well no one — except maybe Carter — knows their gender. Thank you very much. 'Go figure,' as Doctor Cookie would say.

Jacko then takes an eagle feather out from his sleeve and touches Kevin's back with it to draw out apparitions and then taps the plume toward the ground to send any harmful spirits back into the underworld where they came from. Flick. Flick. Flick.

The ashes have already been placed among the roots because The Celebration Committee agreed with Elmore that making too much of Grayson being smooshed into the dirt like that might upset some of the elder or up-tight residents who may not even appreciate watching Jacko as he finishes shoveling dirt until it reaches level with the surface.

And then The Hacienda moans.

The joints are slipping, and the wood is making a popping sound usually only heard at night. Usually only heard by me and Grayson. Yet even though no one else seems to notice, Kevin looks up toward the exterior of the attic as if he has heard.

And since no one else is doing it, I take up the role of the banshee to honor the dead by moaning, chanting, and crying loud enough for The Hacienda to hopefully settle down before we adjourn for milk and cookies.

Other Books by Howard Wallman

A Socially Distant Man
Novel

Baby Blues
Novel

Senior Shorts
Short Stories

Life Coach in the Jungle
Novel

Afterlust
Novel

WHATEVER Happened to Alec
Novel

Dying to be Good
Novel

Liberate Your Gifted Self
~ Become Your Own Therapist
Self-Help

A Big Man's Little Book of a Few Very Short Heartfelt
Poems
Poetry

Visit
www.HowardWallman.com

Made in the USA
Middletown, DE
13 September 2023